FINDING JACOB, BOOK 2

TRACIE PODGER

COPYRIGHT

Be the better person, DON'T take part in piracy.

CHAPTER ONE

My phone beeped, indicating I had a message. I checked my watch and swore. It was one in the morning. I had an early start, but I hadn't wanted to be woken that early.

I picked up the phone and saw it was from my friend, Nathan. I shook my head and smiled. It had to be urgent for him to message me at that time, he knew I was in New York.

I opened the text and frowned.

Mate, I know this is strange but trust me on this. Anna is going to call you. She needs 'a' Jacob. She's in New York or will be in a few hours. Can you take her call? You won't regret it. Do it for me? She'll call on this line.

He ended with a wink.

"What the fuck are you on about?" I said, rousing the female lying beside me.

"What time is it?" she mumbled.

"Time for you to get up and leave, I'm afraid," I replied, knowing how shitty that sounded.

"Are you kidding me?" Her New York accent ground on me to the point I gritted my teeth.

"Yeah, sorry, I have to leave."

I swung my legs over the side of my bed. I rarely brought anyone back to my apartment and could only blame the fine whisky I'd consumed for my error. I didn't even know her name. I was sure she'd told me, but all I'd wanted was to fuck her.

"Bastard," she said, throwing the covers back and standing.

She had a fine body, for sure, and somewhere in my recollect, she was a dancer. Probably at the casino I'd attended that evening. I'd been invited as a guest of a client in town for a meeting, and he'd lined up a row of beauties to entertain his friends. I wasn't into that kind of entertainment and quickly left. However, it seemed one of the girls wasn't into that either, and left at the same time. We found ourselves commiserating at the bar. One too many drinks later, and.... The memory had started to form, and I closed my eyes against it.

I was ashamed of myself, I didn't behave in that way, usually. But it was an anniversary that, every year, I wanted to blank out and getting drunk and fucking some random was my way of doing that. It didn't feel like cheating on my wife's memory, it was meaningless. Just a way to focus on something other than her death.

I headed for the shower as she dressed. I heard her slam the apartment door and hoped my wallet was still in my trousers.

I stared at myself in the mirror, I looked rough. I ran my hand over my stubble and laughed.

"Fuck, get yourself together, man," I said to my reflection.

I had a quick shower and returned to the bedroom. I stripped off the bottom sheet and replaced it with a fresh one, then climbed back under the duvet. I replied to Nathan.

Care to expand? You want me to take a call from a random, why?

He replied quickly.

This isn't a random, this is Anna. Her fuckwit ex is marrying her sister and she said she'd attend their wedding. Trouble is, she said she'd attend with her boyfriend, Jacob.

He left a row of laughing emojis and I sighed.

So you want me to pretend to be her boyfriend just because my name is Jacob? I typed.

Yeah, I did it for you, remember? And this is Anna, my Anna.

I laughed. I did remember. Nathan and I had been in the Army together. We were close, brothers in all but blood. It was one tour of Gibraltar when my then-girlfriend flew out as a surprise. Only, I was also seeing a local. The local girl knew of my other woman and when she turned up at a barracks dinner, Nathan pretended to be with the local. It hadn't worked and I was dumped by both that night. I was young and very stupid at the time. I had no respect for anyone, including myself, and Nathan did like to remind me of my one indiscretion.

What do I have to do? I asked.

Just talk to her, maybe pretend to be her date at this wedding, you're back home then anyway, I checked.

Nathan and I were in business together. We owned a very successful company, a lucrative one that had earned us millions over the years we'd been doing it. We were in high demand because we only employed the elite. Ex-military who had either been forced to retire or came to the end of their 'useful' life serving the Queen and government. He knew I was in New York for a meeting, and he knew when I'd be back in England.

Although Spanish by birth to a Spanish mother, my father was English. I say English, he was born in the UK, but his parents moved him to Spain when he was a child. I was fortunate to have dual nationality. I managed to get out of conscription in Spain but joined the UK Army instead. More because I had nothing to do, no formal qualifications since I'd flunked out of school and hated the thought of working! I never did figure out why I thought the Army would be easier.

Okay, but you owe me. And I take it you still haven't told her you want her, have you?

I knew of Anna; I'd never met her. Nathan spoke about her all the time and whenever I asked, he denied any relationship and any feelings towards her. He insisted she was just a friend. I wasn't so sure. He called her 'my Anna' often.

That old chestnut! Call me later.

I placed the phone back on the nightstand and linked my fingers together behind my head.

Nathan and I could tell each other anything. I had been married to his sister once, his twin. We were bonded before, and more so after the tragedy that had occurred. I pushed the thoughts from my mind, but they bubbled away.

Twenty years ago, my wife had been murdered because I'd fucked up. I could never remember the exact day, I think I'd blocked it from my mind, but I knew it was early in the month, that month. So, every year, there was one day where it hit me hard. Perhaps that was the day she'd died, who knew.

I'd taken on a job, despite Nathan telling me not to. It wasn't safe, or secure, and his gut was telling him we were being led on. I didn't listen to him. We stopped a militia from taking over an island owned by the French at the northern end of the Mozambique channel of the Indian Ocean.

We had been contracted by the French government to oust a bloke they'd put in to oust the previous one. Except, this one had done the exact same as the one before. He was as corrupt as they came, claiming money for islanders who had long since died, not paying the nurses and teachers, until such a point civil unrest ensued. We were supposed to send in a team to take him out, which we did successfully, but it meant his brother, another dictator, took revenge. My house was burned to the ground with my wife in it.

I hadn't noticed the lone tear roll down my cheek until it splashed on my hand. I angrily wiped my face. I had no more tears to shed, I'd convinced myself. I'd locked the box on that memory, knowing it was overflowing and would one day burst open, but I'd deal with it then.

Like Nathan, I had the capability of shutting down emotion. It had been crucial to our survival. And like Nathan, I had blood on my hands when I personally slaughtered every member of the brother's family. It was Nathan who pulled the trigger on him, though. One clean shot straight between the eyes had ended his life, and a part of ours to a degree.

I never dated seriously after that, and although it was unspoken, I guessed I just never wanted to get close enough to have my heart destroyed again. As for Nathan, he believed he'd done way too many bad things to deserve anything good. He often said it was when he lost his bollocks to cancer that he'd decided never to marry, but I knew that was bullshit. He had seen first-hand what our *profession* was capable of, and he didn't want to put anyone at risk. He'd lost his sister. He had nearly lost his friend when I'd sat with a pot of pills wanting to end it all, he wasn't risking anyone or his heart again. I carried a level of guilt around with me for that. So, when he asked me to do anything for him, which wasn't often, I usually did.

There was no point in moping around, I decided, and I climbed out of bed. I walked naked into the living room and fired up my laptop. I googled Anna.

I liked what I saw, not about her looks, although she was gorgeous, but she was an independent businesswoman, not some airhead. Nathan had spoken about her a lot in the past, and there was always a little bit of me envious he had that friendship. She sounded perfect, perhaps too perfect. I searched for flaws.

The woman didn't even have a parking ticket! She didn't owe money; her company was successful, even if she did have a model who seemed to love the limelight too much. She owned property in London and was friends with royalty. She was often pictured with Princess Dorothea, someone who was about fifth in line to the throne.

I found out details of her family, and, importantly, an engagement announcement for her sister and the ex. I checked him out. I knew Nathan always kept a file on everyone, and I brought that up. He was a salesman, fairly successful it seemed, as I scanned his tax data. I also discovered he had a separate bank account and I laughed at the Pornhub and Only Fans subscriptions. He also had one to a foot fetish site. I wondered if Nathan had ever told Anna those details. Probably not. His way would have been to engineer something so she would have found out herself. I went back to her. Despite me believing that Nathan liked Anna, there was a small flutter in my stomach when I stared at her. It was a feeling I hadn't had for a long time. I shut down my laptop.

"Mmm, Anna, I await your call," I said, starting to actually look forward to our 'date.'

I didn't have to wait long. She called later that day.

I proposed dinner and delayed my flight to Dubai for my next meeting. I called down to housekeeping to inform them I'd be staying one more night and asked for the apartment to be cleaned.

I logged into my business and tracked some teams positioned around the world. We had one currently on a ship in the Suez protecting its contents from pirates. I fired off a couple of emails that would be heavily encrypted and untraceable.

I confirmed the details of my flight to Dubai. I usually chartered a private plane, not wanting the option or expense of owning one, but I did own a helicopter. I also had a licence to fly it but chose to employ an old army buddy instead. I emailed him my movements over the next couple of weeks so he could file flight plans. I hated to delay departures, as I'd just done for Anna, but sometimes a friend's request was more important. I had just the one meeting in Dubai and I knew the guy well enough to reschedule the time without any problems. Some of our clients were heads of state and those were trickier, but what I offered wasn't something one could pop online and order. So, I was often afforded the luxury of commanding my own meetings within my own time frame and changing them without much notice.

As the sun began to rise, I stood at the windows and drank my coffee. My apartment was on the top floor and although people walked through Central Park below, I highly doubted anyone could see me.

A little later, I took a second shower and dressed. Breakfast was yet another coffee and a plain omelette I cooked myself. I stacked the dishwasher and then settled down at my desk to get some serious work done.

I filtered through my emails, forwarding what I didn't want to deal with to Philip, my assistant. He was based in London, either from his own home or my London apartment that had become an office with bedrooms and a kitchen! The company didn't own offices anywhere, we all worked remotely. I believed that to be the best for everyone's safety. Once a month, however, we met up. Once every six months, depending on missions, I met with all my team leaders, often in Crete, where I owned another home. I had missed the last meetup and that sprang to mind. I needed to reorganise.

I had invested in property in places where I did the most business. Crete, however, was simply a holiday home. Nathan often questioned why I didn't visit my homeland, Spain, but after losing my wife there, it wasn't somewhere I wanted to live again. I still owned the charred remains and the land it sat on. The intent had been to build a bigger house, but we'd hadn't gotten around to it. Crete gave me the same feel as Spain. The same climate, food, the friendliness of the locals, and it was about the same distance away.

Time slipped away but periodically, I thought of Anna. I returned to the image I'd downloaded of her. I felt like I knew her through Nathan and my research, and now I could put a face to the stories. I could see the attraction.

Never before had Nathan and I liked the same woman. I had a feeling that was about to change. I wasn't sure what it was about her that had me intrigued but she did. I liked the *idea* of her. I think, I'd always liked the idea of her.

An independent woman with her own wealth, yet in need of a man. It was a heady combination and the more I sat there and read about her, the more I was up for the challenge.

Whatever the circumstances she found herself in, I was amused by her need of me, well, a Jacob anyway.

That afternoon I took a walk, I headed to my tailor and picked up a couple of new suits. I liked to walk around New York. It was full of individuals with no time for niceties. It suited me. I like to observe people, keep my skills in tune. I could pick out a threat from a mile away. Without it being a conscious decision, I found myself in the area I knew Anna to be. Nathan had detailed her schedule, as he always did, in our system. Every now and again, he'd instruct a covert operative to watch over her. And yet, he insisted he had no feelings for her? I'd chuckled at that.

I remember when he'd caught her ex cheating on her for

the second time, long before she did. He didn't want to be the one to break the news, so he made sure she'd find something of her sister's to confirm her suspicions. I wasn't for that kind of thing, I'd have told her outright, but for some reason he felt like he couldn't, and I wouldn't question that.

I had been busy with some personal chores when my phone rang. I smiled as I saw the number and took a seat on a nearby bench.

"Hello, Anna," I said. I didn't mean to put her on the back foot, but it was second nature for me to have the upper hand.

I invited her to dinner that evening, knowing her time in New York was short and said I'd send the details. I texted her the name of a restaurant I liked, and the time, and then I walked back to my apartment.

I spent the next few hours in front of my laptop, but my mind was on Anna.

———

I arrived at the restaurant before her, as was my way. I liked to choose where to sit before my guest so I could scan my environment better. It was another habit brought over from army days. When she arrived, she was everything I expected, and more. She was like a breath of fresh air. Despite my assumption of her confidence, she was nervous. She played with her napkin and chatted endlessly. She twisted a ring on her thumb, and nearly knocked a glass over by talking with her hands. But she was someone who I'd never met. Someone who didn't see my wealth, didn't know who I was, and fun. She seemed a lot of fun.

I hid the laughter when she told me what she wanted so as not to embarrass her. And not to give her any clues that I knew. Nathan and I often batted off awkward questions about our friendship, how we knew each other.

I was to play the role of a pretend boyfriend just to piss off her family and her ex. I readily agreed. It would be fun, I thought. And in the meantime, I'd get to spend more time with Anna.

She fascinated me, she said I intrigued her. There was an instant connection, and I believed she felt it as well. I needed to come up with some ideas to prolong our meeting, for sure. I could have listened to her voice for hours, stared at her face for days. I wanted more than just to take her to bed, although that idea was on my mind, and in my crotch, I wanted to get to know her better.

I ordered for us, knowing that there were some amazing dishes not listed on the menu, and it pleased me she allowed me to do that. I didn't want a submissive woman, but I was an old-fashioned man. I needed to take care of my dates, even if they often ended up as no more than one-night stands. We ate and chatted more. After a glass or two of wine, she started to relax. She flirted back with me, picking up on my suggestive comments and inuendo. I liked that about her. She wasn't afraid to banter. She'd lick her lips and her cheeks would flush. She'd look up under her eyelashes and from her, it wasn't stupid. I wasn't even sure most of it was deliberate. When she wanted to flirt back, she was very direct about it. It was the subtle signs that drew me closer to her. The scent of her arousal. The fidgeting in her seat.

When our meal was over and I'd helped her on with her coat, I brushed over her skin and noticed the goosebumps and slight shiver that followed. I smiled, and my cock twitched. Reading body language was a speciality of mine, and hers was screaming for me.

I walked her to a waiting taxi and asked her where to. I knew of course, Nathan had told me where she would be staying. Since I didn't want the evening to end, I asked her to join me for a drink.

The confusion started when we entered The Plaza. First, I was greeted by name, and I saw her frown at that. Then I met a couple of old lesbians who also had an apartment on the same floor as me. They were a fabulous couple, only God knew how old they were, but they'd been partners for over seventy years. I loved spending time with them, listening to their tales of sneaking about to stop from being arrested for being in love. They'd survived the war, fled Germany, worked in brothels, and eventually made a fortune in stocks and shares. They spoke many languages, one being Spanish, and liked to practice whenever they saw me. Despite it being a little rude, they launched into a grumble about the food in the restaurant that evening. I had a quick chat and asked their forgiveness as I was on a very rare date.

"Clients?" I heard, and then Anna laughed. I frowned, not understanding the reference at all.

Things got hotter when we entered the gin bar.

"Do you drink gin?" I asked. "I guess it's a little late to ask that, isn't it? I just imagine all Brits do."

"No, actually, but I'm willing to try anything."

I stared at her, and she held my gaze, challenging me. "Anything?"

She leaned forwards slightly. "Yes. Anything."

"Then let me guide the rest of your evening," I said, and my cock hardened in my trousers, painfully so. I hoped her version of anything was the same as mine.

Whether she verbalised it or not, she wanted to be close to me. I could see a pulse race in the side of her neck, and she wetted her lips. She wasn't the 'doe-eyed, bite the lower lip' type, what she did was unconscious, I believed. But, fuck me, it worked. I could feel my palms start to sweat. I wanted her.

I didn't just want to fuck her, I wanted to spend time with her. I got the attraction Nathan felt, and although I knew what I was doing was wrong, I didn't seem to be able to stop myself. I pushed all thoughts of my friend to the back of my mind, knowing how fucking shitty that was.

We had never competed for a woman before, but I knew that was all about to change.

I wanted to know about her ex, hating him already. She

was straightforward but there was an element of self-doubt, of blame, for their relationship ending. That pissed me off. I wanted her to learn that it wasn't her fault, she'd done nothing wrong. The ex was a fucking idiot to have messed around on Anna. The more I thought about that, the more I was up for the challenge of being her plus one. I began to hope it wouldn't just be the once, however.

We drank and she asked lots of questions, most of which I couldn't answer. I had a policy to be evasive to *randoms,* one-off dates as Nathan and I called them, normally, but there was a part of me that didn't want to do that with her. I did, of course, not really having any idea if I'd see her beyond the wedding. I also liked to listen to her voice. Her words, the sounds she made, washed over me and it was calming. For so many years there had been an uncomfortable fire in the pit of my stomach, a soul burning, and she seemed to douse those flames just by being near me.

I was very reluctant to let that go. When I wanted something, I got it, I took it. I intended to do that with Anna.

"Do you dance?" I asked. It was a random question that came out of the blue for her, but after a moment planning for me.

She was confused, of course.

"Dance?" she replied.

"Yes, dance. Do you?"

"Well, sort of. Why?"

I explained we'd have to dance at the wedding, it was

customary that, after the parents, the siblings joined the happy couple in their first dance. Well, it certainly was when I'd attended weddings, of course.

I took it a step further. "How do you like to be held?" I asked.

"Held?"

"Yes. I don't want you to tense every time I touch you." I shifted closer to her.

She held her arms by her side, opening herself to me. There was nothing *closed* about her, which I liked.

"Perhaps we should practice beforehand," she said, raising an eyebrow in challenge.

That was it, permission granted. I stood and held out my hand. She placed her drink on the table and took it. A shock coursed up my arm, I didn't need to look to see the hairs had stood on end. We walked in silence to the lift. It was then she asked me where I lived.

"Here," I said, leading her into the lift and pressing for the top floor.

I could smell her arousal in the confined space. I could hear her swallow as nerves started to kick in. She shifted from foot to foot and looked up at the illuminated numbers climbing higher as we ascended. I could have pushed her against the wall and kissed her, as clichéd as that was. I purposely looked anywhere other than her initially. She was too tempting.

I would dance with her, of course. I hoped that dance led to another kind. One where we were both naked.

I opened the door and let her walk in first. She hesitated and looked around. I could see her smile before she took a step forward, and I hoped it was because she felt safe. I had one moment where my heart sank a little. Anna stood in front of a photograph of a derelict building. It seemed to fascinate her. I watched her face, her brow furrowed as she cocked her head to one side. I knew she could *feel* that image. She was empathic, and she floored me a little when she also described it as tragic and sad. It was, had been. A tragedy occurred there; one I didn't want to dwell on.

"My childhood home," I said, and it had been once.

I had stood close behind her, wanting her to feel the heat radiating from my body, for hers to acknowledge my presence. It pleased me to see her lean back slightly. I could have so easily wrapped my arms around her then. She would have melted into me, but I took a step back, needing to be away from that image.

I walked to the sideboard and lowered a record on the player. Music wafted around the room.

"Practice," I said, walking back to her.

She laughed and nodded. "Practice dancing," she said. The thought that, once again she was on the back foot, not only amused but aroused me.

It was the push and pull that I loved. I wanted her desperate for me, as desperate as I was for her.

I deliberated about how close to have her, but then decided the obvious bulge in my trousers was going to be felt one way or another. I chuckled.

When she wanted to *practice* a kiss, I nearly came. She'd said it would be normal for us to kiss in front of her parents, so we ought to be okay with that. Of course, I knew it had nothing to do with her parents or practicing of any kind. I pulled her close, forgetting the dance.

She wrapped her arms around my neck, tugging at the hair curling over my collar, and my heart missed a beat. My stomach flipped, and I knew I had to claim her as mine. I kissed her as if she was the last person I would do so. I tasted her, I absorbed her. I crushed her to me, and she moaned. When she did, a pang of guilt smacked me straight in the chest. I slowed down, ending it with a kiss to the tip of her nose, not wanting to, but feeling that I had to.

She should be Nathan's. I should still be married. I wanted to growl in frustration and confliction. One minute I was all *damn the consequences* and the next, wracked with guilt.

The two thoughts collided in my head. I found it hard to reconcile them, to think rationally. My wife was dead, and Nathan kept insisting he wasn't in love with Anna, despite every inch of him screaming he was. Or had I got it wrong about them? Perhaps it was more a case of hoping I was wrong and since he hadn't confirmed, did that give me free rein?

But I couldn't let her go, I would not end our evening there.

I could see her take in a breath and steady herself. "My parents would definitely think we're a couple after that," she said, chuckling. Her eyes were bright, and her cheeks flushed.

"Do we need some kind of cue for our kiss?" I asked, wanting her to find one and then we could *practice* some more. I felt like a fucking teenager, one inching an arm along the back of a chair for a cuddle.

Anna suggested levels of kissing. I was happy to do that. Perhaps one after I would hand her a drink, she'd said. I smiled, knowing how I was going to keep her for a little longer. I headed to the kitchen and opened a bottle of champagne. It wasn't my favourite drink, and I was sure I'd been given the bottle as a gift one time. I popped the cork and poured two glasses.

Before I handed her a glass, I lowered my face to her cheek. I inhaled her scent before kissing her heated skin. It pleased me to see the effect I had on her. If only she could see what she did to me as well.

I needed some fresh air, the atmosphere in the room was charged and heady. And if I didn't take a minute to refocus, I would have ripped the clothes from her body and fucked her on the floor. And then probably embarrass myself by coming way too quick. I opened the curtains and French doors and then stepped out onto the balcony. She followed me.

The charged atmosphere also followed us. So much that I

needed to make a move. I asked her where we would be staying the evening before her sister's wedding and mentioned that it would be fun to stay at her parents'.

"Why would staying at my parents' be fun?" she snorted.

"Because when I make you scream all night, it will be kinda funny to see their reaction the following morning."

When her eyes widened and she spat her champagned all over me in shock, I thought I'd taken it a little too far. There was a pause of embarrassment from both of us, I felt. Anna didn't disappoint, however. She dropped the glass, shattering it across the balcony and straddled my lap. She took what she wanted, and I was happy to hand it to her.

I carried her inside and took my time with her. I could see how agonising it was for her, but she had no idea it was the same for me. If I'd done what I wanted, which was to throw her on the bed and fuck the life out of her, she might not have come back for more. And her coming back was what I needed.

I teased her, I tasted her. Her heady scent of arousal was intoxicating. My mouth watered at the thought of burying my tongue, fingers, and cock inside her. I wanted all of her, I wanted to give all of me to her, as well.

My heart pounded and my senses were on high alert. My vision narrowed so it was just her I saw. Just her I focused every ounce of energy I had on.

She was dangerous. In just the short time I had known her, I knew I was hooked. I'd want more, and I've had to reconcile my feelings in the morning. That night, she was all I needed. She was addictive, she quelled all the irrational feelings I'd had that night. She did what no other woman had ever been able to do.

She took my mind away from my nightmare and it was just about her and me. It was just about us and our scent and taste, our wants, and desires. It was just about satisfying two bodies who knew nothing about each other.

CHAPTER TWO

It was the following morning when things got weird. For some reason, Anna felt she had to pay me.

To say I was insulted was an understatement. She thought I was some kind of hooker!

I did my level best to conceal my shock. She was mortified, of course, and I was annoyed it had spoiled an amazing night. She rushed off with a promise to text over the details. I hoped she would, but I also needed a moment to get my head around how wrong the evening had been.

If she thought she was paying me for sex, did she feel nothing for me? Had I read her all wrong? Was I just a toy, a *random* for her? I didn't like how it left me feeling, and it certainly pulled me up short on my behaviour in the past. I felt used, and I didn't like that.

More so when her text never came.

I checked my phone constantly at first. Every day, a couple of times. I had two phones, one for personal use and one for business. The only calls or text messages I received on the personal phone were from Nathan, Philip, and, I hoped, Anna. I started to get angry. Not just at her, but how I'd let my guard down as well.

"Hey, mate, how's things?" I heard when I answered a call from Nathan.

"Good, I'm in Dubai. Thanks for checking the time zone," I replied sarcastically.

"What time is it?" he asked.

"Three in the fucking morning." I was a grumpy fucker when I wanted to be.

He laughed and I shuffled up the bed.

"So, how's things?" he asked again.

"Good, I've turned down two contracts and taken on one. I'll email all the details. I don't trust this guy out here. Slimy fucker if you ask me."

I was meeting a politician, James Harvey, the business secretary. He was very keen, overly keen, for us to work with a sultan and I wondered why.

"Too much of a kickback?" Nathan asked.

It wasn't usual for anyone, politicians included, to expect a 'matching fee.' Most times, we didn't play those games. We weren't struggling for work and if we didn't work at all, Nathan and I were wealthy enough not to.

"I think it's more than that. He looked very uncomfortable, as if he'd promised something he can't deliver. Anyway, I'm walking away from that one. But I also met with Odessa, they want another crew on a third ship."

Odessa was a shipping company that contracted our services on a regular basis to ensure they had safe passage and didn't lose either their cargo or staff to pirates. The Sudanese pirates were the worst, no fucking qualms about killing everyone on board a ship if their demands weren't met. It paid for businesses to invest in companies like mine rather than pay the ransom. None of them could get insurance anymore, so machine guns and armed men covered that.

"Have you heard from Anna?" he asked.

"Not a fucking thing. I'm surprised and disappointed. And annoyed. She played me, I don't like being played," I replied.

"She didn't, mate. Why don't you text her?"

"She didn't leave her number. Anyway, I don't play games. If she wants me to accompany her to this bloody wedding, then she needs to tell me the details."

"How old are you?"

"Old enough not to chase after women. She embarrassed herself, and me, she probably doesn't want to run the risk of that again. Leave it, Nate, it's fine." I hadn't had time to tell him all the details, there was also a part of me that didn't want to. I'd said enough about her, and I had to remember he liked her.

"It's not fine. She thinks you're ignoring her."

"Did she say that?" I asked, surprised. What the fuck did she think I was doing? I had no means of contacting her.

"Yep."

I wasn't sure if Nathan was just saying that to convince me to call her. I knew if I asked, he'd send me her number, but I didn't and wouldn't. If it was just the one night, then so be it. I was too busy to be chasing after her.

"Well, too busy, Nate, right now. I'll be the Jacob she wants for her wedding if she bothers to send me the details. Other than that, I'm heading home when I wake up."

"You are awake," he said, chuckling.

"When I get back to sleep and wake up again," I said, and then cut off the call.

I placed the phone by the side and laughed, remembering back to the days when we'd deliberately call each other when we knew the other had company. We'd simply say, "Does your phone do this?" and then cut the call off again. We were young, and it was funny at the time.

Once the deals were done in Dubai, I headed home. Home for me was Hampshire in England.

I'd arrived home late in the evening and, without unpacking, I headed to bed. I took a quick shower and climbed under the sheet. I had a duvet on top that was permanently folded back. I hated to have anything that restricted my movement, anything that was heavy on top of me. Although I made an exception if it was a female body, of course.

I had a strange feeling while I lay there trying to adjust to the time difference. Usually, the shorter the trip, the easier it was to adjust, and I had been in and out of Dubai pretty quick. But being in the same country as Anna, and only a couple of hours away, had me agitated. I slept for a little while and dreamt of her. I woke with a raging hard-on after an erotic dream.

One thing that annoyed me when being awake in the dead of the night was I had time to think. And I didn't like to think. My thoughts started about the house I was in and how it came about.

I remembered when I'd bought the land, it had been as a surprise for my wife. I knew she hated being in Spain. She was isolated and unhappy. She wanted back with her brother, her twin. I'd told Nathan what I intended, and it was meant to be a third anniversary surprise. The land already had a substantial house, but it wasn't the house of her, or my, dreams. The land already had planning permission for a second house, which I started to have built. When it was done, I bulldozed down the original.

The plan was to come back to the UK for a holiday and I'd carry her over the threshold of our new home.

She never got to return, and she never saw the house.

It had been so many years ago, I struggled to remember key details about her. Her scent, for example. I was reminded of what she looked like when I saw Nathan, but not the small details. The things that set her apart.

I shook my head to rid myself of all memories. For me,

once I woke, there wasn't much point in languishing in bed. I got too annoyed. I showered and threw on some sweatpants and a T-shirt. I walked downstairs with just the dimmed hall lights to guide me and into the kitchen. Once I'd made a coffee, I headed to my office.

My office was a secure environment. It contained a lot of sensitive information, and I'd installed a safe room should it be required. Thankfully, I'd never had to make use of the safe room. I opened my laptop and fired up my monitors. I watched the stock market, happy that my broker was working well for me. I scanned the CCTV, nothing flagged up other than the odd fox crossing the lawn. I then set about to work. Working through the night was often beneficial because I could catch up with my teams easier. It seemed there was a couple of hours when all the clocks seemed to align, and everyone was around at the same time. I brought each team leader up on a monitor and we chatted, laughed, and caught up on where they were in their contracts.

I heard Sadie, my housekeeper, come in and I glanced at my watch. I was surprised to see it was eight in the morning, and my stomach grumbled. I'd been working for four hours straight.

"Good morning, coffee?" she asked as I walked from my office.

"Something to eat would be lovely," I replied.

Most of the time I cooked for myself. I like to cook; it was something I found relaxing. But nothing beat a good old English breakfast made by Sadie.

"I'll get right on to that," she said, with a smile.

Sadie and her husband, Bill, had been with me from the time I settled in England. They had a bungalow on the grounds, free of rent and for the rest of their lives regardless of their time working for me. As well as a generous salary, for the rest of their lives. They were like family, as loyal and caring, if not more. They had one son, Philip, who also worked for me. He was my assistant and due to visit that day.

Nathan and I employed a work from home policy. We'd found it more productive, but more importantly, safer. Having a group of people in one place posed a high security risk, we felt. And other than Nathan, myself, and Philip, no one person knew everything we did.

"Philip is on his way," she added.

"Shall we wait for him before eating then?" I asked.

"I'll start to get it ready. I'll call you," she said, before heading off to the kitchen.

Sadie had been an accountant prior to retiring. But she got bored, and those skills came handy when managing my house. She dealt with all the bills, saving me money where she could, despite it not being necessary. She organised maintenance, decoration, everything. She made my life a heck of a lot easier, for sure.

She was also an amazing shot. In her youth, she should have been in the Olympics for shooting, but, being a girl, she could never get the funding. I'd been hunting with her and was amazed at her accuracy. Often, when bored, Nathan and I would challenge her at target practice. She always beat us, which pissed him off to no end. She was in her late sixties, a little under twenty years older than me, and energetic. It often amazed me how she kept going. She was on her feet most of the day. Time and time again, I'd tell her to sit, have a cup of tea, and she would for a few minutes but then get up and wipe imaginary dust.

"Ants in my pants, my dad used to say," she'd tell me.

I gave up trying to tell her what to do a long time ago.

I refreshed my coffee, made her and Bill a cup of strong 'builder's' tea, as they called it. I left hers at the sink and took one out to Bill.

"Oh, lovely, thanks, Son," he said.

He had always called me 'son,' and I liked that about him. There was no pretence with him. He'd been a builder all his life, a master stonemason in his prime. He had rough, calloused hands, and a happy face. I didn't think I'd ever heard him mad. Sadie could shout from one end of the estate to the other when she was riled, but Bill? Never a bad word from him. I liked being around him when I was agitated, he calmed me.

"You okay?" he asked, peering at me.

"Sure. No, not really. Got a minute?"

I found Bill was easy to talk to, more so than Nathan, who

always had an answer. There were times I just wanted to vent without an opinion on what I was doing wrong.

"I met someone in New York, she's English. Anyway, I felt something for her."

"And you don't like that?" he said, knowing about my wife.

"I felt guilty, and I know that's irrational. She hasn't contacted me, and Nathan is pushing me to call her."

"What do you want to do?"

"I want to contact her."

"Then you'll find a way to do that," he said, and smiled at me. "Take your time."

He patted my shoulder, his advice given, and went back to repairing the terrace wall.

A man of few words, but they were always thoughtful and wise.

"Ah, there you are. Hello, Pops," I heard. Philip had arrived. "Mother has grub."

We walked to the snug where Sadie had laid out breakfast. Philip and I ate, and then we headed to the office to work.

It was a few weeks later that I found the way to contact Anna and I smiled. It was probably something Bill would have done.

———

I didn't remember the last time I wrote a letter, in fact, I wasn't sure I ever had. I'd sent cards, but never sat down and wrote.

Nathan had been nagging me to contact Anna. He'd told me she wasn't right, sad, and unhappy, that she needed me. He never elaborated, even when pushed. I often retorted with, "If she's so unhappy, why doesn't she call me?" and he'd sigh and tell me to grow up.

I opened the newspaper to see an article about a model acting up. I rarely read newspapers, but the headline caught my attention. They mentioned Anna's agency. I saw a picture of her, and she looked unwell. Her cheeks were sunken, hollow. She looked poorly and instantly I felt a pull to her.

I penned a very short letter to her at her company address. I wrote three versions, screwing the first two up. What I signed and placed into an envelope might be seen as curt and 'professional', but I wasn't about to show my hand only to be spurned a second time.

Anna,

As you haven't texted, and I felt it intrusive to ask Nathan for your number – I don't want to assume you want to hear from me – I did the old-fashioned thing and wrote you a letter.

I'm in London for a month from end of June. I have no idea of your sister's wedding date, but I'd like to still offer my services as your plus one, assuming you're still attending.

You'll see my mobile number above, perhaps you could just confirm if you need me or not. It's perfectly okay if it's a 'not,' but I do like to have my diary arranged.

Jacob.

I sealed the envelope and then wondered where on earth I'd get a stamp.

"Sadie, I have a letter to send," I said, walking into the kitchen.

"Put it with the rest," she replied, waving to a pile of mail in the corner. I left it on the top. "When are you away next?" she asked. "There is some confusion in your diary."

"Confusion?" I asked.

"Yes, you're in London and New York at the same time."

"Oh, am I? I didn't realise. I'll have a look," I said.

I managed my own diary online, but Nathan and Philip, plus Sadie, had access to it. I didn't recall adding a New York appointment.

When I looked, I saw that Nathan had added it. I called him.

"What's this New York appointment?" I asked.

"And a good morning to you, as well," he replied.

"Have you ever wished me the same?" I chuckled as I spoke. "Anyway, enough being the nag, what's this appointment?"

"I thought you might like to block a couple of days out. I think Anna was meant to be in New York then as well."

"She's meant to be at her sister's wedding, or is she running away now?"

He laughed. "She might have to be in New York as an excuse not to attend the wedding, since she doesn't have the required plus one anymore."

I sighed. "Now who's being childish?"

He laughed some more. "Lowering myself to the age you like to live at, my friend. Now fucking call her or I'm going to intervene."

"You sound like it's urgent," I said, curious as to his tone. "Anyway, I wrote her a letter. It's going in the post today."

"Good man, finally, and thank fuck," he said, sounding relieved.

"What's the rush, Nathan?" I asked. Something wasn't right.

"All in good time. I'm out and about today, speak tomorrow," he said, cutting off the call.

Out and about meant he was with Anna.

I'd been surprised when he first took on the role to look out for her. He'd been asked by her friend to do so. It seemed Anna was being hassled by a photographer. We didn't do private security usually, but he'd met her friend while covering a team leader involved in royal security. I remembered him telling me there was something about her, and having met her myself, I got that. But he never made a move. He always denied how he felt about her. I knew why, I didn't get that he would deny himself. He fucked around. He had women throwing themselves at him. It used to irritate me, it had been that way since we were seventeen, and perhaps I'd been a little jealous. The girls hadn't liked me as much because I was always sullen looking. I had anger issues back then. He had all the charm.

I stared at the phone for a moment, only being interrupted as Sadie called out she was off to the post office.

I wasn't going to sit around, however. I wasn't a workaholic, but I enjoyed what I did. I also knew that time out was required for a clear head. Having spent many years in the military, I cherished the time spent at home. My time out, however, seemed to be consumed by Anna. If she responded to my letter to tell me my services were no longer required, then I could move on. It was the being in limbo that pissed me off.

I didn't have to wait long.

The following day, I was in my car heading to London when she called. Her name came up on the dashboard as my phone's Bluetooth connected to the car.

"Anna," I said, when I answered.

"How do you know it's me," she asked.

"Because you're the only one who has this number, other than Nathan, and his name would show. It's good to hear from you."

"I owe you an apology, Jacob," she said and then paused as if she didn't know how to proceed. I could hear the nerves in her voice causing her to stutter a little.

"You do," I said, and then mentally cursed myself. "How about you offer that apology over dinner?" I asked by means of a recovery.

"Okay."

"Have Nathan bring you to my house, say seven o'clock?" I said.

"Okay," she said, again.

I paused and then took in a breath and exhaled slowly, trying to calm my nerves and excitement. "I'm glad you called; I didn't think you would."

"I did text, you didn't answer and then—"

"Tell me this evening." I cut off the call, knowing it probably came across as rude and spun the car around. "Yes," I said, punching the air.

I made another call. "Sadie, can you give Marcus a call and ask him to cook tonight?" I said, when she answered.

"Of course, I can cook if you want," she replied.

"No, you're out tonight, aren't you? I have a guest. Tell him I'll text over a menu later."

"Off to a play, but it's nothing I can't rearrange."

"Honestly, it's fine. Marcus can cook."

She promised she'd call him. He wasn't a permanent member of the *house team* as I called them but came and went when needed. He worked in the local pub as well and was an amazing chef. I'd bought the pub simply so I could put him in the kitchen. I wouldn't ask him on a busy night, but I knew that evening was always a slow one. He would leave his assistant in charge, as he'd often done in the past.

The second call I made was to James. "Hey, mate, Nathan will be bringing a guest over tonight, can you pick them up at Biggin Hill?"

"Sure, want to send me times so I can file a plan?"

James flew helicopters. In fact, he could fly almost anything except a commercial airliner. When we weren't on airborne reconnaissance, his main role for my company, he would fly my helicopter for me. It had been Nathan's idea to get the helicopter. We spent so many hours on the road and that was money lost, he believed. Flying back and forth from the UK to Europe and around the UK was way quicker and much more convenient. It wasn't cheap, however, and I'd wince at the annual fuel bill, but convenience cost money, I was constantly told.

I had planned on heading into London for no real reason. There were a few restaurants I liked, and I knew I could call on any number of women to accompany me at short notice. A small part of my mind, however, kept telling me I was doing it to be closer to her. She didn't look well in the photograph I'd seen. That bothered me. I didn't like to see her not vibrant or laughing.

"For Christ's sake, Jacob, will you get out of the kitchen? I know how to cook, you know," Marcus grumbled after I'd checked on him for the tenth time. "Go get a glass of wine. You need to unwind, my friend, you'll scare her off."

"I didn't think I was wound up," I replied, knowing what he said to be true.

"Like a fucking spring. Sod off, I've got this," he replied, waving a spatula at me.

I walked into the snug and set the table. It was a small room off the kitchen and the entrance to the terrace. It was the most used room in the house. I ate there, sat, and read, drank my morning coffee while looking out over the lawn and woodland beyond, and used it as an area to just be.

I set the table for two and then headed to the wine cellar. The basement cellar was cool, climate-controlled and accessed through a glass trap door in the hallway. People walked over the glass hatch without even noticing the staircase beneath it. Wine was an indulgence of mine. I had many bottles that were sitting gathering dust and increasing in value massively. At one end was a glass room for the white and champagne, rosé, and blush. I enjoyed a cold Chablis with fish and selected a bottle of my favourite from Portugal.

I took two bottles back up and placed them in the fridge in the kitchen before scuttling off again. I headed upstairs for a shower.

As I stood under the cool jets of water, my mind wandered to Anna. We'd had unprotected sex that first time. Usually, I'd make sure I was protected, but desire had overtaken rational thinking. When I stepped from the shower, I made sure to grab some condoms from the bathroom cabinet. I'd leave them beside the bed, *just in case*. I hated wearing the things, much preferring to feel her around my cock, to have her wetness coat my skin. The more I thought, the more aroused I became. I sat on the end of the bed and held my cock in my hand. I watched myself in the mirror as I slid my hand up and down, seeing what she might see. I closed my eyes, however, it wasn't me I wanted to see but her. I brought her image to my mind, I could smell her, taste her even, and my mouth watered as I pumped harder and faster.

When I came, it was her name I breathed out.

I was unusually nervous about the evening. More when I got a text message that they had left. It would take under an hour from Biggin Hill to Hampshire and perhaps I was showing off a little in sending James. Nathan could have quite easily driven but I didn't want a quick getaway. If I could persuade her to stay the night, I'd be happy. Of course, it hadn't occurred to me she wouldn't have clean clothes or toiletries. I took a second quick shower to clean up and then dressed.

James sent a message they were a couple of minutes away, and I headed outside. I liked to walk across the cool tiled terrace and then the grass barefoot. It reminded me of days as a child, always barefoot in the dirt, and it grounded me, literally.

I watched the sky. When I saw the helicopter, I backed a safe distance away and waited until it had landed, and the blades had stopped spinning. All the time, she looked at me, even after James opened the door. It took a nudge from

Nathan to prompt her to move and I wasn't sure of her reluctance. I swallowed down the nerves as I took her hand to help her down.

"It's good to see you again, Anna," I said.

"I owe you an apology," she replied, and then smiled. "And it's more than good to see you again,"

I heard Nathan cough, and he looked over her shoulder at me. He gave me a wink then announced he'd be off. He'd spend the evening at the pub with James, no doubt reliving wars and old times, and then come back later, I imagined. He had a key and his own room in the house. Although he owned an apartment in the same block as me in London, he was a nomad. He could never set down a permanent base anywhere and liked to camp wherever he was. Consequently, he had a closet of clothes at mine as well as his own.

Thankfully, he was at the other end of the house. If either of us brought a woman back, we wanted to make sure we didn't *bump* into each other. Two fifty-odd-year-olds living together never looked good in a woman's eyes.

Anna stumbled in her heels, so I picked her up. She laughed and it was a delightful sound. Like Bill, her voice calmed me. Unlike Bill's, hers affected me to the core. She gripped the back of my shirt, bunching it in her fist as I carried her to the terrace.

"You smell nice," she said, her voice ghosting over my neck.

I turned my head slightly, so her face was at my cheek.

"And you smell edible," I told her truthfully. I felt her shiver in my arms and I smiled.

I led her into the house with the intention of showing her around. She came to stand in front of a collection of images on the wall. I'd arranged photographs of my childhood home in Spain in a square around one of the house we stood in. It was my daily affirmation of how far I'd come through sheer will and hard work, and a reminder never to forget that. Of course, the home ended up a pile of charred debris in the last image. Again, a reminder never to take anything, or anyone, for granted.

"My childhood home," I said.

"You told me in New York. You said it was...tragic," she replied.

"I'll take you there one day." I wasn't sure why I offered that.

It was bare charred land now, the burned down house having been removed many years ago. Ironically, nothing grew in its place. The fire had been so fierce that it remained a dark patch of earth. I couldn't bring myself to sell it, however. The land had become my wife's grave. And my child's. She had been pregnant at the time of her death. The fire had burned so ferociously, there wasn't a body left to bury. A small plaque was attached to a tree, a tiny indication my wife and child lay there. I'd never been able to do anything more. Not even for Nathan, who had no resting place to visit and mourn his sister.

I needed to move away so I offered her a glass of wine. I didn't want the past to cloud my evening. We arrived at the kitchen, and I introduced her to Marcus. I finally brought up the subject of her silence.

"I'm happy you responded to my letter, Anna. I wasn't sure you would."

She took a deep breath in. I hadn't wanted to make her feel uncomfortable but felt it needed to be said, to get it out of the way, I guessed.

"I texted you, the following day, after..." she started and then paused. She looked from me to Marcus, who had his back to us. "I thought I'd offended you more than you'd said. I didn't realise until I showed Nathan and he compared the number I'd used to the real one," she babbled as I poured the wine.

"So when you didn't hear back from me, you left it at that?" I asked.

She didn't reply immediately. "Yes. Wouldn't you have?" she asked defensively.

"No. I would have texted again." I smiled as I placed the wine in front of her and took the seat beside her. "Marcus has prepared a nice meal for us. I hope you'll like it."

"I'm sure I will, let's hope I don't have any food allergies," she said in a rather brusque tone of voice. I guessed she was a little annoyed at my earlier comment.

To diffuse, I raised my glass, encouraging her to do the same. Just before I took a sip, I said, "I checked with Nathan."

"Can we start again? Without the escort references?" she asked.

"I'd like that. I also recall that I still have some homework to do. I'm looking forward to meeting your family." I smirked. "Assuming that's still going ahead, of course."

That was it, from then we were back to *normal*. No awkwardness, no pauses, or sighs, just chat and laughter. We talked about getting a background story together, how we met, when, how often we dated, and where. I committed everything to memory, knowing I'd be able to recall it when necessary. It was nice to see her laugh, and to see the spark return to her eyes. However, I had noticed the pallor of her skin beneath her makeup. No amount of concealer had covered the dark circles around her eyes.

Marcus informed me dinner was ready, and I led her to the snug. I wanted an intimate area, and I never used the formal dining room. I didn't invite people to my house often enough to have a use for it, and I had a plan to use the room for something else.

Although Anna ate her starters, a dish of fresh asparagus from a local farm coated in parmesan cheese, she seemed to struggle with her main. Marcus had prepared a chicken dish with a cream sauce, and although it looked heavy, it was in fact a light sauce and a favourite of mine. She pushed her food around her plate, citing fullness as an excuse to leave it. She poured herself some water and I watched her gulp it down.

When Anna asked me about my business, I avoided a direct answer. I didn't want to talk *shop*. I wanted it to be about her, the up-and-coming wedding. I was never comfortable talking about myself, in case I had to mention my wife. Most women thought they needed to take pity on me at that point, and I hated it.

I scooted my chair closer to hers. "I want to talk about you, Anna." It hadn't been a conscious decision to lower the tone of my voice, it was pure lust showing through and I knew she'd felt the same as well. I saw her pupils dilate.

"I gathered that, but it feels a little one-sided," she replied.

So, I told her. She seemed a little surprised, I guessed talking to a man who 'rented out' private armies wasn't your everyday kind of business. Then she became fascinated. Something clicked in her brain, she'd connected me to Nathan at that point. She'd only said his name, but she'd cocked her head to one side and narrowed her eyes. She pursed her lips as if she'd just discovered a secret. Nathan and I rarely told anyone how we met, or even that we were best friends. It didn't pay for the enemy to know too much, it made us vulnerable and that, I guessed, just followed us into our personal lives as well. Neither of us had family, so if someone wanted to get to one of us, it could easily be through the other.

"His story is his to tell," I'd said firmly. I didn't want to go into what we'd done together. It was an unwritten rule among servicemen. Acknowledge a connection, leave it there. We'd gone through too much shit to accurately tell another's story.

I couldn't remember what I'd said next, but something affected her. Her hand flew to her stomach, and she paled significantly. Her cheeks flamed. I placed the back of my hand against her skin.

"You're glowing," I whispered.

"I'm hot," she replied.

"For me?"

"Yes."

Anna stood from her seat and pushed herself between my legs. I placed my hands on her arse, sliding them up and under her shirt. Her skin goose-bumped at my touch, and I could feel my cock twitch with a need to be held. I leaned forward and kissed the smooth skin of her stomach, feeling her muscles contract beneath my lips. I kissed again, running my lips across her. She moaned with pleasure.

The sound spurred me on, I kissed farther and farther up until I had bunched her shirt around her chest. I pulled down her bra, freeing a nipple and closing my lips around the hardened bud. She moaned again and her fingers tightened on my shoulders.

Then she took a step back. Her eyes were wide in surprise at something.

"Anna?" I asked, concerned.

"I need the bathroom," she said, and started to look from side to side.

"Urgently?" I asked stupidly. Obviously, it was urgent.

I took her hand and led her back to the hallway and the toilet. I waited outside while she locked the door behind her. I hoped it hadn't been the meal that had upset her. It would be awful if she felt she had to leave. I heard her mumble.

"Anna, are you okay?" I called out. I was worried, and since I hadn't heard the toilet flush, I was concerned about what she was doing in there.

I breathed a sigh of relief when I heard water gurgle and then the tap turn on. She opened the door a moment later. I stepped towards her, cupping her cheeks in my hands.

"What happened there?" I asked.

"Would you believe that I desperately needed to pee, and I didn't think you'd appreciate me doing that over your lap." She smiled and shrugged her shoulders. "Although I under-stand there are some men that pay for that kind of thing," she added, then clamped a hand over her mouth.

I laughed, enjoying the unfiltered Anna I'd met in New York. Although I didn't believe her, I didn't question it. If she had a need to not tell me, then that was fine. For the moment.

"I'm sure there might be, but I'd appreciate if you didn't," I said, moving closer to her.

Once again, her pupils dilated and whether it was inten-tional or not, she wetted her lips.

She reached forwards and grabbed my shirt, pulling me to her. We stumbled and I steadied myself by placing my hands on the wall beside her head. I happened to also like the position of dominance I found myself in. She was *held* against the wall, unable to escape. Mine to do what I wanted with.

"You have no idea what you do to me," I whispered, staring at her.

Her *show me* was all the permission I needed. I slid my hands down the wall cupping her arse and lifting her, she wrapped her legs around my waist, and I told her to hold on. I walked us both upstairs as she nuzzled into my neck. I felt her tongue, her mouth, taste my skin and it caused a growl to leave my body. I fucking wanted her with such passion, I felt I was on fire. My fingertips tingled and my heart raced. I'd never felt that way before. The pull to her, the want, was overwhelming. So much so, I couldn't wait to get to the bedroom. I needed her there and then, exactly where we were.

A carnal rage took over me. I let her legs go and clawed at her clothes. I heard her trousers rip and she scrambled out of them, pushing her panties down as well. Her kiss was demanding, claiming me as much as I was doing to her. It was a competition, as such. Who could get the most. She would never win, for sure. I was more powerful, but she was giving it a go. She clawed at me, tugging my clothes to get to what she wanted. She needed me it seemed as desperately as I needed her. My vision blurred and it became just about being inside her. Nothing more, no foreplay, just being buried balls deep inside her soaking wet pussy.

I grabbed at her legs, lifting her again and pushing my

cock inside her. I paused, teasing until she demanded I fuck her. I slammed into her. I could feel heat and wetness around my cock, her muscles contracted sucking me in deeper. She demanded faster and harder, and I complied. I forced my body so close to her, holding her against the wall. It wasn't enough, though.

I lowered us to the carpeted floor and fucked her more. She had hooked her heels over my legs, and I parted them. In doing so, that gave me better access to her pussy. The scent was intoxicating, I could taste it, small beads hung in the air, and I'd breathed it in when I dragged in air. I wanted more. I needed to get lost inside her, to have all normal thought extracted from me. I wanted to revert to that Neanderthal man inside who took. I panted, forcing air through my nose, and gritted my teeth in an effort to control my need to come.

My heart pounded in my chest. She screamed out my name, tightening her grip on me, digging her nails into my skin. Every muscle became taut, the veins at the side of her neck were prominent as she arched her body off the floor. I came so hard my stomach ached. My cum pumped into her over and over. I wanted to curl in a ball, but I was held in place by her. It was delicious and painful at the same time. And all the way through, I wanted her again.

"Jesus, Anna," I said, finally pumping my last load into her.

She started to laugh. "God, I hurt," she said, finally opening her eyes to look at me.

"Same," I said, raising myself on shaking arms. I looked down at her torn clothes. "Your clothes are torn."

"So are yours," she replied, then we both laughed. It wasn't that what was said was overly funny, I think it was that last release of endorphins.

"I can't get enough of you," I confessed, resting my forehead on hers. She nodded in agreement. "Can we stay like this for a little longer?" I asked.

We laughed when she asked me how clean I wanted the floor. I liked her sass! I slid to the side and rested on my back, tucking my cock back inside my trousers. When I stood on shaky legs, I helped her to do the same. For the first time, she seemed a little shy. She was naked from the waist down and looked around for the rags that were once clothes. She had tried to cover herself and I laughed. I reminded her I'd seen her naked. I wanted to remind her I'd had my tongue, my fingers, my cock inside her pussy, there was no need to hide it from me. And I fully intended to have it again. But I thought that a little crass.

"I think I need a shower, and then some clothes to go home in," she said, and I hoped she wasn't serious about the going home part. At least not soon.

I led her to the bathroom and while she stripped to shower, I returned to the bedroom. I found the smallest pair of sweatpants I could, not recognising them as mine, but they were certainly men's, and laid them on the bed. I found a fitted T-shirt to add. The thought of her in my clothes aroused me again. I then joined her in the shower. I wasn't done with her yet.

She came again, and then, once I'd got her into my bed, once more. I didn't think she could get more beautiful, but as she came apart beneath me, on top of me, I fell in love. It surprised me, it pained me, but it had happened. I didn't believe in love at first sight, and I also didn't believe this was a *first sight* type of thing. I knew her, I'd learned of her years ago from Nathan. The connection I felt, the pull towards her, gave me an ache in my chest. There was no way I'd tell her that, it was too soon. And it was going to be way too complicated, I thought.

When she fell asleep, I watched her for hours. She belonged by my side in all her post fucking glory. She was sweaty, her hair stuck to her cheeks that were still flushed. She smelled of arousal and cum. Her body had tinges of red from scratches and bites, markings of ownership. I studied her fully, pulling the tangled sheet from her body. She was perfect to me, from the small scars I spotted, the blemishes around one nipple, and the birthmark on her inner thigh. Her lips were plumped from biting and her mascara had smudged around her eyes. Just the sight of her aroused me again. I should have woken her, but I didn't. I let her sleep and pleasured myself.

I finally fell asleep but only for a few hours.

Despite being so exhausted, I woke in the early hours. I missed her beside me. Perhaps, unconsciously, I'd heard her rise or hadn't heard her breathing. I pulled on a pair of shorts and headed downstairs, hoping she hadn't left.

I paused at the entrance to the kitchen, she sat with her back to me holding her phone. It illuminated her face. She wore my clothes and that pleased me. It was stupid, but it added another dimension to her being mine.

"Hey," I said gently. Although I hadn't wanted to scare her, I obviously did. She spat her water out.

"Jesus," she said, lifting the T-shirt to wipe her mouth. I glimpsed the smooth skin of her back and side.

I chuckled. "I didn't mean to scare you."

I walked over to the fridge and pulled out a bottle of water. "Here, the tap water isn't cold."

"Thank you. I woke and... I was thirsty."

"Disoriented as well, I bet?"

I took the stool beside her, swivelling until I faced her. I reached forward and tucked some hair behind her ear. I wanted to touch her.

"Did I wake you?" she asked.

"I missed your body beside me. I knew you were gone before I even woke. I just hoped you hadn't run for the hills," I replied, smiling.

"Why would you think that?" Confusion laced her voice, she squinted her eyes and frowned at me.

"We've met...what? Twice? And each time we've had the most unbelievable sex. Yet, you don't even know my full name."

She let out a laugh, and I was filled with relief. I thought my statement might make her think and back off. "You're right, on all counts. Although, you did give me your card, remember?"

"The name on that card is my first and a middle name. I don't share my surname often. No reason, other than most people can't pronounce it." I held out my hand. "Jacob Daniel Santiago-Domínguez." She closed her hand around mine.

"Anna Roberts, no middle name and very easy to pronounce. Why Jacob?" I frowned at her question. "It's not very Spanish."

I shrugged my shoulders. "No idea. Maybe after a relative I never knew. I'll celebrate my fifty-third birthday in September."

"That makes you twenty years older than me. Not that you look that old, of course." She fluffed through her words, and I laughed. It was one of those, *should I have said that*, moments.

"I should hope not. Does that bother you?"

"No, not at all." She stifled a yawn and I stood.

"Back to bed, I feel. We can talk more in the morning if you have nowhere to be." I hoped she didn't, I wanted to spend more time with her.

She stripped and climbed back into bed. I pulled the sheet over us and we, initially, lay on our sides looking at each other. She reached out and ran a finger down my nose, one that I'd broken many years ago in a bar fight. Of all the fights

I'd been in, of the danger I'd been exposed to, a bar brawl had been the only thing that had scarred my body. I wanted to suck her finger into my mouth when she traced my lips, but I saw her eyelids flutter. She was tired. I slid one arm under her neck and pulled her close. We fitted together perfectly, and I watched her quickly fall asleep. I could have stared at her for hours, and I was glad I had for as long as I did. When I drifted off to sleep myself, she was the only image in my mind.

CHAPTER THREE

I woke before Anna and slipped from the bed. Even showering and dressing hadn't stirred her. I kissed her forehead and she grumbled, frowning in sleep-anger. I chuckled as I left the room. I could hear Nathan downstairs; he was an early riser, regardless how long he'd been asleep. I knew it to be Nathan rather than Sadie because he was 'fucking helling' the coffee machine.

"Nate, just put your cup under and dial for what you want," I said, walking in.

"Just get a fucking kettle, will you?"

"There is one, it's called a hot tap. Not my fault you're still stuck in the eighties."

I took the cup from him and placed it on the tray. The digital display came up and I selected a black coffee. Once it poured, I handed it to him, taking a second cup from the rack above the machine.

"See, don't need a degree for this," I said, taunting him.

He grumbled an expletive. "Anna still asleep?" he asked, and it wasn't hard to detect a slight bitterness to his tone.

I nodded, and then turned to him with my coffee. "If it's a problem, believe me, I'll back off now," I said quietly. I knew we needed a proper conversation, but I didn't think I could bring myself to have it just then.

He stared at me, and then shook his head. "No, you're good. You can offer her way more than I can."

I frowned. "What do you mean by that?" I asked. It couldn't have been wealth, he had enough of his own.

"I... I don't know. I can't commit to her, and she'll need that."

"That's bullshit, Nathan. What aren't you telling me?"

He sighed and I knew there was something he was holding back. "She needs to tell you," he said quietly.

"Is it bad?" I pushed. I hated to have to wait for news.

"No, I don't think so, but it's for her to tell you." Finally, I understood what it must have felt like to tell Anna that Nathan's story was his to tell. Annoying and frustrating. I bit my lip so as not to demand more.

He shut me down, however, by picking up his phone. "Did you see this?" he asked, sliding it over to me.

I looked at a news report to see that James had been sacked. He'd been caught watching porn on his phone and an accusation from a male colleague had surfaced. It seemed he like the boys and had touched him up.

"What the fuck?" I said.

"Just came up on the news. Will it have any effect on us?"

"No, don't see why it should. Unless the silly fucker declared our payment," I said.

Nathan rolled his eyes. "Could become uncomfortable if we have to defend ourselves."

"Let's wait and see what happens."

If James Harvey had declared the payment we gave him, he would have lied about it, for sure. If he hadn't and it was discovered, sure, it would become *uncomfortable*. There had been times in the past where we'd been brought in front of parliamentary committees to defend ourselves. War and employing private armies was a dirty business, but a necessary one. There weren't the armed forces readily available in the UK for all the shit thrown at them. In all wars, the regular army was shored up by private individuals. It just wasn't spoken about and if the current government could throw us under a bus, they would. Our contract was signed by the previous one, and it would be way too expensive for them to get out of.

"We can erase all records anyway," I added.

Everyone was paid via various corporations dotted around the world. Money moved through loads of channels before landing in the recipient's bank. It could be traced, of course, but it was a lot of work to do so. It depended how determined they were as to whether they traced it back to us.

"So, Anna?" he said, smiling at me. Knowing him for as long as I did, I knew the smile was genuine, but it wasn't the largest he'd normally produce.

"Amazing. Why did it take this long to introduce us?" I asked, taking a seat at the breakfast bar.

He shrugged his shoulders and I wanted to take back the words. It took this long because he'd wanted her for himself. I knew that, he denied it, but something had changed now and waiting to know what it was wasn't my best trait.

"Don't fuck her about," he said, and that took me aback.

"I've never *fucked anyone about*," I replied, and I stared at him hard.

He broke the stare first and nodded.

There was no time to add any more, we both turned at the sound of footsteps across the hall to see Anna approach. My stomach knotted. Her hair was bunched on top of her head, her breasts filled the T-shirt, and it was clear she wasn't wearing a bra underneath. I wanted to kick Nathan, he stared at her too long for my liking.

The pants were too long, obviously, and she had them rolled over at her waist. What that achieved was to define her pussy and I knew she wasn't wearing any panties, either. If only we were alone...

"Afternoon," Nathan said, smiling at her.

"Shit, what's the time?" she asked.

"Nearly one, I didn't want to wake you," I said.

"Sadly, Boss, I did," Nathan said, then proceeded to show her a news report about one of her models.

I was pissed off he hadn't told me first. I could have warned her, prepared her. I stared at him. If he was going to play games, we'd fall out pretty quick.

Anna read the report, one of her models had gotten drunk then had a fight with her boyfriend, so it seemed. That wouldn't have been a problem, I guessed, had he not been a member of the royal family. It meant that she had to leave. I scowled at him; he winked back.

"Fuck off," I mouthed, and immediately smiled when Anna turned to me.

"I have to go," she said, and her voice was full of regret. Had she not been looking at me, I would have smirked to Nathan.

She stared at Nathan, as did I. He got the message and left us alone to say our goodbyes.

"I don't know where my clothes ended up," she said.

I pulled her into a hug and nuzzled her neck. "I like you in mine," I replied.

"If you keep on doing that I might not leave," she replied breathlessly. I did it some more.

Reluctantly, she pulled away. She asked after her shoes, and I told her they were by the front door. I'd joked that her clothes had probably been cleaned up by Sadie and she gasped. I laughed.

"I'm joking. They're in the bedroom. You can collect them another time."

"There'll be another time?" she asked quietly.

"I hope so," I replied, my voice a little unsure.

She laughed. "Listen to us, we're like a pair of teenagers!"

I made her promise to call me once she'd got to grips with her model and walked her to the door. When she bent to pick up her shoes, my sweatpants rode up her arse. I was envious of them. I chuckled to myself.

"Come back soon," I said, running my finger down the back of her neck. She shivered at my touch. I kissed her forehead.

I stood at the door watching her leave, and it was only when she was totally out of sight that I closed the door and headed back to the bedroom.

I picked up her torn garments and put them in the bin. There was no recovery for the trousers, I didn't think. I laughed, having never torn the clothes from a woman's body before.

———

It was late that night when Anna called. She told me about the model and her day, fielding press calls, and rebooking appointments. She sounded tired. I was going to propose that I drive up, take her for dinner, but instead I told her to get an early night. We'd catch up the following day.

I didn't sleep well that night. I tossed and turned and realised it was because the bed was too big without her. I reached out for the pillow she'd rested her head on and pulled it close. It smelled of her. I laughed, not believing myself. I was hugging a fucking pillow, inhaling her scent. I picked off a hair, pleased she'd left something of herself in my bed.

"Get a fucking grip," I said aloud.

I climbed from the bed and pulled on some shorts, then headed downstairs. It was a muggy evening, the daytime temperature had been in the mid-thirties, a rarity for the UK. I grabbed a cold bottle of water and walked outside. The grass was cool beneath my feet, having been watered from the underground sprinkler system. I sipped from the bottle as I walked to the pool. In the distance, I could see a light on in the gatehouse, as it had been called. Sadie or Bill were also struggling to sleep in the heat, I guessed.

I stripped off my shorts and placed the water on a rock, and then I waded into the cold water. I took in a sharp breath and then released it slowly as I acclimatised. It was a natural pool, part pond with fish and plants. The water was kept fresh by a filtration system and the planting around the edge. I dove under and swam the length, resurfacing only to take a breath. I was comfortable in the water, having spent many years scuba diving, initially in the military, and then for pleasure.

For me, there was no better feeling than swimming naked in cool water.

It also had the added effect of cooling my brain from thoughts of Anna.

I rested my back against a smooth edge, placed my arms along the ledge, and looked up. The moon was full, probably why I couldn't sleep. Full Moon Syndrome, it had been called. I laughed. I used to go off the rails when it was a full moon and that was an official army medic's diagnosis. The sky was clear, and I could see millions of stars. It reminded me of being abroad, where the light pollution was way less. Although I lived in the countryside in Hampshire, there were still lights from the nearest village visible in the distance. I continued to look up and wondered if we were the only planet occupied.

I was a deep thinker, sometimes too deep, according to Nathan. I thought of Anna and what our future held, if there was one. I'd met her twice, that's all, but in those two times I felt a real connection to her. I'd laugh at the love at first sight shit, normally. I didn't believe it was possible. Maybe as I aged, as my time on earth lessened, my feelings for someone became more pronounced quicker.

I chuckled. Could feelings become pronounced?

Whatever it was, it was happening. I missed her, longed for her even. I wanted to hear her voice, feel her body close to mine. Fuck knows how I'd cope if Nathan declared his hand. I knew I'd be the one who should step back, but I wasn't sure I could.

I swam some more, a couple of lengths before climbing

out and picking up my shorts. I walked naked back to the house. Traipsing water over the tiled floor, I crossed the hall and back up the stairs. The water had cooled my body significantly. I grabbed a towel to pat myself dry and climbed under the sheet. The swim had done the job, I guessed. I didn't remember falling asleep, only waking to a phone call the following morning.

"Did I wake you?" Philip asked.

"Yes, but I should have woken anyway."

"I think we have a slight problem. I'm proposing to be with you within the hour."

He was very precise, Philip, having been extremely well educated. He'd attended Sandhurst, passed out as an officer, and saw active service in Iraq. When his platoon was ambushed and he was captured, it totally fucked him up. He was tortured for days until his rescue.

When I'd got to the house he was being held in, I didn't recognise him. He had been chained to the floor like a dog and beaten. A headless body lay beside him. He'd witnessed that execution, knowing he would be next. Understanding he would be videoed and that played around the world as his head was sawn from his body, finished him where active service was concerned. It was no wonder that for months, a year, he fought and screamed like a madman. It was only when I intervened, having employed his parents at that point, that we got him in a hospital. He was there for another year before he was fit enough to leave. He'd worked for me ever since and, in all that time, only once had he relapsed. He was highly contained, tightly coiled, one day he would release that, I was sure, and I could only hope I'd be around to catch him again.

"Okay, see you then."

I texted Nathan. When Philip used words such as *slight problem* it usually meant more.

Philip says we have a *slight problem*. He'll be here in the hour. You out and about?

I waited for his reply.

Fuck, yeah. I'll try to get there but it won't be within the hour. Any ideas?

No. Don't rush. I'll let you know what it is later.

I strode to the bathroom and showered. Once dressed, I headed down. Hearing me, I was greeted with a cup of coffee from Sadie.

I kissed her cheek. "Exactly what I needed," I said. "Philip is on his way over."

Sadie and Bill knew what I did, knew Philip was my assistant, but that was all. They had no idea of any details. They also were never told exactly what Philip had gone through in Iraq, other than it was bad. So bad, they *lost* their son for a while. They would often say how grateful they were to me for rescuing him, and I wasn't comfortable with that. I was doing my job and I knew Philip. He was a fair officer, a likeable one who got his hands dirty with his men. I respected him, even if he was much younger than I was.

"Oh, lovely, I have some of his washing. I wish that boy would meet someone and settle down. I get fed up ironing his shirts."

"Sadie, he is more than capable of ironing his own shirts."

She chuckled. "If he did, he wouldn't need me as much, now, would he?"

I shook my head and laughed. "We all need you, Sadie," I said.

I took my coffee and headed to my office.

I saw Philip arrive on the CCTV and opened my office door ready for him. He strode in, rigid in his back, with his briefcase. He should have been born in the fifties, such was his manner. He wore a brown suit with matching coloured tie and brown brogues. His glasses were framed in tortoiseshell, and he carried a brown briefcase.

"It's a brown day, I see," I said, smiling at him.

"Huh?" Philip didn't get it.

"It's a brown day?" I waved my hand over his attire.

"It's called colour coordination. You should try it," he replied, waving his hand over my torn jeans, flip-flops, and scrunched up white T-shirt.

"It's dress down Friday, didn't you get the memo?"

He raised his eyebrows at me, rolled his eyes. "It's not Friday. Does my mother know I'm here?"

"She sure does, I imagine she'll be bursting in here any..."

In she came with a tray. "With coffee for her baby boy," I added.

Philip laughed and winked at me. "Thank you, Mother," he said, taking the tray from her. He kicked the door shut behind her.

I sighed. "Don't kick the fucking door."

"Chill. Now, as I said, we have a slight problem."

He placed the tray on a small table between two armchairs in front of an open fire. The fire wasn't lit, obviously, but it was a nice place to sit, less formal than my desk.

When Philip talked work, his demeanor changed. He became very businesslike. Back to the officer body stance.

"James Harvey has been sacked; this you know. There is going to be an investigation into *alleged* backhanders from the Saudis, they'll find some hefty payments to him."

"What are the payments for?" I asked.

"Arms contracts, mostly. Our wonderful government sells a lot of guns to the bad boys. Anyway, they are also likely to find a payment from Benedictine. I have taken the precaution of erasing all trace, but my man in the know says information is going to be leaked to the press, and they might add that payment to it since they have no idea who or what Benedictine is. The hope is, enough questions will be asked about it and the gutter press will try to solve the riddle."

"Can we stop that leak?"

"No, prearranged. You know how it is."

I did know how it was. It wasn't unusual for another

government department or official to leak information to speed up the demise of an individual. And by demise, sometimes it was exactly that. Where Harvey was concerned, I suspected they wanted to discredit him immediately, he had information that could embarrass the government. Although, it was pretty much public knowledge the government sold arms to the Saudi government, it wasn't pushed into the public eye. It was a little distasteful.

What I didn't want was any reference to Benedictine to be made public.

Benedictine was a company based in the Bahamas. It was a front, of course, and one of mine. There was an office, it wasn't manned. Money travelled through its bank account, most of which was untraceable, I hoped.

"And you're sure there is no trace back to us?" I asked.

"I can never be one hundred percent sure, as you know. But I believe we're safe."

"So what's the *slight problem?*"

"It appears that our man, James, was rather cute and recorded a statement on tape. Everything he knows, all the deals he's done for the government are on there. He doesn't mention us, he says, but the government will be looking for a scapegoat should that get out."

"Where is the tape?"

"I have no idea. That's the *slight problem.*"

I pursed my lips and nodded. "Mmm, I see. Yes, that's a problem."

"So, I'll leave that one with you. In the meantime, I have these contracts that need signing." He reached for his briefcase and took out a folder. Every section was separated with a coloured tab, and I flicked through signing where he'd placed a sticker. I trusted him implicitly. I had no need to read any of the contracts.

He sipped his coffee, wrinkling his nose at the strength. "You'd think, in forty years my mother would remember I don't like strong coffee."

"The machine is programmed that way," I said, pointing and without looking up.

He chuckled, and I carried on signing.

"I spoke to Nathan this morning," he said.

"So did I. What did you tell him?"

"Just what I've told you. He seems rather preoccupied at the moment."

"There's something on his mind that he's not telling me. I'm sure he will when he thinks the time is right."

Philip nodded and I handed back the signed folder to him.

"T10 is heading out to Mozambique tomorrow. All arrangements have been made," he said.

I nodded. T10 was heading out to help with the recovery of over one hundred girls and women who had been kidnapped by the militia. T10 was a crack unit of men and women who would move in undercover for recovery of people. Most times, they'd be there to deal with a kidnapped child of a wealthy parent. Occasionally, it would be on the request of a government.

"I'll leave you now. Perhaps you might like to get dressed," he said, standing and smoothing down the front of his jacket.

"I bet you sleep in silk pyjamas and a night cap, don't you?" I replied.

"Of course, one has standards, my dear man." His fake accent made me laugh. "Perhaps I could recommend a tailor."

I laughed and shook my head. "I have one, now fuck off," I said.

He gave me a salute in jest, even though he had been higher ranked than I had and left. I heard him calling Sadie. He'd spend a half hour with her and Bill before he headed back to London, I imagined.

I moved to my desk and pulled up all the information I had on James Harvey. We never did business with anyone without knowing every single skeleton in their cupboard. I had a piece of information and a photograph I knew he wouldn't want to be made public, that I was searching for. When I found it, I printed both off.

Perhaps Mr. Harvey needed to be reminded that he kept my company's name out of the press, always. I didn't care how he did it, either.

I stared at the image of him getting a blow job in a public toilet from a male prostitute, someone who looked a lot younger than they were.

"It was a pleasure doing business with you," I said, laughing and folding the papers.

Blackmail was part and parcel of my business to ensure the level of secrecy required. And we'd never been outed before. I had no intention of allowing the slimeball James to wreck that statistic.

I checked some stocks and shares, satisfied I was still making money, and switched to my diary. I had nothing in for the next couple of days, so I texted Anna.

If you're free, how about dinner tomorrow or Sunday?

Oh, yes please. Tomorrow would be lovely; I could do with the distraction.

'Tomorrow' never came, however.

The following morning, I received a call to say that James Harvey wanted to meet me. I had to cancel my plans with Anna, although I hated to do so. Philip was right when he'd said meeting Harvey was a priority.

We met in a backstreet pub in London. I had Daniel, a member of my team, station himself at the bar long before James or myself arrived. He would continually scan the room for any security or threat.

"I'm glad you could come," Harvey said, sitting down.

"I hear you're in a little trouble," I replied, not offering to buy him a drink.

"It's a fucking stitch up. Anyway, I want to reassure you that any dealings we had can't be traced."

"I have no idea what you're talking about," I said. Not for one minute assuming he wasn't wired.

"You know, our deals." He winked and seemed to be vague.

"Sorry, James. We haven't had any deals. What's this all about?" I asked.

"I'm under investigation, I thought you could help. I need money."

"Why would you think I could help you? Are you asking me for a loan?" I asked.

He started to look very uncomfortable. "Mr. Harvey, I have no idea why you would come to me. We have never had business together; I know you only in the capacity of the Business Secretary and that you've been sacked for misconduct. I have no desire to be involved in whatever it is you intend to propose. And I have no intention of loaning you any money. I will leave you with this, however." I left the envelope with the photograph in it on the table.

I stood and glanced to Daniel. Daniel nodded and slid from his stool, we both walked from the pub.

"Did you get all that?" I asked.

"Yep, all recorded."

The following morning, Harvey went missing, so it was reported. It was assumed he'd left the country because of the pending investigation. It pissed me off I had missed my date with Anna for him. But I had achieved what I wanted, so I believed. I knew he hadn't 'gone missing.' He'd been taken into custody somewhere, placed in a house for his safety.

Anna and I rearranged, and then she had to cancel. It seemed we weren't destined to meet until the eve of the wedding.

CHAPTER FOUR

I was late to Anna's the evening prior to the wedding. I'd flown in from New York after an emergency meeting regarding the T10 team in Africa. It seemed not everything was going as planned out there. I landed at Heathrow and had Daniel meet me in the car. He had collected some clean clothes from Sadie and would drive me into London. What he'd also done was to bring a charger for my phone. It had died mid-route back to the UK. Obviously, there were charging pads in the car, but not for the brand of phone I used for Anna. I wasn't stupid enough to use a smartphone for business or her. I could hack one of those fuckers in seconds, as could lots of other people. I had a bog-standard analogue phone for calls. Daniel had use of my apartment and would collect us the following day. If I was to play a part, then I wanted to play full-on. Her family needed to see her chauffeur driven to the wedding.

I stood outside her house and called her as I finally got some battery charge.

"Hey, I've woken you, haven't I?" I said quietly, not wanting my voice to echo along the narrow street.

"Yes, but that's okay," she replied. Her sleep-fuelled voice sounded even sexier than normal.

"I'm outside. I'm so sorry to be this late. I'll explain if you still want to let me in."

"I'll be right down."

I heard her rush down the stairs and chuckled. She opened the door for me, and I smiled. She was holding up her pyjama bottoms.

"You look exhausted," she said, holding the door wide so I could come in.

"I had an emergency abroad. Literally, just flown home. Battery died, didn't have a charger," I said, holding my phone aloft with the charger attached. "Until just now," I added for clarification.

"Blimey. Nothing too serious, I hope?" she asked.

"Nothing that seeing you doesn't make better," I replied with a smile.

"Smooth, Jacob, very smooth," she said, closing the door behind us. "Do you want coffee?"

"No, I want sleep. We must look the super couple tomorrow."

I didn't want sleep, I wanted to get into her bedroom as quick as possible. Sleep was the last thing on my mind. My cock was already rigid in my trousers. As I followed her up the stairs, I adjusted myself to a more comfortable position.

When we entered her bedroom, I chuckled. I left my suit carrier on a chair and walked to her nightstand.

"Started without me?" I asked, picking up a vibrator. Her cheeks flamed but she squared her shoulders.

"Of course. We don't hang around for men anymore, you know?" she said, staring back at me.

"Did you come?" I asked, my voice had taken on a gravelly tone. She swallowed hard and her pupils dilated. It pleased me to know just the sound of my voice could affect her.

I took a step towards her, raising the vibrator to my lips. I poked out my tongue and tasted.

"You did," I said, answering my own question.

I wrapped an arm around her, holding her still, and slid the other down the front of her PJs. She was still wet. I swiped my fingers over her opening, coating them in her juices. I could feel her legs quiver and she closed her eyes. She dragged in a breath through her nose.

"So wet," I said, mumbling the words.

"I wasn't, but I am now," she replied, then told me her battery boyfriend didn't compare to me.

She pushed her PJs down and I lowered to my knees. I wanted to taste more of her. I buried my mouth in her pussy, licking and sucking on her swollen clitoris. I wanted to absorb all she could offer, to have her coat my lips and nose. I could have covered myself in her scent, it was that enticing.

Instead, I rose and stepped back. I slid off my trousers and pulled my shirt over my head. I wanted her on my cock. I stepped back and sat on the bed. She understood. When she straddled me, lowered herself onto my cock until I was buried so deep inside her, I felt like I was home. Her hot flesh surrounded my cock, tighter and tighter as she contracted her muscles. I held her hips, wanting to lose the T-shirt so I could watch her naked form ride me. She seemed way too preoccupied to remove it.

She dug her nails into my chest and my heart rate spiked. My breathing was laboured. I wanted the pain, to have her draw blood, to mark me as hers. She rode me harder, her muscles squeezing on every rise, I met her with my own thrusts halfway. The sounds of skin on skin spurred us on further. Moans, heavy breathing, and whispered names swirled around the room.

As I was about to come, I sat up and kissed her. I forced my tongue into her mouth, claiming it. I bit her lips as she moaned and came with me.

We lay for a little while, she rested on top of me, and we caught our breaths. I didn't think I could ever get enough of her, and it seemed she felt the same. I smiled, but then a thought hit me.

We hadn't done much but eat and have sex. "Is this just

about sex?" I asked. She hesitated. "I hope not," I added, forcing her answer.

"I hope not, too." It was the answer I wanted. I smiled at her and then asked for the bathroom.

I showered and when I returned, she was back in her PJ bottoms and under the covers. We held each other and slept.

———

I was woken by the smell of coffee and a dip in the bed. Anna had brought me a tray with coffee, cream, and sugar.

"Good morning, after all the sex we had, I still don't know how you take your coffee, so I made you a tray," she said, laughing.

"Black, strong, and lots of it," I replied, patting the bed beside me. "Come and sit for a minute."

She placed the tray on a unit and handed me the mug. I smelled it and sighed, then took a sip. "Other than you, this is my only drug."

"Other than me?" she asked, sitting beside me.

"I meant what I said in that I hope this isn't just about sex. I can't help but think about you all the time. You're very distracting," I said, chuckling.

"Sorry about that." She smirked at me.

"Is there anything you want to tell me?" I asked, shifting slightly so I could face her. I was hoping she'd say something along the same lines. However, she looked panicked. Her face had paled, and she blinked rapidly.

"Erm, I'm not sure. There is, but..." She paused.

Her smile slipped and I remembered what Nathan had said, about her needing to tell me something. My heart missed a beat and I hoped she wouldn't confess she had a month to live, or something similar. I didn't think I could deal with losing her. Since she didn't continue and had started to look very uncomfortable, I decided to push it aside.

"Later. I don't want to move into a relationship with secrets."

She nodded, and then finally smiled a little.

I kept my voice gentle and soft, although I didn't do 'waiting' very well. I knew she wasn't married, there was no husband or children about to be sprung on me. I decided to change the subject.

"Now, however, we need to blow the socks off your father, charm your mother, and destroy your ex and sister!"

Back to the play, and it immediately cheered her up.

Anna lowered herself to her knees and cupped my balls. Stroking my cock, she said, "I do owe you one."

I'd take that, but I filed her attempt at a distraction away for another time. If she didn't tell me soon, I'd have to bring the matter up. I wasn't going into a relationship until I knew whatever it was. I doubted it would change my feelings for her, in fact, that would be impossible. But it might reflect the kind of relationship we had. While she blew me, I wracked my brain trying to recall anything she might have said that would give me a clue.

I dressed and went downstairs, cursing the narrowness and pitch of the stairs. *Fuck knows how Victorians ran up and down those things,* I thought. Anna was just finishing up her makeup and gathering all the crap she needed in her bag. I waited for her to join me outside. Daniel had arrived with my car, and when she joined me, he held the rear door open for us. I patted him on the shoulder as she climbed in.

"Nice car," she said.

"I aim to fuck you in here one day," I told her. I'd never fucked anyone in a car before, but for some reason, I wanted her to be the first and in my favourite car.

Wide-eyed, she glanced at the driver. Her mouth opened in shock.

"He has earphones in," I said. He often listened to music in the car, his music, which I hated. And for that reason, he'd put earphones in.

"Why?"

"Why do I want to fuck you in this car?"

"No, why does he have earphones in?"

"So, he can't hear me." It was meant to be a joke, but she seemed to accept it so easily.

"Ah, okay. Why then to the other bit?"

"Because I love this car, and... And I want to." I very nearly slipped up and told her I loved her. I couldn't do that until I knew what her secret was. Or until I had resolved my feelings myself, considering it was so quick.

We stared at each other, her pink tongue ran over her lower lip and my cock hardened. She had to know the effect she had on me. I couldn't believe she wouldn't have.

"Then I can't wait," she replied.

I picked up her hand and kissed her knuckles.

We arrived at the church and standing to one side was, obviously, her mother. No one else would wear the outfit and hat she had on, next to her were the bridesmaids. I checked my watch to see if we were late. We weren't. Surely, they wouldn't normally arrive until all the guests were seated.

Game on, I thought.

"Are you ready for this?" I asked, smiling.

"No, can we go back home?" I was taken aback, she looked genuinely anxious.

"We can, if you want to." Daniel removed one earphone, waiting for instructions.

She sighed and swallowed hard. "No. Let's get this over with. Where did we meet?"

I laughed and we recapped our story. Daniel exited the vehicle on my side and opened the door. I slid out, nodded to the waiting party who peered into the car. I paused, looking around, then buttoned up my suit jacket and held out my hand to her. She exited so slowly and so perfectly, as if she'd done it a million times before. She looked up at me as she stood, we were close, I stared down to her.

"Anna!" her mother squealed, and her voice immediately grated on me. I flinched.

The mother rushed over, and I frowned. Her shoes appeared too large for her, or she had a strange gait. She didn't pick her feet up but dragged them across the gravel. Very odd. The sleeves of her dress were too long, covering half her hands. Whoever had dressed her needed shooting.

"Mother, I'd like you to meet Jacob. Jacob, this is my mother, Alma."

From the look on her mother's face, I knew that whatever it was Anna had said wasn't the right thing.

She turned to me, her thunderous look a little late to change into the fake smile. "It's a pleasure to finally meet you, Alma," I said, using the most seductive tone of voice I could. I stared intently at her and clasped my hand around hers. She melted in front of me. Inwardly, I was laughing.

She rambled on about not using that name and the more I stared at her, the redder she became. *Score one to Anna,* I thought, she'd used her mother's real name, one that her mother hated and rarely used. I intended to keep using it as well.

I like this game, I thought. Alma then tried to introduce me to the bridesmaids, one of whom was desperate to be introduced. She pushed her way to the front, bustling and jutting her breasts out of her ill-fitted dress. Mutton dressed as lamb sprung to mind.

It was strange. Perhaps the fashion gene had missed

everyone but Anna. There wasn't a shred of class among them. Their hair was sprayed to within an inch of its life. It couldn't move even if a tornado hit them. Their clothes were ill-fitting, didn't compliment their shapes or skin colouring at all. The makeup was *clownish*, as if they didn't wear makeup usually and had just copied a magazine without the knowledge of how to apply it. I never criticised women, usually, but these ones had hurt Anna and I wasn't going to see them again. When one of the bridesmaids leaned forwards to kiss my cheek, I backed up. I'd be covered in fake tan, I thought. I did lift my hand to point to her eye, though. Not even I could let her stand in front of the photographer with half an eyelash. I quickly looked at my jacket, hoping the other half wasn't crawling around on me. In the meantime, Alma constantly talked about how handsome the men were, how beautiful her daughter was, the other one. Not once did she actually ask after Anna at all. My blood was boiling. Forget why we were there, to show off to the ex, her whole family needed a wake-up call. Anna was perfect, she was beautiful and kind. How the fuck she could end up with a mother like that baffled me.

Alma was a walking, talking, perfect dictionary example of a narcissist.

The icing was when her mother complimented my car, and I told her it was Anna's. She blinked multiple times, having not spoken to her daughter since her initial greeting.

Anna smiled at her mother, in what I thought she believed was a very innocent way.

Her mother's mouth fell open. "Oh, well. You better get in. I'm sure there are a couple of seats reserved at the front with the family." It was said so dismissively that I bristled again.

She had taken hold of my hand again and I had to prise it from hers. I used my other hand to remove her fingers. She was sweaty. I retrieved a napkin from my pocket and wiped my hand with it. I took hold of Anna's hand, raised it to my lips and smiled at her.

"Shall we?" I said with a gesture towards the church.

She fell in step beside me, and I could hear her trying hard to contain her laughter.

As we walked through the door, I said a quick prayer. I wasn't overly religious, I had been born into a Catholic family and attended church as a youngster, but it was an old habit. Churches gave me peace, not from a religious point of view. They were often serene, calm, and cool. And in the heat of the Spanish sun, when I was a kid, it was a sanctuary from other kids or angry parents. The children from my village could always run to the church and by the time their parents found them, they felt they couldn't punish their children in such a place of worship. For me, when my mother caught me praying, she assumed I was asking for forgiveness for what-ever I'd done wrong that day. Instead of the slap to my arse I should have received, she'd tell me how proud she was I'd decided to chat to Jesus. I'd inwardly chuckle at her naivety.

It was noticeable how many people turned to look at us when we walked in, and their whispered echoes. Anna chose to dart into the first empty pew. I would have wanted her to walk to the very front and sit, but she was calling the shots.

I leaned down to her. "So, we've started the play now?" I asked, kissing her temple, and making sure to be slow about it so enough people saw.

"I guess so, but carry on doing that, I like it," she replied.

A woman staggered past clearly drunk, and I was amazed she didn't turn an ankle on impossibly high heels. Anna whispered that was the model she'd been dealing with. I thought I'd recognised her. She looked wretched. She had way more than just alcohol on her plate, I thought. Anna told me the prince had hit her, and I bristled. I didn't know the woman, but the one thing I hated was weak men who beat them.

Alma bustled down the aisle screeching the bride was here. I chuckled and shook my head. If there was ever someone who wanted to be centre of attention, it was clearly her. I felt Anna stiffen and I followed her gaze. The groom came into view. He looked about as wrung out as the model and most certainly didn't look like he wanted to be there. He didn't have a smile for anyone. But, for me, the best bit was when the bride came down the aisle and Anna laughed.

"That was my wedding dress," she said, covering her mouth to quell the sound.

I stared after the bride and noticed the sewn in panel at the side, the colour was slightly different to the rest of the material. The dress clearly didn't fit her.

"Your dress?" I asked.

"Yes. It's been at my parents' since I'd kicked him out. I never bothered to collect it."

I did my level best not to laugh as well. She waddled in white high heels, hugely pregnant, and looked about to drop her baby in the church. She had the audacity to curtsey to the Virgin Mary and cross herself. I highly doubted the woman had ever set foot in a church before. If she had, and was religious, she ought to be in the confessional, not at the altar, pregnant before marriage.

We sat through the service and held in more laughter when the wedding ring was dropped. I felt a little like I was watching a comedy. I expected the bride to hit him with her flowers, or her mum. She was fuming! When it came time to sing a hymn, I picked up the order of service. It wasn't a hymn that they'd chosen but a fucking Britney Spears song. I stared at Anna, who returned my stare and was wide-eyed. She bit down hard on her lip to not laugh aloud, and tears ran down her cheeks. I dabbed at them, not wanting her makeup to spoil.

It was a farce, a comedy sketch, and I looked around for cameras.

Not once did the groom look at the bride, even when they exchanged vows. He kept his gaze firmly over her shoulder and when I followed it, a tearful bridesmaid was staring back at him. I guessed his bride wasn't holding his attention so much, anymore.

We filed out of the church once the not-so-happy couple had made their exit and then stood to one side. Only one person came over, the best man, I guessed, since he was dressed the same as the groom.

"So, Anna's new boyfriend, huh?" he slurred his words, and the stench of stale alcohol was rather overwhelming. I took a step back.

"Yes, although I think the term 'boyfriend' is a little juvenile, don't you?" I held out my hand. "And you are?"

He stumbled through who he was and announced proudly he was hungover, as was the groom. I guessed that accounted for some of his lack of enthusiasm, although, I thought it extremely disrespectful to his guests, let alone his intended wife.

We stood for one photograph before heading back to the car. Daniel was beside the car with the door open ready for us, but before he could get in, the model arrived. She smelled about as bad as the best man, and I saw Anna look into her open bag. A silver hip flask sat on the top of her purse. The sadness that radiated from Anna hit me. I closed in and placed my hand on her back.

"Well, that was odd," Anna said as we climbed into the car.

"She looks very troubled," I replied, and I caught Daniel's eye in the rear-view mirror. He gave a very subtle nod.

I hadn't liked the way the model shifted from foot to foot. She was nervous and it wasn't just alcohol. Her body language screamed alert to me and Daniel. It wouldn't take him long to look into her background and see if there was any threat to Anna there.

The wedding meal was being held at the most god-awful venue, a mock Tudor building that was nothing more than a working men's club. I had nothing against those types of clubs, of course, but it seemed cheap and shabby. The carpet was heavily stained and sticky. We walked over to the table plan, and I picked up two glasses of water from the table. The champagne looked flat and warm.

As Anna scanned the table plan, I saw her father walked towards us. He had a broad smile, and his arms were outstretched. He called her name.

"Ah, the elusive boyfriend," he said, chuckling. "We didn't believe you existed."

"Oh, I'm real all right," I replied, and shook his hand.

"They want us to sit down so your sister can make her entrance," he said, smiling at Anna.

"We won't be, I'm afraid. It appears we don't have a place to sit," Anna replied.

"Huh?" Her father seemed extremely confused.

I didn't comment, but just looked at Anna while her

father stepped over to the plan. "That's not right. I know you were on there. Your sister fitted you…"

"Fitted us in?" Anna asked when her father didn't finish his sentence.

"No, you know what I mean. She wasn't sure you were coming, and she'd made these plans a long time ago."

"Before or after she had yet another affair with a taken man?" The bitter tone in Anna's voice was obvious. She tried to hide it, particularly from me. She glanced over to me and then back to her father.

It was time for a recovery. "Darling, it's perfectly okay. You thought this would happen, so I've reserved us a table at Albarello's," I said.

"No one can get a table there," I heard. Anna's sister came up behind us. She had a nasally tone, one that would irritate easily. "Dad, you need to sit down." She spat the words, clearly annoyed she hadn't made a grand entrance.

"Hi, Aimee. I'm never refused," I said. "Lovely dress and thank you for inviting us both. It was a… nice service." I made sure to add a look up and down. I wanted to chuckle, feeling like a teenager.

"I didn't get your RSVP in time," she said, as if that excuse was an explanation.

"What's going on?" Alma said, bustling over. "People are looking!" She was another that hissed out her words.

"Just wondering why Anna and Jacob aren't on the seating plan," Anna's dad explained.

Alma waved her hand. "Can we talk about this later?"

"Of course, Alma. No need to make a fuss about something so trivial," I said. I wrapped my arm around Anna's waist and kissed her temple.

"It's Freya!" She hissed back and looked around.

I dipped my head in apology. Harry sidled up to join the *party*. "Can we just fucking sit down already?" he said.

"Anna and I were just leaving," I replied. "Shall we, darling?" I held out my arm to lead the way. I had no idea just how awful her family was, until the next words hit my ears.

"Congrats on the baby," Aimee said, spite and spit leaving her mouth.

"What baby?" Alma asked.

"Oh, Anna's pregnant. You're going to get two grandchildren this year, Mum." Anna stared at her, her face frozen with shock. "Jules told me." She then looked up at me. "You did know, didn't you?"

Without missing a beat, I replied, not wanting for one minute for her to have any kind of upper hand. "Of course I knew, Aimee. It was a delightful surprise. We agreed not to spoil your day and leave our announcement until another time. Did you think I didn't know?" I asked.

"Shame you won't both be at St. Mildred's at the same time," the father said, obviously not getting what was going on at all.

I shook my head at his utter stupidity. Alma looked shocked and Aimee, having not received the desired response,

I guessed, looked close to tears. I smiled at them all, squeezing Anna to pull her back to the present.

"Anna will be at The Portland Hospital. Only the best for my girl. Now, we really must go, I don't like the thought that Anna may be hungry, and we could do with something a little nicer to drink than tap water. You never know how healthy that is in these cheap places, know what I mean?" I said, smiling at her father. He returned the smile, still clueless.

I didn't give a fuck who I offended at that point. I took Anna's hand and led her from the room. I couldn't speak, I'd clamped my jaw so tight, my fucking teeth ached.

I should have known. How the fuck had I missed that? It was obvious when I thought about it. She'd had a slight rounding of her stomach, something she didn't have before. Her breasts were enlarged, her nipples darkened. She often covered her stomach with a floaty top, keeping half dressed. The rushing off to the bathroom that time.

"Fuck!" I whispered.

I wrenched open the car door and she slid in silently. I closed the door and then walked to the other side. I needed to take a deep breath. I needed to compose myself. Daniel looked over the roof of the car to me and I nodded to him.

"Alberello's" I said, knowing I needed to be in a public place with her.

I climbed into the car, my mind in a whirl. I hadn't planned on children, my life in the armed forces wasn't conducive to being a family man. And then, when my wife was killed, I vowed never to replace the child she was carrying. Ever.

"What hideous fucking people," I said, needing to say something as I took my seat.

"I'm so sorry. I... I didn't want... I don't know what to say," she blurted out. The pain in her voice stabbed me in my chest.

I turned to her and held up my hands. "Say nothing at the moment, other than clarify that the child is mine?" I did my hardest to keep any kind of emotion from my voice. I imagined that was hard with a jaw so rigid as I tried to contain my emotions.

"Of course the child is yours," she replied. She frowned as if I'd just asked the dumbest question ever. I supposed it was. Her voice had hitched, part in anger, I guessed, that I'd asked that, and part in dismay.

"Yes, I'm sorry. I shouldn't have asked," I said. Despite not knowing her really, I didn't believe for one minute if the child was someone else's she'd be fucking me.

"New York," she said, shrugging her shoulders gently. "I am that one in a million, first date, on the pill, that kind of thing."

I saw tears fill her eyes and she tried desperately hard to swallow them down. I picked up her hand in mine and ran my thumb over her knuckles. She struggled to not let the sob escape from her chest. It was her turn to grit her teeth, I could see. She held herself rigid.

We continued the journey in silence, even though I knew she wanted to openly cry. She'd look out the window and I'd see her reflection and feel her move to wipe her eyes when those tears finally fell. I hated my reaction had done that. I hated more it had been her vile sister to break the news.

I thought back. Anna had said she would tell me something after the wedding, I hadn't, in my wildest dreams, thought it would be that I was to become a father. So many thoughts rattled through my head. I was afraid, and I hated that feeling. Fear of losing her, fear of losing the child flooded me. I wanted to punch the fucking window out, but I kept my composure, I didn't want to scare her. Thankfully, before I burst, we arrived at the restaurant. A public place, somewhere I knew I wouldn't explode. I hoped.

CHAPTER FIVE

We walked in, and still I held her hand.

"Mr. Santiago," I heard. Andréa walked towards us.

"A table for two, and I'm sorry I haven't booked," I said to him. "My partner, Anna," I added by way of an introduction.

Andréa bowed to her. "It's nice to meet you, Anna. I have a lovely table for you." We followed him to a roped-off area reserved for his special guests.

We sat and received menus, a bottle of sparkling water was placed on the table, and still in silence I poured two glasses. I took a sip.

"So, pregnant," I said. She nodded. "When were you going to tell me?" I asked.

"After the wedding," she replied.

"Why not immediately when you knew?"

"First, I had to get my own head around it. It was an accident, Jacob, not planned. A mistake."

"No pregnancy is a *mistake*, Anna!" I couldn't stop the fierceness in my voice and hoped I hadn't startled her.

"A mistake on my part in not taking my pill at the usual time. I forgot about the time difference. As for the rest of 'why,' there just never seemed to be the right time."

"I think I would have rather heard it by text than from your sister," I said, taking a moment to breathe and calm down.

"I had no idea she was going to do that."

"How did she know?"

"Jules, I think."

"So, your employees knew but not me?"

She nodded. "They had to know—"

"Before me?" I questioned, and again, swallowing down my anger, I leaned back needing some distance.

She apologised, and her voice cracked. I softened immediately. I didn't want to add more upset to what had already been a shitty day. I reached over and took her hand in mine, and then I sighed. I gave her a smile. She asked me if I was angry.

"Yes, I'm angry, but only about the way I've discovered I'm going to be a father. I'll get over it. We now need to discuss what you want to do."

"I'm going to keep the child, obviously. I'm over three months now and have a scan on Monday."

I released one of her hands and picked up my mobile phone. I dialled Philip.

"I won't be available on Monday, sort my day out, please?" He confirmed he'd heard my request, as was his usual. Then asked me if I was okay. I didn't reply, I couldn't.

'You didn't need to do that," she said, and I felt that anger return.

I raised my eyebrows at her. "You're carrying my child, Anna. Do you think I'd leave you to deal with it on your own? I have a responsibility to you, whether it was an *accident* or not."

"I meant, I didn't want you to feel obliged." Her voice was small. I needed to check myself before I spoke again. She deflated in front of me, and I hated I'd done that to her.

"I don't. I'd be honoured if you allowed me to be part of this journey. You are carrying my child. Mine. Well, ours, but you know what I mean. I'm sure it's going to take me some time to adjust. I hadn't contemplated on being a father at my age, and we'll have lots of things to sort before the due date, of course." I felt my smile widen a little. It wasn't that I was overly happy, but something inside was warming up.

"Slow down, we have months," she said. "Nathan knows."

"I'm glad. If there was ever a man to confide in, it's him. He is my keeper of secrets," I said, not actually glad at all.

I blinked a few times. Of course he knew, that was why he was pushing me constantly to contact her. It must have been hell for him.

I told her we'd have to discuss logistics, I guessed, I'd gone into work mode, planning, and running scenarios through my head.

"Logistics?"

"Where to live, that kind of thing. My house isn't exactly child friendly and yours isn't large enough for me. So, we need a new home."

"A new...?"

"You weren't expecting us to live apart, were you?"

I'd cocked my head to one side as I'd spoken. It was a challenge, not a question. I didn't believe in broken families where possible. And I'd fucking never allow another man into her life to bring up my child, regardless of whether we made it or not.

"I hadn't thought about it. Like you, I think I need to get my head around a few things as well. I had expected to go into this as a single parent."

"That's not going to happen. Let's eat, this revelation has me starving." It hadn't but I wanted to just calm myself. I knew I was coming across as an arsehole. I was giving her mixed messages, I was sure. I had smiled, and I had scowled.

I scanned the menu. Well, I didn't really because I knew what I wanted to eat. I ate the same thing every time I visited, which was often when I was in London. I'd even had Andréa come and cater for parties.

She stared at her menu, but her eyes hadn't moved. She wasn't reading anything. It did, however, give me a minute to study her. She was beautiful, if sad at that moment. Her skin was clear, and her cheeks had a little glow. With the news I had, of course she was pregnant, she looked fucking pregnant.

I could have kicked myself for not picking up on it. I was an expert at body language and all I could imagine was that she floored me, that had 'camouflaged' her. I hadn't seen it, and I should have. What kind of soldier wouldn't see that, normally. I was immediately taken back to Iraq to times when I'd have to decide on whether to pull the trigger or not. Was it a child, or an adult pretending? Was it a pregnant woman or an insurgent in disguise? I closed my eyes for a moment, needing to clear those thoughts from my head.

"Stop thinking and start ordering," I said, desperate for the distraction.

"I can't stop thinking. I have a lot to think about," she said quietly.

"I know you do. But no matter what, I'm not letting you go through this alone."

"That sounds very...demanding," she said, smiling slightly at me as if she wasn't sure she should, and I was actually glad I'd managed to make her smile.

"I'm a demanding kind of guy. I've gotten my own way for over fifty years; I highly doubt I'll change any time soon."

The waiter appeared and waited for her to speak.

"Order for me?" she asked.

I ordered a selection of dishes to share, another bottle of sparking water, and a large glass of red wine for myself. I remembered my manners and asked if she wanted to join me with a glass of wine, she declined.

"What do you want from us?" I asked. It was a thought that had popped up in my head.

"I'm not sure what you mean."

"I think we've both hinted that we'd like for this to become a relationship, but how serious?" I stared at her.

"I'm not looking to get married, if that's what you're worried about."

"I was married once," I said, my voice lowering. "She was killed, and I don't think I've ever fully gotten over that."

"I don't expect you can, Jacob."

"She was killed because of me, Anna." My voice broke and I coughed to regain my composure. I didn't like to lose control in front of her. "I made a wrong call, took on a job I shouldn't have. Your safety will be paramount to me."

"Okay," she said slowly. "Is it likely to happen again?" I could see the uncertainness creep into her eyes.

"No, I don't think so."

"You don't *think* so?"

I paused, staring at her. "The person who killed my wife, lost his life." If she were to spend her life with me, bear my child, she needed to know a few things about me.

"As much as you should feel free to talk about your wife, and I'd like to know about her, I don't want to know any more right now."

It was the right answer for the moment. Anna would

never know everything there was about me. I'd been a killer, a paid one at that. I was soulless when I worked, and sometimes, I would take that home.

"So, my house is too small for you?" she asked, clearly wanting to change the subject.

I chuckled. "Yep. I need an office, a secure room, and I like space and greenery."

"And if I don't?" she challenged.

"Then we compromise, obviously," I said, knowing full well compromise was something I'd need to learn to do.

I didn't like her house, not that I would tell her that. It was too small for my liking. I needed space and light. Large windows and adequate security. Not that she would have known, but every pane of glass at my house was bulletproof. The perimeter fence was electrified. Cameras were everywhere, alarms could easily be tripped. No one was getting into my house without me knowing about it, not even from the air. The whole roof had pressure pads that would alert me should anything weightier than a bird land on it.

Plates of food were laid on the table and we ate. I kept the conversation general from that point. I guessed, we ought to actually get to know each other since we were to become parents.

"Why did the card you gave me say Jacob Daniel?" she asked.

"Easy name to use. I don't use my full name very often. I

don't want people to know too much about me. Other than Nathan, and now you, of course."

"The guy here, he just called you Mr. Santiago," she added.

"Yes, for reasons I've just explained."

"Okay, one last question. You said you'd be in London in June, but it was end of May when I came to your place."

I raised my eyebrows and shook my head. "End of May, beginning of June. Did it really matter? And, just for full disclosure, I wasn't in London when you visited me, I was in Hampshire. Now, I know I'm not from this country, but I have lived here for a while, and I know Hampshire isn't London. I also have an apartment in London, but I allow colleagues to use that."

She laughed. "So, your main residence is in Hampshire?"

I nodded. "Yes. I've lived in England mostly, for about twenty years. Although I'm sure I could find the actual date if you require it of me." I smirked at her. "You know, we're asking all the questions we should have before we produced a child," I said, and then chuckled. The initial shock was wearing off.

She shrugged one shoulder. "I guess, I've never been conventional."

"I like that about you," I said.

She laid her fork down. "What else do you like about me?"

"Fishing for compliments, huh?" I jested, also laying my

fork down. "I like how, even if you thought I was an escort, you allowed me to fuck you that first night."

Her face reddened and she visibly cringed, looking around quickly, and hoping no one else heard, I guessed.

"Jesus, Jacob," she hissed. "I don't like that. I mean, I *liked* it, but not how I fell at your feet so quickly."

"I like that you fell at my feet and sucked my cock," I replied.

I then proceeded to tell her every detail of her body I liked, and what I loved about what we'd done so far. Her cheeks reddened further, and I saw her breath hitch. She was aroused, I could smell it.

I leaned closer. "Phew, it's hot in here," she said, fanning her face.

I was done with food, I wanted something else to eat. I stood and took her hand, leading her from the restaurant. Once outside, I held out my hand to Daniel who chuckled and threw the car keys at me.

"Get in the front," I demanded, and once she had, I told her to remove her panties.

I'd said I was going to fuck her in my car, and I fully intended to do it as soon as I could find somewhere half decent.

Anna teased herself, she opened her legs so I could see. I struggled to keep my eyes on the road, and I was desperate to free the raging hard-on in my trousers. She slid on the seat, pushing her wet pussy closer and I swerved. A driver beeped his horn at us. I plunged two fingers inside her, finding that spongy spot that had her moaning. I twisted and stroked, needing her to come on my seat. She grabbed my hand, forcing my fingers in deeper.

"God, I need more," she said, her breath ragged, and I chuckled. I liked the wanton Anna who sat beside me. I needed her to come undone.

I found a car park and swerved the car in. I drove up a few floors and then headed to the darkest corner. I turned off the engine and locked the doors. Before I could even get my cock free, she was straddling me. I'd pushed my seat back, but I highly doubted it was comfortable for her. She didn't seem to care as she lowered herself on my cock.

I dug my fingers into her arse cheeks as she rode me hard. She demanded more, clawing at me. She was coming undone, and it was a sight to see. Her cheeks flamed, her eyes were glassy, her lips plumped. Her nipples were so hard, not even a bra and her flowing dress could conceal them. Her hair started to fall around her face, strands were stuck to her sweaty cheeks. She looked beautiful to me.

As she came, she kissed me. I could feel her stomach contract, her muscles grip my cock harder as her body shuddered.

"Oh God," she croaked, her voice hoarse.

I smiled. "No, just Jacob," I said.

She rested her forehead on mine. "There is nothing *just* about you," she replied.

I fell in love for sure, then. Whatever I thought about the pregnancy, about how I felt for her, it paled against the emotion I was feeling then.

It was overwhelming and confusing. I kissed her lips gently and encouraged her back to her seat.

She slumped against the leather and closed her eyes. The tops of her thighs shimmered with my cum as it gently slipped from her. Before I'd even turned the engine back on, she was asleep. I was grateful, I needed the quiet to gather my thoughts, again.

I gently woke her when we arrived back at her house. I climbed from the car and opened her door while she adjusted her clothing. She stood on tiptoes to kiss me.

"Come in?" she asked.

"I would love to, but I have some things I need to do."

She looked disappointed. I cupped her face. "I'm not going anywhere, Anna. I'll be honest. I'm feeling very over-whelmed, I think we both need just a little space. Just for tonight." She nodded and smiled.

"I appreciate that," she said.

After one final kiss, she walked away, and I drove back to Hampshire. I wound down the window allowing the fresh air to flow through the car. The sun was setting and the red and gold hues as the landscape changed from city to countryside settled me. Daniel texted to say he was staying in London unless I needed him.

I sent a voice message, asking him to look out for Anna, discreetly. He didn't reply, he didn't need to.

I didn't rush home, opting to actually stay at the speed limit, a rarity for me. I wanted that time to think. I wanted to keep the smell of our cum currently soaking into my leather seat in my nostrils. I was a mass of conflict. I loved her, I knew that. I wanted her, desperately, to the point of being hard again. I was upset at the delivery of the news, the anger had subsided. I wasn't sure what I thought about being a father. My thoughts went back to my wife. I remembered when she'd told me she was pregnant. I'd picked her up, swung her around. She'd laughed and cried at the same time. I knew then that we had to return to England. She couldn't give birth, be a mum, in Spain where we lived. My parents loved her, but they didn't speak much English and she was still learning Spanish. My heart lurched.

How the fuck was I going to not compare the two?

How was I going to separate out the experiences, so each was individual?

How was I going to keep Anna and my baby alive? That thought pulled me up so sharp that I struggled to breathe. I pulled onto the hard shoulder. I needed to speak to someone just to bring me down.

"I found out about the baby, thanks for giving me a heads-up," I said, when Nathan answered the call. I heard him sigh.

"Jacob, what would you have done in my position? I've been telling her to tell you since she knew. I've hated it, mate.

She had it in her head you weren't interested in her to start with, and she would be a single parent. Then she said she never found the right time."

It was my time to sigh. "I'm not sure how I feel about it. Obviously, I'll be stepping up, but…"

"But what, Jacob?" he said quietly.

"What about you?" I replied.

"She's not mine to have. She's carrying your child. I'll always be in her life, and yours, obviously. She's into you, not me."

We both fell silent for a little while. "I don't suppose she'd be up for sharing, would she?" he asked and then laughed.

"Don't even joke, Nate," I said, knowing it had been said in jest.

"Sorry. How do you feel about being a dad?"

"It was a shock, and I'm still fucking pissed off at finding out the way I have. But…" I sighed. "I think I kinda like the idea, but I can't help but go back in the past right now. I pulled over to call you because I'm a mess. But…" I started to smile. "I feel like I have a second chance here."

"Don't fuck it up, because I will step in then, mate. I won't hesitate to take your place if I need to, and I will bring your child up as my own," he said sternly, and that time, he wasn't joking.

Again, we fell silent. I could hear him take in a deep breath. "Sorry, that wasn't called for. I know you won't let her down."

I nodded. "I'm scared."

"I know. It's not the same, okay?" he said. "What happened.... It won't happen again because I won't let it. You're not on your own here, Jacob."

We both sighed.

"Understood, and signing off," I replied, then cut off the call.

I continued my journey home.

———

The following morning, I showered and sat in the snug with my laptop catching up on news. I called Sadie and Bill to join me.

"I have some news," I said, and smiled. "It seems that I'm about to become a father."

Both sat in stunned silence. "How?" Sadie asked.

I raised my eyebrows at her. "Well, there's this stork..." She swiped at my arm. "Let me start at the beginning. You know I've been seeing Anna? Well, she's pregnant. How's our luck, she fell pregnant the first time we... You know what I mean."

"Are you sure you're the..." Bill started and then didn't continue.

"Yeah, I am."

"How do you feel?" He started to smile at me.

"I was annoyed, terrified, but I'm growing to like the

idea."

"I'm so happy for you, Jacob. You'll make an amazing father," Sadie said, and she reached out to hold my hand. Both she and Bill knew about my deceased wife.

I nodded my thanks. "I'm going to see if I can persuade her to live here. So I need some help in making the house seem more child friendly," I said.

"Oh my God. It will be wonderful having a child around," Sadie said. "Assuming you still want us to help," she added with a little hesitancy in her voice.

"Don't for one minute think I want you to go anywhere," I replied sternly.

She laughed, and then slapped her thighs. "I can't wait. Bill, let's get a list going, come on." She stood and dragged her husband to his feet. He smiled at me and dutifully followed her.

I continued to sit in the snug. My phone lit up with an incoming message.

The model, Jules, took her own life last night. Something stinks about it. I'm with Anna, taking her into the office to sort things.

Nathan's messages were often to the point and blunt. I replied.

What's off about it? And thanks, I'll message her.

She didn't do heroin and that's what it looks like. Gut feeling.

I replied.

Want me to do anything this end? All resources are open, you know that. Is this the woman you were fucking?

Despite his feelings for Anna, Nathan still fucked other women. Although, he hadn't said anything directly, I'd seen her with him.

Not much gets past you, does it? Yeah. I'm gutted to be honest. I kinda liked her.

I sighed and thought about my words before I replied again.

I'm sorry, Nate. If there's anything I can do, you know I'm here.

There was no point in me telling him I knew how he felt, because it wasn't the same, but it sort of was. The death of anyone close hurt.

An hour later, an email came in. Nathan had detailed everything he knew about Jules, her background, and recent movements. He had sent the email to one of our IT guys but copied me in. It wouldn't take too long for IT to have a full financial report, family details, any public CCTV footage of that evening, and details of all known contacts.

I then sent a text to Anna. I thought it better than trying to call her, I was sure she'd be up to her eyes in calls.

Hey, I'm so sorry to hear the news. I expect you're inundated. I won't call to add to your busy day but know I'm thinking of you. I'd like to

meet up this evening if you've got the time. Just a night in, perhaps. I'll cook for you and be a shoulder to cry on.

I headed back up to the bedroom to change my clothes. I wanted to be in London, to be close. Even if she didn't want dinner, I wasn't going to let her spend the evening on her own. I texted Daniel I'd be in town, not that he had to move out of the apartment, of course. There was plenty of room.

Daniel had reported in that Anna hadn't left her house and Nathan had collected her a little after lunch. I thanked him and told him to stand down for a while. All the time she was with Nathan, I wasn't worried.

What made Daniel perfect for us was that he was so unassuming. He didn't stand out. His ability to blend in was amazing. I'd had him standing in the middle of Kings Cross Station one time, and not one person thought it odd. At no time had he been approached by the police, despite standing opposite some gates for three hours with no attempt to get on a train or leaving his position. He could have stood outside Anna's house, and no one would have noticed. Nathan had nicknamed him Adrian, after H.G. Wells's character, Adrian Griffin in *The Invisible Man*. Nathan was extremely well read! His favourite book, one he'd read time and time again while in the army had been *The Count of Monte Cristo*. He knew the words and would never see the movie in case it deviated.

I drove into London and through the barrier to the private

underground car park. My apartment was one of ten in the exclusive block, the other apartments were mostly owned by Arabs who rarely visited. Occasionally, I'd seen their mistresses but never their wives or families. I knew everyone who lived on the same block, of course. The mistresses wore western clothes, carried bags of shopping in every day, all designer of course.

I let myself in. Daniel waved from the lounge. He was sitting in front of a laptop with headphones covering his ears. I walked to the kitchen to grab a bottle of water and then joined him. He was moving through some drone footage detailing the events he saw. It appeared that our James Harvey may have been moved from safe house to safe house, something not uncommon when the security forces wanted to protect a witness. They hadn't protected him well enough from Daniel, however. He pointed to the screen, to a figure that left a building in the dead of night. That figure was helped into a car and then driven off. The drone ascended and we could see the car drive through country lanes. We lost the car once it headed up the M1, but Daniel was confident he could pick him up on CCTV.

"Is that him?" I asked, and Daniel nodded.

"Good work. Keep on him."

I wanted to find out what agency was protecting him, and for what reason.

I pulled my phone from my pocket and noticed a reply to my earlier text from Anna.

Thank you, Jacob, I needed to hear that. Yes, to dinner, my place? I've no idea what time I'll be leaving but I'll try to give you as much notice as possible. Or, I could have Nathan send over a front door key for you?

I quickly responded.

I'm in London, I'll get the key from you, be there in about an hour.

I fired off some emails and diverted the rest to Philip, then left the apartment. I headed to a nearby deli to buy some groceries and returned. I wanted to make Anna lunch. I didn't do the shop bought sandwiches, not only were they full of crap additives I didn't want my child absorbing, but they were also expensive! I prepared a sandwich, cut some fruit, and bagged it up, then added a napkin and fork. I piled it all in a paper bag.

When I arrived at her building, I wasn't happy about the lack of security. I knew she rented out a couple of the floors to other fashion-related companies and a start-up magazine. I just walked in through the large wooden front door into a tiled floor hallway with a staircase in front of me. Someone had left a bike, there was a table with mail anyone could look through. The building had clearly been a grand house back in its day but had been repurposed as offices. I didn't know if that was something Anna had done herself. I imagined so, considering how informal the whole place was. I stopped and scanned, placing cameras in my mind for when I suggested my security firm come take a look. Anna would probably block that, but being in the business I was, she joined Nathan as a potential target to get to me. And the thought I had a child in the mix was fucking terrifying. Whether she liked it or not, I was getting a team in that building to ensure they were safe. I had to admit though, it was a magnificent building. I wondered if I should, via another company of mine, rent the ground floor. There were two rooms at either side of the hall. They'd make for great security offices, killing two birds with one stone. I made a mental note to talk to Nathan about it.

I took the stairs two at a time and then entered her office. It was open plan other than two rooms at the back, one was hers, the other was a meeting room come photo studio, by the looks of it. I watched her lean back in her chair and close her eyes. She looked tired; I was concerned at her paleness. Eleanor hadn't suffered with any kind of sickness. One day she wasn't pregnant, the next she was, and nothing changed other than her stomach expanded so I had nothing to compare. Not that I wanted to do that, of course. I was concerned about Anna, however. I didn't like how tired she was all the time. Again, another mental note was made to speak to my doctor about her. Perhaps I'd persuade her to see Saul for a check-up.

I walked across the floor, and it annoyed me not one person, and there were many, in the company challenged me.

No one knew me, many looked up though. I simply walked across the room and stood in her doorway.

"I bet you haven't eaten, have you?" I asked.

She shook her head, and I handed over a brown paper back. "Did you make this for me?" she asked, peering in.

"Yeah, just a simple chicken with a citrus dressing. I'll need to learn what you can and can't eat, I guess."

"I didn't know you could cook."

"I'm an excellent chef when I have time. Now, how are you?"

Her bottom lip trembled, and her hands shook. I guessed she'd been holding it together for the sake of the guys loitering outside. I walked around her desk and crouched down in front of her.

While she cried, she asked, "Why?" I held her, telling her that no one knows why someone takes their own life. I kept my arms around her until she'd stopped. When I leaned back, I stared at her. She cupped my face and kissed me. I ran my thumbs under her eyes, removing the smudged mascara.

"You are so beautiful," I whispered. Although I meant the words, I found them hard to say. Watching her cry had my stomach in knots. I desperately wanted to take her pain away for her, make things right, but not even I could turn back time.

"So are you," she replied, and smiled gently at me.

I kissed the tip of her nose. "I'll get out of the way now, and wait for you at home, okay?"

She nodded and handed over a door key. "Eat, please. I know this is a distressing time, but we must still think about the baby," I said sternly.

She smiled at me. "Is that your demanding voice?"

"No, you'll know when I'm demanding because you'll be hot and wet for it," I whispered in her ear, wanting to give her something else to think about.

I kissed her cheek and walked away. I saw Nathan enter and stopped. "She okay?" he asked.

"Sort of. Make sure she eats, will you?" I asked. "Also, we should take over those rooms downstairs. Not one fucking person has challenged me walking in here.

"You got a lot of eyes on you," Nathan said, scanning the room. I chuckled and followed his gaze. Some looked away, some raised eyebrows and pouted lips, and some just smiled.

"Yes," I heard called out to the office. "Meet my baby's daddy."

I turned to face her, blew a kiss, and then carried on. I chuckled, she was telling all to back off, I was hers.

I drove to her house and left the car outside. There was no designated parking, and the only other car was a vintage Rolls Royce a few doors down. It was immaculate, and I wondered if the owner had bought the car new. I appreciated the car, stood, and looked at it for a little while. It was a thing of beauty, for sure.

I jiggled the key in the lock and then let myself in. Her house was cool, a Victorian townhouse, in great condition. I removed the groceries from their bags and put them away. I'd brought my laptop with me so I could do some work while I waited. After making myself a coffee, I headed for the small courtyard outside and sat in the sun. It was a perfect work area with a high wall. There was a small alley that ran down one side and then along the back of the properties and I scanned for any security. As with the office, Anna didn't even have a functioning alarm. I made a note to get that rectified. I could see neighbouring properties had cameras, but none focussing on the alley. I'd hate to be their security consultant should they get burgled.

I prepped the meal, then worked until I received a text message from Nathan that they were leaving.

I heard the car pull up outside and opened the front door. She hugged Nathan and I invited him to share dinner with us. He didn't want to. He gave her some bullshit story about wallowing and television, but I didn't believe it. He was struggling with seeing us together, I thought. I sighed, not knowing how to rectify that.

"I'm worried about him. He and Jules had a *thing* going on," Anna said as we watched him drive away.

"Call him, see if you can persuade him to return."

We walked inside the house. "I already tried that. I offered for him to stay but he didn't want to," she said.

"I hope that's not because I'm here." I wanted to see if she'd picked up on that, if she had any thoughts on the situation.

"No, I think he actually wants to be on his own. He does that, hides away when he needs to." I smiled at her; she was genuinely so naïve.

"How are you?" I asked, turning her to face me.

"Okay, hoarse from all the calls, and sad, of course."

"Go and have a bath, or a shower. I have a nice cold white wine, I'm sure you can have one glass, and dinner will be ready in a half hour."

I smiled as she walked away. A few minutes later, I heard the bath run. The pipework in the old house gurgled away, that would drive me nuts, I thought. A little while later, I took a cold drink up to her.

"Here," I said, handing her the glass. "It's a fake mojito." I sat on the edge of the bath, looking at her and detailing what was in her drink. It was very clear she was pregnant, and for the second time I could have kicked myself for not noticing. She had a perfect bowling ball tummy. Slim at the sides, round at the front. Her breasts were larger, as were her nipples that had changed colour, darkened, I'd thought.

"Pregnancy suits you. Maybe we should do it again after this one," I said, meaning every word. I hated being an only child, and I didn't want that for my own. I'd keep her pregnant for years if I could. I inwardly smiled.

"We haven't quite gotten over the fact or made any plans about this one yet," she said, chuckling.

"Yeah, I guess we ought to. Perhaps we'll sit with my lawyers after the scan tomorrow?" There was a lot of financial issues to be dealt with, wills to be changed, and I wanted to make sure my child wanted for nothing.

School fees would need to be set aside; my child wouldn't be attending the local state school. Medical and travel insurances. I hoped she'd had dual nationality, like me, and a fleeting thought crossed my mind. If Anna gave birth in Spain, our child would automatically have Spanish nationality, because I was Spanish. I wasn't sure on the procedure if the child was born in England. I also wanted my child to be bilingual. There was a lot to discuss.

"Or my lawyers," she replied, raising an eyebrow at me.

"Both, then. Do you think we could get them in the same room at the same time, or will they all want to double the fee for double the unnecessary appointments?" I laughed and she joined in. I wanted to take her mind off her sorrows just for a few hours.

"Let's get the scan out of the way, and then let's decide before involving the vultures, shall we?"

She handed me her drink and stood, water sloshed over the sides of the bath, and I had jumped back to not get soaking wet. While she stood, I admired her.

"Are you enjoying the view?" she asked.

"Oh yes. I didn't think I could get more turned on by you, but that stomach of yours is going to be sorely missed." I could feel my cock pulse in my trousers at the sight of her wet naked body.

I picked her up and carried her, dripping wet, to the bed,

where I laid her down. She moaned about wet bedding and dinner. I silenced her with a kiss.

While I continued to kiss her, I unzipped my jeans and slid them off. I only broke the kiss, reluctantly, to pull my T-shirt over my head. Then I climbed on the bed and kissed her chest, down and over her stomach. I paused, emotion was threatening to spill out.

"Hello, baby," I whispered.

I kissed her some more, trailing my lips and tongue down to her pussy. Fuck dinner, what I had in front of me was plenty to satisfy my hunger.

When my cock was straining enough and became painful with the need to be buried deep inside her, I stopped. I hovered over her, plunging inside until I was balls deep. I fucked her hard and fast, she wrapped her legs around mine and raised her arse from the bed. She came, I came, and when I was done, I fell to the side.

"I need to get back to the gym, gotta build these arm muscles up," I said, flexing my biceps.

"I think you look fine exactly as you are," she replied, rolling onto her side to face me. "Did I tell you I used to be an expert equestrian? I need to ride more often, I think."

"Anytime you want, baby, anytime you want," I said. "But not now. I don't cook often, but when I do, not even your pussy will distract me." I laughed at my obvious lie. I'd been totally distracted by her no more than twenty minutes prior!

I rolled to the edge of the bed and, as I did, she knelt up

beside me. She kissed my neck before I left, and she parted her legs to show me what I was about to miss. I laughed, called her a witch, and left the room.

Witch, it was the perfect name for her. She had bewitched me, all right!

Anna joined me some ten minutes later. I'd cooked a light white fish on a bed of spinach. I wanted iron rich foods for the baby, not that I had any idea how much spinach one would need to eat to really gain any benefit from its iron levels. I made a lemon and garlic sauce, opting not to add any cream after the last time.

We ate and it pleased me to see she still had her appetite. Although the bump was growing, I began to think she was losing weight elsewhere. She wasn't as rounded over the hips as she had been, and her ribs were visible. I worried about her. Her clavicle bones were protruding beyond what was attractive. Her cheeks were getting sunken. It didn't detract from her beauty, if anything, she became more haunting, mesmerising, but she shouldn't be losing weight.

"You are an amazing chef. Where did you learn to cook?" she asked.

"The army initially, although I can assure you, we didn't eat like this. I enjoy cooking. I find it relaxing." Most of my *skills* came from the fact that, prior to Sadie, I had to learn to cook for myself and I found some comfort in it. I experimented until I knew exactly what I liked.

"You can cook anytime you want," she said. "Me and this

little one certainly appreciated that." She patted her stomach, and it gave me an opening to ask a few questions.

"What are your thoughts about us, Anna?" I asked.

I believed we needed a firm plan going forwards. I wasn't a *drifter*, even if I hooked up with someone, I knew it was a one-night stand or short-term engagement. With Anna, I needed to hear her tell me she wanted long term, a forever-type relationship. I couldn't say it, even if I'd wanted to.

"I want you in my life, in our lives," she said. "I'm not sure how we'll manage our living arrangements. Perhaps we should just commute back and forth between both houses for the time being?"

I nodded but sighed. "There are things I need in a house that this won't accommodate. I know this is close to your office, but how about we buy something in London that suits us both a little better. I mean, do you really want to be carrying the baby up those stairs each evening?"

The time I'd spent in her house that afternoon had given me a good insight into how problematic it would be for me.

"What things do you need?" she asked.

"I need an office, a large one. I need a secure room for...things. I need a gun room."

"Oh, I don't know about the gun room, Jacob," she said, and I saw her place her hands instantly on her stomach protectively.

I owned guns, shotguns mostly, and some military wear that was kept *unofficially official*. It was known I had them by the relevant agencies but ignored. Those needed to be stored correctly. I enjoyed hunting, often bringing home deer or rabbit, a pheasant or partridge, for Sadie and my local butcher to cut up and freeze. Stage two of my home development, that I'd never gotten round to, was to set up a vegetable garden and build a cold room to hang meats. I wanted my child to enjoy those outdoor country pursuits as well. I envisaged us on our quadbikes, shotguns over our shoulders as we stalked for the day.

"I can promise you this, our child will be safe, Anna. Come home with me next weekend, let me show you around my home. You never got to see it before. I'm not pushing you to move in with me. For now, we'll go back and forth if you really want, but, in the future, we do need to address this again."

She paused, and then smiled. She nodded. I couldn't do what she wanted, go back and forth. I'd be driven mad with a need to know my child was protected. I knew I'd suffocate Anna if I felt she wasn't as secure as I'd want. She'd end up hating me calling all the time to check on them. It made sense to move in with me, my security was full-on and very subtle.

"I'll set up a trust fund for uni or...whatever. And I'll need your bank account details so I can deposit a monthly amount. I don't want our child to go without anything, Anna."

"You know I can afford to pay for our child myself?"

There was a slight tone of indignation in her voice, and she squared her shoulders.

I was an old-fashioned man to a degree, and I also blamed my Spanish heritage. No, she wouldn't be paying for my child. That was my responsibility. As was it my responsibility to care for her, make sure she had all she needed. It wasn't like I couldn't afford it. But I had to remember we were still getting to know each other. I conceded, for the moment. I knew when to pick my fights, and which one I was going to win. But sometimes, I would take a step back until I found another route to get my own way.

"No, I don't know what you make, but I would like to do this. If you don't want the money in your account, I get that. I'll just open one for her."

"It's a girl now, is it?" she teased, smiling at me, and the tension was immediately gone.

"Yeah, I think so. Now, can we get back to planning?"

Later that evening we had agreed on a list of items that needed to be bought, and we doubled up on them opting for two nurseries, one at mine, and one at hers. It appeased her for the time being.

When it was time for bed, she climbed under the sheet and was asleep before her head even hit the pillow. I lay looking at her for a while before tucking my arm under her neck and pulling her towards me.

CHAPTER SIX

I was surprisingly nervous the following morning. We were sitting in the waiting room, and the midwife was running late. I didn't do lateness. I paced, my agitation showing. I didn't do state hospitals, even if it had an amazing maternity suite. It wasn't for any snobbish reasons, just many failings of colleague and ex-army friends who had been severely let down by the NHS over the years.

"What's taking so long?" I asked.

I heard a reply from behind the reception desk. "First baby?"

I shook my head and grumbled some more as Anna chuckled. Another thing I didn't do well was being surrounded by women who all had something to say when I was anxious. I smiled to myself, knowing I sounded like a complete dickhead with that thought. I loved independent women, just not when I was being an impatient prat.

"Sit down, you're making me tired just looking at you," Anna said, and I glared at her. She patted the seat beside her, staring back at me, challenging me to say something.

"We should have gone to The Portland," I whispered, while looking at the most god-awful posters of baby development and birthing on the wall.

"My midwife is here, and I like her. You're not the one pushing a bowling ball out of your fanny, so be quiet," she whispered back angrily.

I chuckled and took her hand. "I'm nervous," I confessed, hoping that would also excuse my shoddy behaviour.

"What for? Nothing has shown as untoward on previous scans, the baby is kicking around in there like he... or she... is training for the World Cup. I'm healthy, you're healthy, all is good."

"How can you be sure?"

"Because I am. When miracles happen and you can carry a baby, you'll know as well. Call it mother's instinct." Her face was stern, and I wanted to kiss the pout from her lips. Or put her over my knee and slap her arse. The thought aroused me.

We were called through and I knew Anna had seen the crying woman being led away. My stomach knotted in fear. I hated not being in control, and where Anna and the baby were concerned I was a fucking bystander, and I didn't like it.

How I was going to cope when seeing her in pain and giving birth I had no idea. I wondered if I ought to desensitise myself by watching some video clips!

Anna removed her skirt and lay on the bed. Her top was pushed up and gel squirted onto her stomach. A probe ran over her skin and immediately I could hear my baby's heartbeat. It was fast and strong. I caught my breath. The sound of a child, *my* child, *my* DNA, stunned and left me breathless.

"Fucking hell," I said. "She's got a strong heartbeat!"

I scooted forwards. Anna had seen our child on a scan, but this was a first for me. I stared at a screen of black and white. I could make out her head, she had two arms and two legs kicking away. She was clearly pissed off at the intrusion of being on the television, I thought. I wanted to laugh. I smiled, biting down on my lower lip. My baby was a fighter, for sure.

I touched the screen. "There's my baby," I said, not meaning for it to be said aloud.

I was mesmerised. Totally smitten. I fell instantly in love, and it hit me hard. I had never had the depth of feeling I felt for anything in my life before. Nothing. What I was seeing on that screen floored me.

"Does she have all her fingers and toes?" I asked, not taking my eyes from the screen. "And what about her ears? Does she have ears?" For some reason, it bothered me that I couldn't see ears. "What about eyes?"

The midwife assured me when she could. Obviously, she

couldn't answer all my questions. I chuckled to myself when she asked if we wanted to know the sex. I replied with a yes, no doubt about it. I closed my eyes and waited.

"You're having a little..." She paused, and I tapped my foot impatiently. "Girl!"

"I knew it!" I jumped from my seat. "I bloody knew it," I said, laughing. I couldn't care less if anyone in the waiting room could hear me.

Anna laughed. By the time they had her cleaned up and we had a copy of the scan, I was wanting to discuss names.

What I hadn't told Anna was my previous child had been a girl. I had been given a second chance with Anna, and for me, now I was being given a second chance with my daughter.

I could have cried, and I instantly thought of the small gold bracelet I had kept tucked away for the past twenty years. It was meant to be worn on my first daughter's wrist after birth, it would be worn on my second. It was something that was a tradition in my family. All girls were given a keepsake piece of jewellery when born. I wanted to keep that tradition going.

Inside the bracelet at home was a small engraving. It just said, 'de papi.'

The midwife was talking, booking the next appointment, filling in a booklet she then handed back to Anna. I wasn't listening. My mind was swirling with thoughts. Most welcomed, some not. I needed a diversion.

"Shopping. Let's go shopping," I said, dragging her from the clinic.

Anna had protested, she needed to go to work but conceded. She'd give me a few hours and I'd drop her off to work at lunchtime. Not having the work schedule that she did, not having a fixed office, meant I had much more free time than Anna. I wouldn't stop her going to work once my daughter was born if that's what she needed, I was more than happy to be a stay-at-home dad, but I hoped she would at least consider going part time or working from home. I'd missed out on the first few months of my daughter *cooking away*; I wasn't going to miss out on any more time.

We headed over to a department store and I really let my excitement flow. We bought two of everything we needed except nappies. Until we resolved our living arrangements, our daughter would have a magnificent nursery at both homes. I didn't care about the cost; my daughter would have the best of everything.

When she said she was tired, I suggested we grab a coffee before she headed back to the office. We sat, I took a call, and then ordered a light lunch. I'd spent ages researching foods for pregnant women and, without making it overly obvious, I'd been introducing those. Anna had chosen a mint tea instead of her usual coffee.

"I asked Nathan to be the godfather, I hope you don't mind," she said.

"Great, what about a godmother?" I asked. If there was one, there had to be the other.

"Do you have anyone you'd like to ask?"

I slowly shook my head. "I'm quite the loner, Anna. My family is long dead."

"Maybe Dory? She has been my best friend for years. I know you haven't met her yet, but..."

She didn't continue. I smiled. "Sure, Dory it is."

Of course I would have loved someone from my side, but there wasn't anyone left. And for some reason, choosing godparents highlighted that. I gave myself a mental kick up the arse. But the thought my genes would continue with my daughter buoyed me up. My line would continue. All I needed to do was to add a son to the mix at some point, and my name would go on as well. When my parents had died, it really had hit home that once I went, that was it, no more Santiago-Domínguez. The name would die with me.

"I wish we could skip forward six months. Still be pregnant and whatever, but...have met six months prior to when we did. We'd know more about each other," she said.

I frowned at her but understanding what she meant. We knew very little about each other.

"My parents were old when they had me, their only child, they died of natural causes, old age, nothing sinister. I had an amazing childhood. My father owned land, he'd been in the air force in his younger days, and my mother was a stay-at-home mum. I sold the main farmhouse and most of their land, as they wanted me to, some years ago. I kept a smaller house and a little land. I did have an aunt, but we weren't close, no idea if she's still alive, I highly doubt it. As for friends. I have friends, I'm not a *people* person, as such. When you've been in the military for as long as I have, and then do the job that I do, cultivating friendships outside of that circle isn't done. Do you understand that?"

She frowned. "Nathan is my brother from another mother, Daniel and I are very close," I added.

She cocked her head to one side. "Not really, but then I haven't been in the military. I'm curious about your company though."

I sipped my coffee, debating what to say. "I supply security to businesses all over the world. You've heard of piracy, haven't you? I supply armed guards on ships sailing in dangerous areas to prevent that. We guard pipelines that get attacked, we provide the government with military personnel. That kind of thing," I said, shrugging my shoulders and downplaying it.

"Are you in danger?" she asked, quietly.

"No, because I live the way I do. I'm not flash, I don't court friends from the wrong side of town," I said, laughing. "Now, let's get back to us. Nathan would have been my choice; he is the closest to family I have. I'm pleased you asked him."

Before she could ask anymore, I, thankfully, received a

text. Nathan was outside. I picked up the bags and waited for her while she slipped on her shoes, and we left the store.

Nathan stood beside the car parked on double yellows with hazard lights on. He ignored the doorman who was gesticulating for him to move up, so at least another car could squeeze, illegally, outside the door as well. There was a row of chauffer driven vehicles waiting to collect or drop off. She climbed inside the car, and Nathan and I loaded the boot. I smiled at him and waved a copy of the scan image before putting it back in my pocket.

"So, shall we tell him?" I whispered as I slid beside her.

She nodded.

"Mate, do you want to know whether you're going to be godparent to a girl or boy?" I asked.

Nathan looked in the rear-view mirror. "You know?"

"Found out today. We're having a girl, Nathan."

We stared at each other, then smiled. Nathan had known his sister was pregnant with a little girl before her death.

"A girl?" Nathan replied. "We are in for a tough time, and she is going to hate us for protecting her."

We laughed. I knew what kind of an uncle he would be because it would be far more than just a godparent. He wasn't religious, anyway. It was nice to see the sadness leave his face as he had something new to focus on.

Anna leaned forwards and placed her hand on his shoulder. "How are you holding up?"

"Okay, I got a call from her sister. Did you know she had

a sister? Anyway, she was going through Jules's phone, and I was the only male listed."

"No, she hasn't got a sister. She has a brother, he emigrated to Canada years ago. That's really odd, Nathan," Anna replied.

"I thought so as well."

"What did she ask?" I enquired.

"She wanted to know what my relationship with her sister was. I said I was a work colleague, nothing more. She pushed to know names of friends, it seemed no one in her phone admitted to being a friend. I wanted to know why she was calling me; she gave some bullshit about the funeral arrangements."

"How do you know it's bullshit?" Anna asked.

"Gut feeling."

"Could it be her brother's wife?" she asked.

"She was English, had a northern, Yorkshire I'd say, accent. Not to say it couldn't have been, of course. I'm going to do some digging."

"Resources are available should you need them," I offered. Nathan nodded to me in the rear-view mirror then quickly glanced at Anna. He would know that I meant Daniel could be spared to do whatever he needed him to do.

"Should I even ask?" Anna said. I picked up her hand in mine and held it, not answering.

We dropped Anna off to work and then headed to my apartment.

"What are you thinking?" I asked him as we entered the flat.

"She didn't take an overdose. Someone did that to her. She was determined to turn her life around. She'd been abused by an uncle, she said she was going to the police. Her mum had made her cover it up, years ago. I'm going to start there. Her uncle is some hotshot in the city or was. It wouldn't be good for his image should that information get out."

I nodded and left him with Daniel while I went to fetch some drinks.

By the time I returned, the printer was whirling out pictures of family members, family trees, and as much as Daniel had dug up the short time it had taken me to get our drinks. I picked up the photograph.

"I know him," I said.

"Yep. Sits on one of the same committees as Harvey," Nathan said.

In the early days, when pitching for contracts, we'd often sit in front of a board to do so. Neither had been in parliament at that time, but both were *attached* to the business secretary as large companies often are, as advisors.

We sat in silence as more documents churned out. "What the fuck?" I said, reading through a news report.

I handed the report to Nathan. "Jesus, how did we miss this?"

The report was from a sleezy newspaper accusing both

James Harvey and Martin Taylor, Jules's uncle, of running a paedophile ring in London. It appears that a young male prostitute had come forward and told the press he had been trafficked by the pair into the ring. He'd been held prisoner for years, farmed out to the rich and famous. His story was dismissed because he was a prostitute, and it died a death. As did the young lad, so it seemed. A follow-up report detailed his heroin overdose. There had been periodic attempts to reraise the story, but nothing could stick. The same journalist had written various pieces in different newspapers, eventually setting up his own blog to expose this ring. We dug further. He had disappeared some years ago. His blog had been shut down, but Daniel believed he could access what had been published. Once it was on the internet, nothing was ever truly erased.

I stared at Nathan. "How close was Anna to Jules?" My guts were churning.

"Pretty close. I wouldn't say best friends, they didn't go out or socialise together, but close enough. Anna is protective of her girls. Also, Jules was Aimee's best friend when they were children. The parents all knew each other."

I raised my eyebrows at that news, not liking that one bit. I couldn't care less about the family, but that was too close, even if they weren't best friends.

"I want security on Anna," I said, and both Daniel and Nathan nodded. "Let's find out all we can about Taylor, and I think we need to finally pay Harvey a visit."

It started to make a little sense. Someone in the know was keeping Harvey in protective custody. Perhaps that person knew of other members of this gang that might be sitting in the fucking Houses of Parliament! Harvey had gone from insignificant to highly desirable. More so, he knew that I knew of his penchant for young boys. That made him also a threat.

"He needs gone," Nathan said, tapping the image of Harvey after I'd explained my thoughts. I nodded.

"I'll take that one myself," I said.

"No you won't. I will. You're about to be a father," Nathan replied.

I stared at Nathan; he stared back.

"Neither of you will, you're both too important. He's under the care of the authorities, you aren't gonna just walk in and shoot him. I'll sort it," Daniel said.

"Is this our *Spartacus* moment?" I asked, and we laughed. "Daniel, you sort it."

"We could *rock, paper, scissors* for it?" Nathan said.

"You, my friend, need to get back out in the field. You're having kill withdrawal," I told Nathan, and we laughed. Me more than him, that suggested he knew, and agreed, to what I'd meant.

And yes, we laughed. Between us we had killed many in the name of war, or for reasons good enough to us. We had an immunity to the emotion. It took a lot to take someone's life, to look them in the eyes and extinguish them. To see the light die, and that wasn't a myth. Close up, everyone's eyes dimmed, changed colour slightly as their heart stopped. It wasn't something everyone could do, and not as often as we had. If we thought too hard about what we'd done in our life-time, we'd crumble. So we laughed instead.

"So we're agreed, both need to go," I said, and they nodded.

Daniel took out a pad from his jean pocket. He licked the end of the small pencil that was attached to the side. Then he flipped it open and made two strokes. I shook my head and chuckled. He was keeping a tally.

"And you are too kill happy as well," I said, patting Daniel on the shoulder.

"I only learned from the best," he said, giving me a wink in return.

He turned back to his monitors, and I reread the printed off paperwork. I fucking hated anyone who abused kids, whether that was sexually, emotionally, or physically. I hoped both would die in agony. Daniel had been the best one for them. Nathan and I would have just shot them, he'd have them writhing in pain, begging forgiveness. He was an evil bastard when he wanted to be.

Nathan left to collect Anna and I took a shower. I always had a sense of *dirtiness* when discussing that type of business. When I returned, Daniel had just taken a call.

"Organised," he said and then stood. He stretched and smiled broadly.

"How?"

"Heroin overdose," he replied, and winked then laughed. "Huge one, but slowly so he's conscious enough to know about it at first." I liked his thinking. "Get back what you give out," he replied. "I'm off, out for the evening, do you need me for anything?"

"No, go have fun."

Although I knew Daniel well, there was a part of him I didn't. He often 'disappeared' for a day or so. He'd tell me he was disappearing, and there would always be a promise to return which was fulfilled. But he had a need to get away. Nathan had many theories, his best being that Daniel holed himself up in some sex club somewhere. Got his fill, and then came back. Neither of us had ever seen him date. I didn't care less where someone got their sexual kicks, I'd visited many a club in my younger days, just as long as it was consensual and safe.

He left the room and headed to his bedroom to change, I assumed.

I had agreed to meet Nathan and Anna at a local restaurant. One of us had to be with her at all times from now on. If Taylor knew Jules had told her their sordid secret, she could be a target.

We made a point not to talk about business or Jules. It was all about the baby, and when she moved, both Nathan and I fought to get our hands on Anna's stomach to feel. By the end of the evening, Anna was complaining her top was grubby. I was sure that, from the outside, Nathan and I looked like the couple and Anna the surrogate.

———

A couple of days later I met Dory for the first time. Anna had asked her to be godmother while they were in the kitchen. When I arrived, she rushed to hug me as well. She took me a little by surprise, to be honest. I wasn't a *hugger* generally. I laughed awkwardly, and Anna laughed genuinely, at my discomfort. Dory was oblivious.

We were standing in Anna's kitchen and Dory was joining us for dinner. While I cooked, Anna took Dory upstairs to show her all the clothes we'd bought for the baby. I could hear them talk but not make out the words. I fully intended to install a security system that included cameras and microphones inside and out, although I didn't think Anna would be too pleased about it. It wasn't that I wanted to snoop on her, but it was important to be able to know who was where and hear them.

I enjoyed talking to Dory. She was totally not what I expected. She competed on horses, had been a competitive skier before breaking her leg. Her mother had been a sports-woman and competed in the Olympics, from memory. She drank, swore, and laughed. She told us some gossip from within the Royal household and I was amazed at how related all the European royals were. She avoided any mention of the prince and Jules, however. She cooed over the baby and demanded to know what her role as godmother was. She wanted our daughter to be well educated, and it would be her role to ensure she had a *coming out*. Fuck proms, she'd said, we're going all out in making sure she mingles with the right people. I began to worry, and Anna laughed.

After dinner and when Dory had left, Anna and I sat in her lounge. We watched the sun setting and she lay over my lap.

"Shall we take a holiday together? Before the baby is born?" she asked, sitting up abruptly.

"Where do you want to go?" I answered.

"Anywhere, close to the UK though. I don't want to be too far away in case anything happens."

I nodded, an idea forming. "Would you like a surprise?"

She smiled. "I love surprises, but I didn't ask you just for you to feel you have to do that."

"I don't feel I have to. In fact, I don't generally do anything I don't want to."

I sat forwards and grabbed my phone. I sent a text message and then rested back.

"That's all settled then," I said, grinning at her.

"Huh?"

"You wanted a holiday, locally, so to speak. So, that's what we're doing. Fancy leaving next week?"

"I don't think I can do that..." She tailed off. "I can do that!"

"We'll go just after the funeral," I said. "Take our bags with us and fly straight out."

It would be the perfect alibi should it ever be needed. Daniel could do his thing while I was out of the country. Nathan just needed to be someplace else as well.

I spent the next couple of days at home. I'd called in an interior designer, a guy I knew from years back, and asked him to make a list of how to 'child up' the house. The first thing he suggested was to add some softness, some colour. He came back the following day with rugs and cushions, things I had no interest in, and he and Sadie argued about where they should all go. Bill spent the day filing down corners and rounding everything. I opened packets of plug socket covers and grumbled about how many fucking sockets we had.

———

The following Friday, I collected Anna from work and drove her to my home. She was staying the weekend, and I hoped she'd be so in love with the house she'd agree to move in with me. I had the house made more child friendly, I just needed to persuade her that she could still work. I'd spent the past couple of days ensuring I got that message over well enough.

I was nervous as I showed her around the house. We walked from room to room, finishing the downstairs tour with a look in the safe room. She wasn't overly enamoured, I felt. I was keeping the best for last though.

It had been a push to get it done in time, but the designers came through good for me. I walked her upstairs and led her into the nursery.

She clasped her hands over her mouth and tears filled her eyes. She looked around, then walked, feeling the furniture we had bought. She opened doors and drawers, each filled with clothes. She looked into the bathroom, then walked to the animal corner. A large teddy, an assortment of stuffed wild animals sat waiting for my daughter.

"You're good at this daddy thing," she said as tears filled her eyes.

"I hope so. I hope I get to do it more than just as a weekend dad," I said. "Do you like it?" I wrapped her in my arms.

"I love it. It's perfect and exactly what I would have wanted."

I leaned down to kiss her. That kiss started off gentle until she didn't want 'gentle' anymore. Her hands closed into a fist gripping my hair. She dragged in air through her nose and pushed herself closer to me. I wanted her, desperately. It was obvious she felt the same. I was going to fuck her in my baby's nursery, and it was only a fleeting thought that it was wrong. Desire took over. We lowered to the plush carpet.

She wrestled with my trousers, and I heard her tut that, for the first time in ages, I had shorts on underneath. I chuckled as she tore at the material to free my cock. Once I was inside her, I slowed. It felt so good, and so right. I never wanted that feeling to go, and no matter what happened to us, I didn't believe I'd ever feel that way again.

"I love you," she said, and I stilled. Even my heart paused for a split second.

I couldn't speak. A lump had formed in my throat, blocking my words.

She loved me.

I wanted to tell her the same, I knew I loved her, but I was frozen. I felt wetness around my eyes.

"I've got you," she whispered. "Always."

With that, I let go. I fucked her hard, I made love to her. I poured my heart and soul into her. We came, we rested, and then she rode me.

"Tell me again," I said, the words no more than a growl. "Tell. Me. Again!"

She did, and I covered her mouth, stealing those words to hold inside me forever.

The sun had started to lower when we finally rose. We'd dozed, tangled in each other's limbs. I winced, moaning that I was getting too old for all that rolling around on the floor. Not that I had any intention of stopping, of course. I watched her walk naked to the bathroom to pee, which she did with the door left open. I headed to my bedroom to shower. It wasn't long before she joined me. She washed my back and kissed across my shoulders. It was a tender moment that I gave back to her.

We finished the tour of the house before I took her

outside and down to the pool. She'd walked past it when she'd visited before, but it was a balmy night and I liked to swim naked most evenings when the weather was good. I stripped and waded in, encouraging her to join me. A naked Anna with the lowered sun behind her was even more enchanting. A poet would say she was bewitching. She'd certainly trapped me in her spell, for sure. She yelped as she jumped in and swam to me. She wrapped her legs around my waist, and I held her.

I stared at her. "Tell me again," I whispered.

"I love you, Jacob with all the names. I know it's soon; I know we're having a baby, and I know we've done everything arse about face, but I love you."

She shrugged her shoulders and smiled at me. Her eyes were shining, she looked healthy and happy. I hoped I had something to do with that.

Naked, and carrying our clothes, we walked back to the house. I saw her looking around, as if she was expecting someone to jump out on us.

"No one here but us. I told you, I like my privacy," I said.

"Who cleans?" she asked.

"I have someone here for that. But not on weekends. I prefer to have the house to myself...ourselves."

We sloshed our way into the kitchen, and I headed to the utility room. I grabbed a couple of towels, rubbed one over my hair and then tied it around my waist. I took the other to Anna.

"Sit, have a cup of tea," I said, pointing to a chair. I made two cups and joined her.

"Tell me about your wife?" she asked gently.

I smiled at her. "We'd only known each other a short while before we ran off and got married. Mostly to piss off Nathan, I should add. He was very protective of his sister. They were twins, I don't know if you knew that." She nodded. "Anyway, it was a whirlwind romance and ended way too soon."

It was a well-rehearsed statement without a lot of detail. "When did she die?"

I huffed and pursed my lips. "Twenty years ago now." It wasn't I didn't want to tell her exact dates, I just didn't want that information to be on her mind each time the anniversary came around. So I kept the actual date to myself.

"Twenty years ago," I said, sighing. It felt like a lifetime ago. I picked up her hand and kissed her knuckles. "And now I have a second chance."

I told her Nathan had information on Hannah, Jules's mum, and would be joining us for dinner. She opted for a nap, and I had an hour's work to do. I wanted to catch up with Daniel.

I heard Nathan come strolling through the front door. He had a key and always let himself in unannounced. I might have to think about that should I be fucking Anna somewhere in the house in the future.

"Hey," he called out.

"I'm on the terrace," I replied.

When he walked through, I handed him a beer. "Something smells good," he said, taking the beer. "We should have got married, mate, you're perfect in the kitchen."

I clinked my bottle against his and sighed. "I'd fucking kill you if I had to live with you," I said, remembering how untidy he was from days in barracks. "How many push-ups did you do?"

He'd been punished time and time again for not keeping his area tidy, or not making his bed properly. He held the record for the number of push-ups in one session as a punishment.

"Eighty, and no one has beat me yet," he said proudly. He took a large gulp of his beer.

"Daniel has everything set up. Harvey first, then Taylor," I said.

Daniel had decided Harvey was actually the easiest to get to. He'd discovered where he was being holed up, unfortunately for Harvey, the UK security forces weren't ever that 'secure.' Hacking into their systems, paying for information from old colleagues, was a doddle. It had taken him only one day to find him and for the past few hours he'd managed to get a positive sighting of Harvey in the garden having a cigarette.

We wanted both to look like suicide, and convincingly. So, at the time Daniel was doing his job, Nathan and I would be leaking the information of their paedo ring. We had emails lined up that couldn't be traced, with photographs. All I had to do was press a button and they'd be sent to every major news outlet in Europe. From there, the story would likely be picked up outside of Europe.

I'd prepared a barbecue for us, and while we chatted, I started to baste the meat. Nathan kept asking how long it would be until it was ready. He was like a child when it came to food.

"Where's Anna?" Nathan asked, as if he'd just remembered she was meant to be joining us.

"Sleeping. I'll go and wake her," I said.

I placed my beer on the outside counter and headed upstairs. Anna was lying naked on the bed, on top of the covers. I leaned down and kissed her shoulder, she didn't stir. I wish I had a camera with me, or at least my phone. She was perfect against the white sheet, and I wanted to capture that image. It would look amazing blown up and framed.

I gently shook her, and she jolted awake. She was disorientated at first. "Jesus, how long have I been asleep?" she asked.

"Only about three hours."

"I won't sleep tonight, now," she said, grumbling.

I laughed. "I can think of lots of things to keep you entertained if you like."

She smiled at me, and I leaned down to kiss her forehead. "I'll see you downstairs."

I re-joined Nathan. "She'll be down in a minute. So,

what's going on with Hannah?" I asked, turning the meat, and noting some already missing. I raised my eyebrows at him, and he shrugged his shoulders.

I'd been furious when I'd found out Anna had met with this Hannah, but thankful that she'd reported that back almost immediately. I'd made a point of not making it too obvious I was concerned about her security, but wasn't being overly successful with that. I knew Anna was starting to get worried. Thankfully, Nathan had taken over talking to Jules's mother about her fears of being stalked.

"Not a thing. Seems a little too coincidental to me. She complains about these calls, very precisely details the sound of a click and yet, the minute we investigate, nothing?" He shook his head as he spoke. "She's lying."

I watched Nathan as he watched Anna stride across the kitchen. No matter what he did, he'd never be able to hide the affection that showed. He smiled a little and his features softened. She smiled back at him. I guessed he remembered I was there, he dipped his head and glanced over her shoulder as if something behind her had caught his attention. She gave him a quick hug, he stiffened. Then she came to me. I kissed her temple and she stood beside me, with her arm around my waist. I didn't want to make Nathan feel uncomfortable, so I stepped a little to the side, pretending to be turning the meat one more time.

Anna and Nathan sat, I grabbed her a beer, and we chatted about Jules and a statement the Palace had released, extending their condolences. Neither Nathan nor Anna believed it. I hadn't known Jules, she was their friend, so I stepped back a little, letting them catch up on their news with each other. I basted and turned the food, prepped the fish, and wrapped it in tinfoil ready to be placed on the grill. I mixed a dressing for the salad.

Nathan told Anna that heroin had been found in Jules's system, I had assumed she knew that, but apparently not. She seemed extremely surprised, stating she didn't believe Jules had ever taken the drug. I would have thought Anna would have seen track marks on Jules had she been a regular user. Same for Nathan. He fucked her, he'd seen her naked I assumed, and he'd said he'd never seen any evidence of injecting drugs.

"So, what's next?" Anna asked, sipping on her drink.

"We'll see if anyone turns up at the funeral and looks out of place," Nathan replied. It wasn't unusual for a murderer to attend the funeral. No idea why other than a sense of pride in ending a life.

The conversation turned to Anna. She felt that her friends had dropped her, and it pissed me off, big time. Nathan had often commented about her friend, Julie, who came on to him constantly. As much as he joked with her, he said he didn't like her. He believed her to be fake, hanging around perhaps because of Dory rather than Anna.

I suggested Anna have her baby shower at the house, turn it into a spa day and invite her friends. That way it was on her terms. Of course, the more I encouraged her to do at the house, the more I hoped she'd fall in love with it, see that it worked for us, and move in.

Nathan gave me a sly smile, picking up on my idea, I imagined. I winked in return. Soon enough, dinner was ready. I laid the salad, fish, and meat on the table. Anna and I chose the fish, I'd only cooked the meat for Nathan, knowing he wouldn't eat any of that 'veggie' type food. I hadn't known him to eat a salad in the years we'd been friends. He was strictly a carnivore.

It was nice to relax and get mildly drunk. Not too much that I had no idea what was going on, of course, I knew my limits and only ever took myself to it. Nathan and I laughed about the old days, trying to outdo each other with stories from our army days.

A couple of hours later, Anna excused herself. I watched her leave. I also saw Nathan watch her leave. I kept my sigh to myself. There was no jealousy, she was having my child and was with me. He was my best friend, but he knew her before I did. So I had to accept his affection for her. I knew he would never do anything about it now.

By the time I climbed the stairs, leaving Nathan asleep on the couch on the terrace, I was more than tipsy. I stripped off my clothes and settled beside her.

"I love you too," I whispered, and watched her smile even though she kept her eyes closed. She'd heard me.

CHAPTER SEVEN

It was the day of the funeral. Anna looked stunning in a figure-hugging black dress, albeit pale. I was further concerned. She was quiet, sipped some tea, didn't want to eat, and I let her be, assuming she was lost in her thoughts. I wanted her to know I was there, beside her, when she wanted me.

Daniel drove us, it would be our last catch-up before he went off on his killing spree and I took Anna abroad. She didn't know where we were heading to, but I'd told her to pack for warm weather. I was taking her to my second favourite place, and somewhere I spent a lot of time, immediately after the funeral.

We were dropped off and I held Anna's arm. She seemed to wobble a little. I frowned at her. She assured me she was fine. We walked along a cobbled road towards the church and some of Jules's family were already there. We waited and watched a hearse and several cars arrived. We fell silent as the coffin was removed.

Hannah came over and hugged Anna. Her grief was obvious, her voice was hoarse, the sound one made after crying for so long. A sound I was familiar with myself. She greeted Nathan and me before moving to other people.

"Thank you for coming," we heard. We turned; a gentleman dressed in black came up to speak to Anna. He smiled at me.

"I'm so sorry," Anna said, her voice hitching, and I assumed she knew the guy.

"Mum said you'd be here. How are you? Jules told me you were expecting."

"I'm well, thank you," she replied. There was an awkwardness between them. When his French-Canadian partner started to talk, I understood he was Jules's brother. Why Anna was hesitant around him, I didn't know.

The whole service was strange. Jules's father spoke in a monotone voice devoid of any emotion. There were no childhood stories, attempts at humour, crying. Nothing, he didn't even look up from his speech. He could have been talking about a stranger, for all anyone knew. I wasn't the only one that thought it odd. Anna glanced at me a few times and frowned.

Thankfully, the service was short. We filed out and just as we got to the car, Anna turned to me.

"I don't feel..." She didn't get to the end of her sentence before she collapsed in my arms.

Nathan rushed over, and between us we got her into the car. I was frantic, so was he. He scooted into the front seat and before I'd even managed to get myself comfortable with Anna lying on my lap, Daniel was off.

We drove straight to the Portland, without Anna knowing. It wasn't intentional, I just hadn't told her yet, I'd scheduled an appointment there. I called ahead, explained what had happened and was told they'd have someone waiting for me. Although they didn't have a general A&E, they did have an emergency centre for pregnant clients. I fully intended for Anna to have her baby there, so we were deemed clients.

She roused a little on the journey, threw up, and then drifted off again.

I carried her into the hospital, and she was taken from me. I was instructed to wait. I didn't do waiting, neither did Nathan. We paced and scowled at anyone passing who dared to look at us.

"Are you the father?" I heard. Both of us turned and I glared at Nathan. He stepped back.

"Yes, how is she?" I asked, not knowing if she meant was I the baby daddy or Anna's!

"She's fine. Her blood pressure is all over the place. I'm surprised that wasn't picked up. We did some blood work, and she has very low iron levels, so we'd given her a little boost and we'd like to just keep an eye on her for a few hours.

Anyway, she fainted, nothing more sinister is showing up, but she's waking if you want to be with her," the nurse said.

I stepped into her room. She didn't look like she was waking to me. She looked peacefully asleep. I sat in a chair and waited.

I saw Nathan at the door, and I waved him in. I needed to remember he was part of her life as well. She roused and looked at him.

"Why did you pick those shoes?" she asked, and then drifted off again.

"She's fine," he said, and sighed. "I'll go get some coffee. There was nothing wrong with those shoes, was there?" he asked, and I laughed.

"They're shoes, mate."

He left and it was a few minutes later that she woke.

"Where am I?" she asked, sitting up.

"You're awake," I said, standing.

"Or I'm sleep talking," she replied, chuckling.

"A proper hospital," I said dryly. "It appears the one you so loved hadn't noticed how erratic your blood pressure had been of late and how low your iron levels were. Hence the tiredness and fainting."

"The baby—" Her hands instantly went to her stomach.

"Is fine. You just needed an IV to bring your iron levels up, and some rest."

"What about my blood pressure?" she asked.

"Rest, and you've been tested for pre-eclampsia."

"Bloody hell."

"You don't have it, or whatever the correct term is, but the hospital wants to monitor you regularly… More regular than your own hospital wanted to."

She settled back in my bed. "So, I fainted?" she asked. "And how long have I been here?"

"Yes, you fainted. You did come round a little, enough to blame Nathan for his choice of shoes." I chuckled. "He's outside, I'll let him know you're awake, and you've only been here a couple of hours."

"I *fainted* for two hours?"

"You're tired. You've said it yourself. The doctor will be round at some point."

"Oh, you're back, then?" Nathan said as he walked through the door with a couple of coffees. He handed one to me. "If you wanted a nap, you could have waited until you got in the car, ruined my trousers catching you." He chuckled. "And you threw up in the car."

"Well, I'm sorry for your trousers," she replied, smirking at him. "Fall to your knees for me, did you?" She smiled sweetly at him. "My hero!"

Before he could reply and while I was laughing, a nurse walked into the room.

"Hello, Anna. Are you comfortable?"

"Hi, yes, very, thank you. Do you know when I can go home?"

The nurse told her exactly what I had, that they wanted

to monitor her and the baby. She was asked if she wanted a cup of tea and, not before batting her eyelids at Nathan, the nurse left to fetch one.

A little while later, Nathan left, and I sat on the bed. "I was so worried," I said, stroking her hand.

She assured me that she was fine. I wish I had the same confidence she had. I wanted to tell her I'd lost a pregnant woman once and I wasn't taking her health for granted, but I didn't. That wouldn't be fair on her.

She'd feel she couldn't sneeze without me panicking.

But she couldn't sneeze without me panicking.

I didn't want to leave her. I told the nurse she'd been sleepy of late, and that was down to low iron, I'd been informed. While she sent a message to Hannah to apologise, not that I thought she needed to, I googled all the iron rich foods I could.

Eventually, the doctor arrived. He cleared her to leave and fly on strict instructions she'd return immediately should she feel unwell. He felt that the sun and good food abroad would do her well and her last blood test came back with levels he was happy with. While I'd waited for her to wake, I'd googled all I could about pregnancy anaemia and thought I was pretty clued up.

As much as Anna told me she felt fine, I still worried though. I would have postponed the holiday, but she kept reminding me that it was the last chance before the baby was born. We were flying privately, could schedule our return whenever, and the doctor agreed with her.

"She's fine, Jacob. You need to trust her instincts," the doctor had told me. I reluctantly agreed.

————

A week in Crete was exactly what the doctor ordered. Anna bloomed. She tanned, she rested, ate like a starved dog, and laughed. We talked constantly. We learned more about each other, or as much as I could tell her in that one week, making up for all the months we should have dated prior to making a baby.

I loved being with her. Her laughter lifted me and the minute we were one day over the same pregnancy length I'd lost my first child, I relaxed. Luck might finally be on my side.

We made love, and the further into her pregnancy she got, the more she wanted me. Of course, I was only happy to oblige whatever the time, wherever we were.

I took one call that week from Daniel.

"What's needed is done," he said. "Nathan will send the emails."

I didn't reply, just cut off the call. Anna looked at me quizzically.

"Wrong number, I guess," I said, and then kissed her to distract her.

I'd find out the full details when I returned, I was sure.

On our last evening, I took Anna to a small local restaurant that only served the fish that had been caught that day. It was family owned, near the beach, and totally unpretentious. It was exactly my kind of place. Everyone was treated the same, whether pauper or king.

Once we'd eaten, I wanted to show Anna a place that held some memories for me. A place I visited for contemplation because I knew I'd be alone, and it was beautiful. I drove that evening and as we headed back, I took the opposite turn from the house. We bumped along an unmade road that crossed my land. I'd bought the land to ensure it was never built on. Crete was getting too built up. We parked up in a small cove at the edge of the sea.

"Let's walk for a little while," I said, taking her hand.

The moon was full and high, it shrouded the beach in a silvery glow. We slipped off our shoes and walked barefoot. I loved the coolness of the sand against the soles of my feet. There was something about walking along a beach at night. The way the waves gently lapped at the shore and the sound they made was soothing.

"This is a beautiful place," she said. I smiled at her; happy she felt the same way.

"Let's sit. I used to do this for hours when I was younger and after..." I didn't finish my sentence; she didn't need to know that.

At the end of the small sand beach was an outcrop of

rocks. They made perfect seats, and one was worn smooth from years of being sat on.

"Does it feel odd for you? You know… You haven't had a partner for a while. Or maybe you have, I don't know, but you know what I mean?" she stumbled through her question.

I chuckled. "I haven't had any serious partners… Until now." I took her hand and raised it to my lips. "And yes, it feels odd, but only in the sense that I didn't think I could feel this way again."

I turned to look at her, wanting to be honest about how I felt. "I didn't think I could love again, and what I feel for you and our child outstrips what I've felt before. I feel guilty for that, but also know that's irrational. I feel like I should hold back, and I don't want to. I guess… I guess I need something, or someone, to tell me it's okay, what I feel is fine and I'm not being disloyal to Eleanor."

She stared at me. She showed no pity or upset in what I'd said. She smiled gently.

"It's okay to feel that way, Jacob. And it's not like you had any time to prepare for this child. I had made my peace with being a single parent at first. I would have told you, of course, but I was building myself up to do it alone."

"If I'm honest, I think I fell in love with you long before I met you."

She furrowed my brow in question. "How?"

"Nathan talked about you all the time. He has feelings for you. Anyway, I guess I fell in love with his version of you."

"He does not have feelings for me," she scoffed. "Does he? That will be awkward. And this *version* of me, is it better than the real thing?"

"A million times better." I leaned forwards and gently kissed her lips. "A million times better," I whispered, repeating himself.

"Tell me again," she said, echoing my words.

I leaned forwards, keeping my face just short of hers. "I love you, Anna, a million times more than I loved the thought of you."

Our kiss was demanding and urgent, a statement of our feelings. As the waves broke around our feet, I pulled her to the sand.

I wanted to make love to her in the place where I'd bared my soul, my pain, and anger.

In the place that then soothed and calmed me.

In the place where I exorcised my demons and gave myself permission to love Anna with all my being.

In the place where I, finally, thanked my wife for her love all those years ago, and acknowledged she would be at peace knowing I was loved again.

I had no idea just how important that last night was to become. How I'd recall those words I'd said to myself over and over, and how I'd look for them when I felt I was in the depth of hell.

CHAPTER EIGHT

I took a call in the dead of the night. It was Nathan.

"Anna's in trouble. Someone broke into her house; she's locked in her bedroom. Police are on the way, as am I."

"Fuck! I'll meet you there," I replied and cut off the call.

I scrambled into some clothes and ran down the stairs. I slipped on trainers and grabbed my keys. The Bentley was in the garage, and I cursed at the slowness of the door as it opened.

"Come on, for fuck's sake," I shouted.

I wheelspinned down the drive, and again, cursed at the slowness of the electric gates opening.

As soon as I could, I hit one hundred and twenty miles per hour and kept that up until I was closing in on London. All sorts of thoughts were running through my head. What if they got to her? What if they hurt her or my baby? Or worse?

I slammed my palm on the steering wheel multiple times, swore out loud, and I then took another call.

"I've got her, meet us at Springers," Nathan said.

I diverted down a second motorway keeping my foot on the accelerator until I saw the sign for the service station known locally as Springers Corner. It had been a regular meeting place of ours, halfway between London and Hampshire.

I pulled in the car park and alongside Nathan's car. Before I'd even turned off the engine, I was out of the car and ran to his. She opened the door and fell out, scrambling to get to me. She cried as I held her. I kissed her hair, holding her as tight as I could.

"Shush, baby, it's okay now," I said repeatedly.

"I don't understand what happened. There was a noise, I shouted, and then someone attacked me. Why would they do that knowing the police were there?"

"I don't know, baby, but we will find out." I looked over to Nathan who nodded.

"We need to get you home," I said.

Before I could lead her to my car, she broke away. She hugged Nathan, who closed his eyes and swallowed hard. Only I saw his display of grief at what had happened to her. I stepped back, giving them space and time, but I lowered my gaze, not wanting to see their affection for each other.

I held her hand all the way home while she told me what had happened. She'd taken a call from a policeman, so she'd thought, and then discovered it wasn't. It was possibly one of two intruders. She shook as she recalled the fear she felt and how she threw things and fought to get out of the room. I couldn't speak for fear of my rising anger clouding my words. I bit down hard on my inner cheek as a distraction and tasted blood. My heart raced and acid burned my stomach.

Whoever had broken into her house would pay and would pay brutely.

Anyone that frightened my woman, would feel that fear tenfold.

When she settled back, coming to the end of her recounting, I called a private doctor I used. He was a discreet man, able to sew up the odd wound without too much questioning. He agreed to meet me at the house. I wanted her checked over. She would have endured a spike in adrenalin, and I didn't know if that was harmful for the baby. On top of that, her blood pressure was elevated. I didn't care if it was overkill, it was happening.

When we arrived home, I ran a bath for her. I wanted her to soak in some warm and fragrant water to bring down her stress levels. I saw the bruise forming on her temple and she had marks on her sides. Again, I swallowed down the anger and bile that rose to my throat. I wouldn't allow Anna to see me angry, not that many people had, but I had the capability of scaring her and I didn't want that.

While she soaked, I went back downstairs.

"I'll fucking kill you," I mumbled, needing to just get those words out from my head.

I opened the door to Saul and detailed what I knew, adding about Anna's brief stay in the hospital. He nodded and rubbed his chin as he listened. If there was ever the TV series clichéd country doctor, it was Saul. Even in the early hours of the morning, he wore a heavy tweed suit, shirt, and tie. I'd often joked that he slept like that. He even carried an old-fashioned cracked leather holdall. I expected he'd owned that from new and when he first trained to be a GP.

We walked upstairs to find Anna in the bedroom.

"Hello, Anna. How are you feeling?" Saul asked, walking to the bed.

She looked up at him. "Like I've been assaulted," she said, and he chuckled.

"You look like you've been assaulted," he added, giving her a kind smile. "Let's have a look at you. Jacob, I'd like that glass of water you offered, please."

I stood staring at them; I hadn't offered him anything. "That's code for, can you give us some privacy, please?" Saul added.

"Oh, right," I replied, hating the fact I'd been dismissed. I hesitated by the door, not sure if I actually wanted to comply or not.

"I'll give you a call when we're ready," he added kindly.

I left the room. "Don't do me any fucking favours, I mean, I'm only paying you," I said, knowing he wouldn't have heard.

I paced the hallway to start with, then ended up in the nursery. I sat in the chair facing the window and looked at the cot. If anything happened to Anna or my child, I'd die, I just knew it. I looked around the room, needing the calmness to destress me. I had techniques I employed when my anger became too consuming, and I went through some of them.

Expressing – Suppressing – Calming

Those three words had been imprinted in my brain from my army days and then again in therapy.

I expressed my anger by making a commitment to find out who had hurt my woman and fucking kill them.

I suppressed that by parking the thought in the box labelled 'Who to Kill' in my head and looked over at the toys in the corner. I needed distraction.

The toys calmed me. The room calmed me. I took in a deep breath and let it out slowly. By the time I had done that, I was thinking more rationally.

I'd always had a temper and as a youngster it had gotten me in trouble. It was why I joined the army, I needed the discipline, someone other than my family to guide me through those years. I fought a lot, but finally, I found myself and another family in the army.

I thought of Nathan and how he might be feeling. I pulled my phone from my pocket and called him.

"Hey, she's okay. She's had a bath and I've got Saul checking her over," I said.

"That's good, thanks, mate, for letting me know."

We paused.

"What was it Princess Di once said?" I asked. "There are three of us in this marriage." I laughed and Nathan joined in.

Laughter was our way, regardless of the severity of the situation. It was our coping mechanism.

"As long as that works," he said.

"It will work," I replied.

I knew he was important to her, and she to him. I'd allow them their space and time without complaint, and I'd temper down any jealously I felt. I knew he wouldn't make a move on her, and I wanted him in our lives as well. That night had cemented it for me. She had two protectors, as would my daughter have.

"He chucked me out of the room, so I don't know what's happening," I said.

"Bet that was hard," he replied.

"Fucking was. I'm sitting in the nursery trying to work out how this fucking monitor turns on," I said, chuckling. "I'm going to have to google it, I threw away the packaging."

He laughed some more. "Give me a call later."

We said goodbye and I disconnected the call. I picked up the baby monitor and turned it in my hands. There was a second one in the bedroom, and a further couple downstairs. They needed to be paired, I thought, but switched the button to on anyway. I caught myself then and turned it off. She deserved some privacy.

I left the room and stood outside the bedroom. I checked my watch and waited some more. Then I couldn't wait.

I opened the door and walked in. "You didn't call," I said.

"So I didn't. Your wife is in good health, despite the circumstances, and just needs a little tender loving care," the cheeky bastard said. "I'm sure Anna will fill you in."

I liked his description of her, and I fully intended to make her my wife soon.

"No concussion or head injury?" I asked.

"Nothing that is presenting itself right now. I'm sure you'll be able to identify anything that crops up later, so keep your eyes on her. Call me or take her straight to A&E if needed."

He said his goodbye to Anna, and I walked him out with a promise to bring her back some tea.

"Are you sure she's okay?" I said as we got to the front door.

"I am positive. Or as positive as my fifty years of tending to the sick and injured, the thousands of hours of medical training in the army, and then as your GP allows me to be," he said, smiling at me.

I rolled my eyes and sighed.

"I'll send my invoice on," he added with a chuckle.

"How about I buy you a new car?" I replied.

"Although my invoice probably will be of the same value, considering the time of call out, I happen to like this reliable old thing." He was joking, of course, and opened the door to his vintage nineteen-sixty-five Hillman Imp in the most disgusting shade of orange.

It choked out a plume of smoke as he drove away.

"Fucking gas us, next," I said, grumbling as I waved the toxic fumes away.

I made the tea and a light breakfast considering the time, and then headed back upstairs.

"Here," I said, placing the tray on her lap. I climbed on the bed beside her. "How are you feeling?"

"I'm okay. I feel utterly exhausted and bruised though. I'm going to have to call a locksmith and the alarm company."

"I'll get that done for you. I want you just to relax and give me a list of what you want from the house."

"I can get what I need," she replied, sipping my tea.

"You're not going back there, Anna," I said, turning to face her and stunned she'd even consider that.

"I have to at some point."

"Why? I don't want you back there. You're at risk until we find out who broke into your house. Anna, do you realise how serious this is? Someone had intended to poison you and my child!"

I frowned; not understanding why on earth she didn't feel the same way.

She picked up my hand. "I'm coming back with you to get my things. No one is going to attempt anything in the middle of the day with you there, are they?"

"Why can't you just stay here and let me deal with it?" I asked, shaking my head in frustration.

"Because if I don't walk back into my home right now, I never will. And I want to be in control, not let whoever that was to be. I'm bloody terrified, Jacob, of what could have been, trust me. *Our* child is my absolute priority, but I have to meet the police, find my phone, and move out. I want to be able to do that, not give you a list. I don't know half of what I have. I'll move in with you, permanently, and put the house up for sale. But I'm not staying here and letting you do all that yourself. It was my home, it's... It's been spoiled by someone for reasons I don't know. I don't want to live there, but I do have to go back." Her voice hitched and tears sprang to her eyes.

I cupped her face in my hands and felt a total shit for trying to run roughshod over her. "Why don't you get some sleep and then we'll head off this afternoon?"

I left her to rest and made my way down to my office.

"I heard about Anna, I hope she's okay," Daniel said when I answered the phone. Although very early, I was pleased he had called.

"She is, Saul just checked her over."

"How is the old bastard? I remember him pouring fucking iodine over a bullet wound once, then telling me to run it off!" Daniel laughed at the memory.

Saul had been an army medic in the field. *Run it off* has

been his standard response and we often joked if he'd use that line to the poor fucker who stepped on an IED.

"Doesn't change. Still driving that old shit heap of a car. Anyway, how did it go?"

"Easy. Remind me never to go into any protection scheme run by our shit forces. Harvey was in the back garden having a smoke. I was fucking able to walk through the bushes and right up to him."

"Did he say anything?" I asked.

"No. Just took a drag of his smoke and closed his eyes. Like he was expecting it."

"And Taylor?"

"Squealed like a fucking stuck pig. Had a man, well a teen, with him, both naked. The kid fucking helped me restrain him." He laughed as he recalled the event. "He was all dolled up in leather belts and shit. Had a fucking metal cage around his dick!"

"Okay, that's good."

Harvey would look like he'd shot himself. The police would spend a couple of days trying to find out why they missed a gun in the water butt, and Taylor would be found having taken his own life with an overdose after penning a rather damning letter of apology.

"Have a good day," Daniel said.

I disconnected the call. He would have a good day. He was the coldest person I'd ever known. No one knew anything about his background, other than it was juvenile prison or the army. He chose to legally kill and took a lot of pleasure from it. He had been up on charges for killing a captive terrorist in his charge. Not one member of his section disagreed with him. Had it been the other way round, we would have been tortured and our fucking heads cut off, slowly, and in full view of the world. We all knew the prisoner and the atrocities he'd done to young girls and women as a means to control their men. He was way better off dead than pandered to in a fucking prison. It was the one thing I hated about Britain after I'd left the army. The way they would hang out soldiers to dry for the sake of publicity or media pressure astounded me. They had trained us to kill, given the okay to kill, been involved in more illegal killings than I'd made hot meals, but they wanted this fake appearance of being fair in war to prisoners, to be following whatever fucking convention they wanted to, to be upheld. I laughed, if only the media and the public knew what really went on. I shook my head; it wasn't a day to think about that. We'd done the country a fucking favour, saved a fortune in taxpayers' money. And ridded the streets of two perverts.

I forced my focus back on Anna.

I sat with Sadie for a coffee break.

"How is Anna?" she asked for about the hundredth time.

"She's going to move in with me," I said.

"Oh, I'm so happy about that," Sadie said. "I can't wait to have a baby in the house."

"I think, to make her feel more like it's her home, I'll let her redecorate or do what she wants with the house. Make it more her style. What do you think?" I asked, genuinely wanting Sadie's opinion.

"Perfect. I think that's a great idea. You must let me know what food she likes so I can buy it in."

I nodded and we both carried on about our day.

Anna slept on and off, showered, and then only came down for an evening meal with me. She told me she felt refreshed and raring to go again. I wasn't sure if that was just for my benefit.

———

The following morning, Anna quietened the closer to London we got. She wore my clothes again, having none of her own. My flip-flops were way too large on her feet, and I worried she'd trip.

We met Nathan at the townhouse. I wanted done as quick as possible so offered to help her pack some clothes. However, when we entered her bedroom, I struggled to contain myself.

"I fucking swear to you, Anna, when I find out who did this..." I rarely swore in front of her, I tried not to, anyway, but I was angry. I clamped my mouth shut.

She walked over and placed her hand on my chest. She cocked her head to one side and looked at me until I calmed. I sighed and wrapped her in my arms. "I will kill him," I whispered, and she nodded, believing me.

We packed as many holdalls as she could find in her closet and then she asked Nathan to grab some suitcases from the basement. It made sense to take as many of her clothes as possible. I wanted to limit the number of times she came back to the house. She had one wardrobe full of evening gowns. We left those for another time.

We packed, well, I balled up shit and she folded it all. She grabbed all her toiletries, makeup, hair stuff, that was enough to fill a cabin bag, and we lined them all up in the hall.

The only sticky moment came when we walked into what would have been the nursery. Boxes were stacked against one wall. Furniture was still covered in its protective polystyrene and plastic wrapping.

"I never got to set this room up," she said, and I could hear the sadness in her voice.

"We'll have this sent to the apartment and you can do that there," I said, referring to the London one. I wanted her to feel free to use that as her base, not her house.

She then said that she'd get a removal company in to box up the rest of her personal possessions and leave the house fully furnished. She'd approached the neighbour to see if they wanted to buy it. As she spoke, I saw the panic starting to rise. There had been a creak on the stair, probably wood settling after being walked on a few times. I'd never known her to have a panic attack, but by the way her eyes shifted from side to side, her breathing escalated, and her body tensed, I knew what was coming. She rushed downstairs and out the front door. I followed, giving her a little space to start with, then sitting beside her and just watching the surrounding area. A neighbour approached and I stiffened. I'd seen him leave his house opposite. He chatted to her for a minute or so before walking away.

I saw the police arrive and we made our way back inside. She was questioned and her statement written down. I'd told the police she wouldn't be attending the station and all information had to be gathered from the comfort of her home. I wasn't subjecting her to the trauma of an interview room. And she certainly wasn't going to be questioned without me present. She had been traumatised when she'd recounted to me what had happened immediately after. When talking to the police, Nathan and I were able to pick up on a few small details that she'd missed out on. Also, being in the house allowed us the opportunity to walk in the footsteps of the intruders, gain a mental picture of their movements.

"We found a ladder on the outside of the wall. One of those collapsible ones," the officer had said. I'd guessed they would have come in from the back, and although she had a walled garden, it wouldn't have been too hard to get over for anyone with the right footwear and half an idea of how to climb. Getting back out was the problem and they hadn't mentioned any means of escape back into the alley.

Anna then mentioned Jules. I hadn't wanted her to, not until we had confirmation that her uncle's body had been found and suicide ruled as the means of death. I nudged her leg, hoping that she'd get the hint. She did, but the damage was done. Nathan answered a couple of questions regarding Jules and the officer said he'd pull her file.

I was also thankful that she got a little agitated at the questioning. Rightly so, the officer asked her the same questions using different words, he needed to know her story stacked up should it get to court. He wasn't trying to trip her up, but ensure she answered in the same manner. She snapped at him, and he took that as his cue to finish up. He was a professional, for sure, and I was pleased about that. Way too many would have continued. I had full confidence in him, at that point. I gave him a card with my full name, address, and contact details. Told him that's where Anna would be living from then on. He added the card to his notebook and then pocketed both.

When the car was packed, we left. She didn't look back at all, just made a call to her assistant that she wouldn't be into work for a couple of days. I'd assumed, the closer she got to giving birth she'd take some time off anyway. She settled back into the leather seat with a sigh. She kicked off the flip-flops and played around with the seat controls until she was more comfortable.

I reached over to take her hand in mine. "Are you okay?" I asked gently.

"Yeah. I'm happy to move in with you, but I wish it hadn't been forced on me. Does that make any sense?"

"Perfect sense. I'll call an interior designer later and you can decide what changes you want to make to the house. Do whatever you want with it," I said.

"We don't need to worry about all that expense. Let's just live in it and then decide if we need to change anything for the baby." She smiled at me. "We should think of names soon."

I returned the smile, pleased she wanted to do something other than think about what had happened. "We should! Spanish or English?"

"Spanish, I think. What was your mother's name?"

I glanced over to her, surprised. "Paloma Santiago."

"Paloma. That's a lovely name," she said, smiling at me. "Why don't we call her that?"

I couldn't answer immediately, and I took a large swallow. I slowly nodded, not looking at her. "I'd be honoured if we called her after my mother," I said. It had always been my wish to honour my mother by naming my first daughter after her.

She placed my hand on her stomach. My daughter was doing somersaults.

"I wonder if every other decision will be as easy as that," I said, laughing.

I told her I'd introduce her to Sadie and Bill. Both had decided to take the day off so Anna could settle in. I explained that Sadie would sit with her and go through the household account and make shopping lists. I'd leave all the house decisions to her.

We arrived home and I explained the car was fitted with a sensor that would automatically send a signal to the gates for them to open. I parked outside the garages and turned off the engine.

"Come on," I said, opening her door for her. We had decided to sort the bags out later. I led her into the kitchen.

"Once a month, you and Sadie will go through all the bills that need to be paid and she'll give you a list of all the shopping she needs. You sign it off, she sorts it out. It's quite simple and efficient. All you have to do is let her know if you want anything added."

"Like what?"

"Your phone bill, chocolate, whatever," I replied, smiling.

"I can pay my own phone bill."

"Then pay your own phone bill. It was just an example. Don't fret over it. You'll love Sadie, and her husband, Bill, takes care of maintenance."

She sat and I made us drinks. She'd never been 'waited on' I felt, but I wanted to do that for her. I wanted to spoil her. I wasn't averse to feminism in any way, it was a good thing, but I also had a need to protect that was instinctive. We'd find a balance, I was sure.

"I'll do some change of address letters," she said.

"When you've drunk your tea, I'd like to formally

welcome you to your new home by fucking you over that counter," I replied.

She spluttered and laughed. "That's a welcome that I'd... Welcome."

And I did just that. I gave her time to savour her mint tea, not that I gave her the chance to actually finish it, though.

Nathan visited later that evening. The three of us sat in the snug.

"So, an update," Nathan started. "Hannah was seen on a neighbour's CCTV at Jules's house the evening she died. When I asked her when she'd last seen Jules, she had said it was a few days before. I called her earlier and asked her again, telling her that I'd seen her on CCTV."

"What did she say?" Anna asked.

"She said, she'd forgotten that she'd dropped off some shopping, but Jules wasn't in. She had a key, let herself in and left the shopping in the kitchen. She also said that Jules's flatmate was there."

"Her flatmate?" Anna asked, clearly confused.

"Yeah, her flatmate, and I'm guessing it's the woman we saw when we visited her. Did you know Jules was bi?"

"No, do you think that woman was her partner?"

"I thought you were," I added, looking at Nathan.

"I wouldn't say we were partners; we didn't have a *relationship* just... You know. Anyway, she told me she was."

"Where is that woman now, then?" Anna asked.

"No idea. Not at the flat, that's for sure," Nathan replied.

"Do you think she could have had something to do with Jules's death?"

"I don't know. But when people disappear for no reason, I start to get suspicious."

"What now?" Anna asked.

"I'm going to keep digging a little. I think Hannah knew of this woman and maybe she can shed more light on where she is. Back to you, though. Preliminary results are the substance was heroin. Now, if you'd have taken a drink from those cartons, I think you'd have tasted it or at least smelled something was off. So, whoever injected that didn't really know what they were doing."

"Why would they have done that though?"

Nathan looked between Anna and me. "Heroin can cause spontaneous abortion."

I fucking wished he hadn't said that, and I scowled at him. Anna looked terrified. "What?"

"Do you think that was the intent?" I asked.

"I've no idea, to be honest. We're dealing with an amateur, for sure. And I do believe there were two people in your house."

"How?" she asked.

I wanted to kick Nathan for giving her too much information. I would have, right or wrong, held back for fear of giving her bloody nightmares. He continued, however.

"Outside the wall was a collapsible ladder. No disrespect to your sex, but I don't see a woman being able to scale that wall, but a bloke might. On the outside there is flint, that makes great footholds. There is a partial footprint, the police took a mould of that. To me, it looks small, maybe a size five or less."

"Do you think the woman had the syringe?"

"Yep. And perhaps the bloke was there just to ensure she could get the job done. Where it went wrong was someone falling over a chair and you alerting them that you'd heard. Which brings me to this... Whoever it was knew you. Knew your mobile number, and it's that person that called pretending to be the police."

"Did you find my phone?" she asked.

Nathan shook his head. "No. I searched inside and out. I've asked the police if they picked it up and it's nowhere to be seen."

"The police have to have it. They searched the bedroom, didn't they?"

Nathan nodded. "So did I, no phone."

"I don't get that," she replied.

"I do. One of the officers has your phone and isn't letting on," I said. Nathan nodded again.

"Stop playing fucking Poirot and tell me what you know," she said, getting annoyed.

"Do you know this man?" Nathan pulled up a photograph on his phone.

"No, I don't think so."

"He's a policeman, obviously. He was at your house; you probably didn't take much notice at the time."

She frowned, trying to work out why that was important information.

"He's also now missing."

"And?" she asked.

"And," Nathan said, dragging out the word. "He drove Hannah to Jules's house the night before she died. When I saw him at your house, I knew I'd seen his face before but couldn't place him. And I knew I'd seen him recently, so I retraced everything I did. I had a copy of the CCTV on my phone, so I checked that. He knows Hannah, he must have known Jules, your phone is missing, so is he and the flatmate."

"What does Hannah say about this?" she asked.

"She doesn't know that I've made the connection yet. It's loose, for sure, but *it is* a connection," Nathan said.

"Why would Hannah know this guy?" I asked, now invested in Nathan's theory myself.

"That's what I want to know. I'm going to visit her tomorrow," Nathan replied.

"This is all too much for me. Where do I come into this?" Anna asked.

"I think Hannah believes that when I said *we* didn't believe Jules took her own life and *we* were looking into it,

179

she assumed you and me. She came to you with her fears, but what if it was more just to find out what you knew?" Nathan said.

"She thinks I know something, so she wants to harm me or my baby?" Anna instinctively covered her stomach.

"We don't know what she thinks the heroin would do. Like I said, I don't believe she knows anything about the drug, but it killed her daughter. Perhaps she thought it would do the same to you."

"You think she meant to kill me?" She sat wide-eyed and with her mouth open in shock, and I was about to fucking jump up and throat punch Nathan.

"The police think someone meant to kill you. There was enough heroin left in that syringe to do some real damage to someone. Maybe they panicked, decided they weren't going to get to you, so opted to poison something instead."

I kicked Nathan hard under the table.

"Oh come on, Nathan," she said. "Just because I thought Jules was murdered is no reason to hatch a plan like that.... Is it?"

"Listen, I can't be sure of anything right now. Other than someone meant harm to you, that's without doubt. Hannah's name is swirling around my gut. I just know she is involved somehow."

Nathan had never been let down by his gut instinct.

"What do I do now?" she asked.

"Stay here," Nathan replied.

It was the most sensible thing he'd told her. She decided that she'd heard enough and headed to bed. I waited until she was out of earshot and then turned to Nathan.

"Don't say it," he said.

"Say what?" I challenged.

"She needs to know. I know her, Jacob. In a week or two, when nothing else happens, she'll find a way to head back to that house or back to work and she's too strong-willed to have security."

It bugged me he knew her better than I did. I shook my head in frustration. "She didn't need to know all of it."

"Trust me," he said gently. "I know this is hard for you. I see you look at me wondering how I'm feeling when you're with her, and I'll tell you this. I'd be fucking devastated if you held back because of me. Sure, I have feelings for her. You know I've denied it. But she's your partner, not mine. But I'll still do whatever to ensure her safety."

I sighed and nodded my head. "Maybe just run things past me first, yeah? I have to reassure her through the night when you're not here. I have to ensure her safety, and my child's, as well. I don't appreciate sitting here not knowing until you deem it necessary to tell me. We are partners as well, Nathan. Don't hold back on me. This isn't a pissing contest; this is Anna and us."

It was his turn to nod. "Okay, I can do that. Now, fill me in on Harvey and Taylor."

"Sounds like a bottle of port," I replied, and the tension

was gone. We laughed.

I recapped what Daniel had told me. "He's not right in the head," Nathan said.

"Nope, and thankfully, he likes us."

"Yeah, I don't think I'd like to get on the wrong side of him," Nathan replied, chuckling. "Anyway, I'm fucked today, I'll crash here, and I have to leave early."

It wasn't an ask; it was a statement. I smiled and nodded. He could stay whenever he wanted.

When I climbed in bed next to Anna, the need to touch her overwhelmed. I curled in behind her and pulled her thigh so her leg was over mine. I swiped my fingers over her pussy and smiled as she mumbled.

"Mmm, I like that," she said.

As her orgasm built, I ground into her, rubbing my cock across her arse, feeling the friction of skin on skin.

"You want more, baby?" I whispered, I know I certainly did. She nodded and turned. "Ride me."

Seeing a pregnant Anna on top of me was a sight for sore eyes, for sure. She overwhelmed me and I bit down hard on my lip to contain the emotion. She rode me hard, slow, and when we both came, she leaned down to kiss me.

"I love you so much," I said. "It hurts sometimes."

She stared at me. "I feel the same."

We dozed, and then we made love, before we finally fell asleep.

As usual, I woke before her. The bed was a tangled mess

and I smiled. There was nothing in the world I enjoyed more than seeing her in my bed still, with that *just fucked* look. Her hair was fanned out around her, her cheeks tinged with red, and a sticky residue between her thighs. She smelled of me, and that made me hard.

I would let her sleep on, she and the baby needed it, but it wasn't easy. Instead, I took a shower and pleasured myself.

I was in the kitchen when Anna came down with a bundle of linens in her arms. Sadie rushed forwards to take it from her and I wanted to laugh out loud at the embarrassed look she had on her face. I knew the linen to be soiled from our lovemaking and I was sure Anna was feeling mortified in handing it over. Sadie rushed off and Anna joined me.

"Oh God, those sheets are rank," she said.

"She's dealt with worse. Tea?"

"What's worse than... You know?" she replied.

"Cum? Maybe lots more of it after I've dreamt of you," I said, feigning an innocent look on my face by widening my eyes.

"Ewww," she said, laughing. "You, you... Over me?"

"I'd wank while thinking of you, if that's what you're trying to say... Lots. Now, tea?"

She nodded and her cheeks reddened. I loved that about her. She was thrilled I'd wank over her but embarrassed at the same time.

"Well, I don't think you should have let Sadie deal with your sheets."

"I promise if I masturbate when you're not here, I'll put the sheets in the wash, okay?" I mocked her, then handed her the tea I'd just made.

Sadie made her some breakfast while I worked on my laptop. She then sat and went through the monthly accounts with her, asking if she had allergies, things I hadn't thought to ask.

I loved listening to them. Sadie was important to me, and it pleased me to see them get on. I hoped that would continue.

We talked some more about the previous evening and the information Nathan had given us. I hadn't wanted to, but she'd broached the subject, so it was still on her mind. She couldn't get her head around why she was a target. She couldn't connect the break-in to Jules or Hannah. I could, as could Nathan, but she didn't.

We chatted some more and then I headed to my office. I had a couple of calls to make. She did the same.

When we broke for lunch, I asked if she'd accompany me to Dubai. Obviously, I didn't want to leave her alone, but I needed to finalise a contract. I could send someone else, but usually the client wanted to deal with me and since we earned millions from this, it was necessary.

She declined, as I thought she would. I offered to postpone, but she wasn't having any of it. I was in a dilemma. I'd speak with Nathan about it, I decided. If I had to go, he had to stay with her.

CHAPTER NINE

Anna headed into work the following day and Nathan and I met. We discussed the Dubai situation and concluded I would fly out for one night and return, he'd stay with Anna. It wasn't that much of a time difference that it would affect me, and I could get done what I needed to.

We parted then, I to my London apartment to meet with Daniel and he to meet with Hannah.

It was a couple of hours later everything changed for us. And not in a good way.

Nathan and I stood at the office block. I was annoyed he hadn't accompanied her to a lunch, and we were arguing. We saw her walk towards us, and we paused. It wasn't the sight of her that caused us to stop, though. It was the car driving part on the pavement behind her. I fucking hated electric cars, she couldn't hear it coming. In the seconds it took before I reacted, I took in as much information as I could for future recall. I also recognised both driver and passenger.

"Fuck," I said. I shouted out to her, "Get out of the way." I waved my arm to indicate she should move. She just smiled as if she hadn't heard me and waved back.

We ran, Nathan got there first and grabbed her. All three of us were in the car's path then. I turned side on to the car and pushed them away as hard as I could. They fell, just out of harm's way, and I took the full force of the car. It smashed into my thighs, and I was thrown first on the bonnet and windscreen, then over the roof as the car continued at speed. I heard Anna scream out my name and I saw her scramble to her feet as I was tumbling. I saw the blood seeping through her clothes between her thighs. I felt the blow to my head as I landed heavily and then bounced along the road. I blacked out then.

———

It was odd. There were times when I thought I'd hear voices, but they seemed so distant. And then there were times when there was nothing but blackness.

I had periods of what I thought was consciousness, but I couldn't move. The strangest part was, I didn't have to breathe.

I couldn't work it out. I made no effort to fill or empty my lungs, they just did. Even when I tried to hold my breath, they still worked. I didn't dream, but I sometimes saw light flash across my closed eyelids.

Some of the voices were female, some were male. I didn't understand words, and I couldn't feel a thing. I drifted, peacefully, pain free.

Until they woke me up.

I'd never suffered with headaches before, but the crushing one I had floored me. I didn't want to open my eyes, and if I could have punched the fucker who was forcing me to, I would have.

"Can you tell me your name?" I heard.

For the first time, I felt like I could move my lips. I swallowed, my throat was sore as fuck, and I was desperate for a drink.

"Jacob," I replied. It took an effort to get just the one name out.

"Do you know where you are?"

I instantly recalled the accident but nothing before it. "No. Hospital?"

It hurt to talk, and I didn't think I could form a sentence. I was guessing at where I was as it was the most logical conclusion. When I finally opened my eyes, I saw a doctor leaning over me.

"Do you know what happened to you?"

"Car ran me over. Anna?"

I remembered she had been thrown out of the way, but I panicked then. I couldn't remember what she looked like!

I thrashed about, or thought I had. I wanted to swing my legs from the bed, but they wouldn't move. No matter how hard I tried, they stayed put. I shouted, started to tear the cannula from my hand until a warmth flooded over me and I relaxed. I knew something was flowing through my veins to sedate me, I could taste it. I welcomed it.

I had no idea how long I'd been in hospital. I hadn't even known that I'd woken a couple of times. I only became *aware* when I saw Nathan sitting beside the bed. I couldn't turn my head, the fucking thing pounded so much I felt sick.

"Hey," he said, noticing my eyes were open. His voice was off. Strange.

I turned to look at him, knowing him, but not understanding why he was crying. I was so confused, still.

"Head hurts," I said.

He rose and rushed to the door, calling someone. It was a few minutes later a nurse joined us. She checked me over, brushed a sponge of water over my lips to quench some of my thirst and then propped me up.

"Your head will hurt for a little while, Jacob. We'll give you something to help with that."

I nodded, not usually one for pain relief but knowing I needed it. She injected morphine into my cannula.

I closed my eyes waiting for the hit to dull the pain.

"I can't move my legs," I said sometime after.

"I know, mate. They work, it's just your brain... You banged your head pretty bad," Nathan said.

I let a tear slide down my cheek. I kept my eyes closed, and then dozed off.

It was a few days later that I came fully round. I was swamped with doctors, scans, MRIs, and physios.

Nathan came every day and eventually he told me about Anna. I'd forgotten she had been pregnant, and I sobbed as he told me I had a daughter called Paloma. She had been born premature and both Anna and Paloma were still in hospital.

"I'm sure I can take you there," he said. I looked at him, and then I shook my head.

"No."

The decision I'd made was totally rational to me. It was a decision I'd made years back when I was a soldier. If I was ever in a state where I needed full-time care, that was to be done in a home, and not at mine.

"Huh?" he asked.

I was saved from answering by yet another neuro specialist.

"Hi, Jacob. I'm glad to see you more with us," he said. "We're going to get you out of bed soon. I know that's going to be tricky, but we need to get your lower limbs moving."

"How the fuck do you think that's going to happen?" I said nastily.

"You need to retrain your brain."

They'd tried to explain to me what had happened a few times, I took it in, but I never remembered what they said.

The pathways in my brain that sent the signal to my legs

were damaged. According to the experts, the brain was miraculous, because we could train it to change the direction of those signals to new pathways. I wasn't as convinced initially.

But I also knew I wasn't living my life in a wheelchair. I'd fucking take my own life before I gave in to that. I certainly wasn't having my family wipe my arse or bathe me.

Nathan didn't push me to visit Anna, and I was thankful for that. I had no perception of time or how many days I'd been in hospital. I didn't even know what month of the year it was. My memory prior to the *incident* was sketchy, but I could remember every detail of the bastard's face sitting next to Hannah, as if it was on replay in my mind. And I guessed it was. I relived it constantly and every time I landed on the road, so my head hurt to the point of blinding me temporarily.

I hated every second of my incapacitation.

I fought all the way, especially when it came to using the bathroom. I slapped arms and hands away from me, determined to drag myself, if I had to.

I hurt, I cut myself on objects in my attempts to regain some independence, and then I gave up.

———

I was sitting in the chair when Anna arrived. Nathan had told me she'd been visiting me when I'd been in a coma, and when I was brought out of it. I didn't remember that, of course, but I did wonder if hers was the voice I'd heard. She walked in and smiled at me. She looked tired, dark circles framed her eyes.

"Hello, you," she said, feigning a brightness I knew she didn't feel.

"Hey," I replied.

She stopped in her tracks.

"You're talking," she said.

"Since yesterday, apparently," I replied.

She sat on the chair beside me and took my hand in hers. "How are you feeling?"

"Like I've been run over by a car." I gave her a small smile, not that I felt like I had anything to smile about. "Not good, Anna, mentally."

"I can imagine that. You must take your time to heal," she said gently. "Paloma is getting stronger by the day. The doctor said she can go home at the end of the month if she keeps improving."

I nodded but closed my eyes against the mounting pain.

"Would you like to see a photograph of her? I've had to send out for new clothes, she doesn't fit in anything we bought yet," she said, adding a chuckle and trying to stay positive.

I didn't respond, and she didn't push.

"Your doctor says you're doing well."

I sighed. I tried hard not to, but I was sick of hearing that statement. "Except I can't fucking walk, Anna." My voice was harsh, and I didn't care.

We sat in silence for a little while.

"You should go, she needs you," I whispered, needing to grit my teeth against the pain and unable to open my eyes because the fucking light hurt them.

"I'll see you in the morning after I've done her morning feed. I printed off a photo for you, it's by your bed. The doctor tells me they're moving you tomorrow, so that will be nice."

She leaned down to kiss my lips. I didn't move.

I heard her sobbing as she left the room and my heart hurt. Tears flowed down my cheeks, and I pushed the morphine pump that had been fitted to me. I needed pain relief and quickly.

I was irritated when the door opened again. By the sound of the footsteps, I knew it not to be Anna though.

"Hey, mate," Nathan said, sitting beside me.

I slowly opened my eyes.

"I need you to do something for me. I'll never ask another thing of you after this," I said, wincing as I spoke.

"Anything, I'll do anything," he said.

"Tell her not to come again."

He didn't respond. "Tell her, Nathan. I can't be with her. She needs you now. This is your turn. You look after her and her... Our daughter. I need you to do that. She is not to come here again, do you understand?" My voice had risen, and an alarm had gone off.

I clutched my head and screamed out in pain as the sound was like needles piercing through my skull.

"Tell her, Nathan!" I shouted.

A nurse ran in and silenced the alarm. She checked my blood pressure, which had spiked dangerously high, and called for assistance.

"I can't," he whispered.

"Then you don't come and see me either."

He stood and I looked at him. "Please, do this one thing for me. I'm begging you."

If I could have gotten on my knees, I would have.

He cried then. And finally, he nodded. I saw him swallow hard. "Goodbye," he said, and I knew that would be the last time I'd see him.

"Call Samuel, now," I said.

Samuel was my lawyer and I'd given him some instructions. Without anyone knowing, I'd had him visit and prepare some documents for me. He hadn't wanted to, insisted I wasn't of the right frame of mind to do so, but he'd relented when I'd asked a specialist to confirm I knew exactly what I was doing.

Nathan nodded again and picked up his phone. He dialled.

"Sam, it's Nathan," he said. He listened. "Okay, I'll get them to her."

I closed my eyes then and waited until he left.

With only the nurse in the room, I reconciled my decision in my mind.

I could not offer Anna what she needed, so I thought. Nathan could.

I could not be the man I wanted to be. Nathan could.

I would love her until I died, so would Nathan.

I would love my daughter forever.

So would Nathan.

I didn't hear from either for a few days, and I was pleased. My mind was in turmoil. I knew I wanted to die, I just had to find the means to do that. It wouldn't happen in that hospital though. I went through the motions; I did what I had to do to achieve my goal. Eventually, I persuaded them a rehab centre was the best place for me. And I wanted one out of the country.

I was told of a centre in Jersey for brain injured ex-military. It was expensive, but that wasn't an issue. I was booked in.

I knew I wasn't going to the facility to recover. I was there because as soon as I had a level of independence, I could end my life. It was all I could think about. I had no intention of living life disabled. I had total awe for those who could, but I couldn't.

I was aware I was spiralling into depression and therapists tried to tell me my thinking was normal for being in that condition. No one could ever understand though, I could not live life dependent on anyone.

I wanted Anna to have the life she deserved. For Paloma to have a father who could run with her, play and jump. Someone who could teach her to swim, ride a horse, drive a car.

More importantly, I wanted someone who could walk her down the aisle when she married, and I knew that wasn't going to be me.

I looked at the picture Anna had left lots. I held it to my heart, I cried on it. The ink smudged, the paper crumpled where I'd slept with it, and I still kept it.

"How are you feeling today, Jacob?" my therapist asked. This would be my last session with her.

"No different to yesterday," I replied, and then remembered my mission.

"No, actually, I do feel different. I'm not sure what it is, nerves perhaps. I feel more.... Lifted," I lied.

She smiled. I smiled back, a broad smile. "Yeah, lifted is a good word for today, I think," I added.

"Do you think you might contact Anna?"

"Not today, but I'm working on a plan for that. I'm going to walk back into my house and propose to her," I lied, again.

I made so many stories up and it always surprised me when the silly bitch believed them. I was a good liar; it had been part of my job for so many years. I was actually looking forward to just being me, being truthful, in my last days.

I chuckled as a thought popped into my head.

Maybe I'd confess my sins.

195

"What's funny, Jacob?" she asked.

"Nothing in particular. Like I said, I feel better. I'm nervous but I'm also looking forward to the clinic, and I want to continue therapy there. It's a shame you can't come as well." I'd learned long ago that flattering a woman who clearly liked me would get me what I wanted.

It wasn't a surprise to me, to acknowledge how calculating I'd become. I was doing whatever it took to achieve my goal.

By then, Anna would have known I'd gifted her the house and money. I'd set up two accounts, one for her and one for Paloma. I knew Anna didn't need my money, but I wasn't going to be buried with it. In my will she'd get everything else but the company, that was going to Nathan.

It was important to me that she had a home and people to care for her. I wanted her to start to hate me, I believed that would be easier for her. And in that hate, she'd turn to Nathan. I couldn't think of any other way at the time.

I forced Sadie and Bill from my mind. Nathan, however, kept returning. Not physically, but he'd send a text message every now and again. Most of the time, I didn't reply.

When my things were packed up and I was transported by car to Biggin Hill. My lawyer kept all the details and had been instructed to deal with all fees. Other than them, I wanted no contact with anyone.

The journey was awful. I was on a small charter plane that bumped around in the air. Each time it did, the cabin pressure changed, and it was like a hammer to my skull. I clutched my head in my hands and did everything to quell the nausea. I wasn't successful. I threw up over myself.

I'd never hit a woman before, but much to my shame I slapped the arms away of the stewardess who tried to help me. Every nerve ending covering my whole body was on fire. It hurt to actually be touched and I didn't want her fucking help.

I wanted to be left alone. I wanted the plane to fall from the fucking sky and take us all into the ocean with it.

When we landed, I was wheeled to the toilets where I changed my T-shirt. I left the sick-covered one on the floor, not caring to pick it up.

I sat in silence in the mini bus that had collected me. I hated the process of being wheeled in and strapped into place. Fuck knows what would happen if we crashed. I wasn't getting out quickly. By the time we got to the facility, I was tired and angry. I hadn't realised just how much the journey would take out of me. I was shown to my room, and I asked to be left to relax for an hour or so. I was hoisted onto the bed, another thing I hated, and the curtains were drawn. I closed my eyes, not getting any sleep whatsoever, but effectively shutting out anyone who wanted to intrude.

———

My room faced the sea. The facility was on top of a cliff and if there was ever such a thing as a perfect view, I had it. I intended to not like it, however. I didn't deserve the room and tried to change it. There were others, I thought, who wanted to get better and would appreciate that view each morning or when they were feeling down.

I was introduced to my new team. I had two physios, a personal nurse, and a therapist. All were male which stuffed my plans a little. I would worm my way into a woman and manipulate, I didn't think I could do that with the guys.

Day two was acclimatisation. I was wheeled around and told about all the different facilities. There was a gym and pool with a wheelchair ramp and lifeguard. I was told I'd do some pool work to strengthen my muscles. I nodded, pretending to be enthusiastic. There was a restaurant, and I was actually taken aback with the menu and wine list. It wouldn't have been out of place in a five-star hotel.

There were therapy rooms, both for the mental and physical side. Art rooms, a photographic studio, and gardens. Acres of land with a veg plot, sheep, and lawned areas with seating. At the edge of the cliff was a bench. I was wheeled beside it, and my nurse sat.

"What do you think so far?" he asked.

"Nice. Can't imagine anyone wanting to leave," I said.

"I'll introduce you to some of the inmates," he said, laughing.

I actually liked him. I didn't want to; I had no intention of getting close to anyone considering what my plan was. Anthony had been in the military, so he'd told me, and when he'd lost a leg, not that it was noticeable, he'd retrained. Most of the *inmates,* as he called them, had recently served. I was one of a handful of old timers allowed to be there. It was thought, Anthony told me, that a mix of generations would help. I had never felt old before that point.

He wheeled me back inside. There was a communal lounge and we headed there. I could hear shouts and cheers; it appeared that a table tennis match was going on. When the ball was hit so hard it thundered past the opponent and bounced towards me, I caught it.

"Good hands," someone shouted.

The room was full of abled and disabled people. Mostly men, but some women. I noticed the women and assumed them to be ex-military as well. One wore her hair in a tight bun, a throwback from her service, I assumed. Another still wore her green regiment T-shirt. She rocked in the corner with her hands over her ears. I'd seen that position from shell-shocked men many times. Although, *officially,* that wasn't the term used anymore, it was exactly that. Bomb after bomb landing so close affecting the hearing. When that happened, the other senses heightened, which also meant so did fear and anxiety. And when you'd seen someone you called a friend blown to smithereens, all you wanted to do was block out the noise, the smell, the taste, and the sight of it all. I felt pity for her and hoped she'd eventually recover to some degree.

I threw the ball back and the game picked up immediately. Anthony introduced me to some. I received some banter about being an oldie and asked where I'd served. It felt strange to talk about the army and I wasn't sure why.

Every person I employed had been in the services in one way or another. Yet I was chatting to a different generation. There were one or two who kept themselves to themselves and weren't so forthcoming when introduced, and I accepted that. I didn't want to make friends either.

I asked to be taken back to my room.

For days, I only left it to sit looking at the sea. Anthony came to me every morning to get me out of bed, showered, and dressed. He'd talk, tell me about his days in the army, and I found him way easier to talk to than anyone else. He would sit with me while I complained and moaned. He'd help me with some coping techniques when my head pounded.

Although my headaches weren't as skull crushing, they were still there. I'd developed migraines that could floor me, and I knew I'd live with those until my last days. I had hoped just for one day, at least, of normal before I ended it. It would be my fucking luck on my last day I couldn't move because of a fucking headache!

I didn't know *when* my last day was, but I knew how it would be. I had begun to like the bench on the cliff. I enjoyed the view, I found that it calmed me. I would think back to that time in Crete with Anna and conjure up the feeling of sand beneath my toes and her in my arms. It was painful and settling at the same time.

I had been keeping back a tablet or two and storing them

in a pot in the bathroom. It was slow going, however. If Anthony gave me my meds, then he'd sit with me while I took them, stay and chat afterwards. I had to wait until he was off duty and one of the other members of staff gave me the pot, and then trusted me to take the tablets. It was those I stored. I wasn't sure exactly how many I needed but I knew I wanted enough not to come back from it. As part of my *getting shit together,* I'd instructed Samuel to prepare a Do Not Resuscitate. Under no circumstances did I want reviving if found before I died.

I also needed to make sure the longer I sat at the bench, the more normal that became and the less I was checked on.

I hadn't heard from Nathan, but Anna sent me text messages. It was often just stuff she and Paloma had done during the day. She'd then send me a goodnight message. She never mentioned Nathan in any kind of romantic way, but I guessed she wouldn't. I didn't read her messages until late at night. When lying in the dark without being able to get up and piss if I needed to, or turn over easily, took its toll on me, I read. My head hurt and I had to squint to read the bright words on the phone, but I wouldn't resort to an eye test or a larger screen. It wasn't worth it, in my mind.

I started to punch my legs in frustration. It was made worse to know I could feel pain. I could bruise and bleed, but I just couldn't get them to move. I felt conflicted. I didn't care about my legs not working, and I didn't have enough time left, I felt, to make them. Yet, I still focussed on the fact they didn't move. I still agonised over the damage in my brain and those fucking pathways I didn't believe in. Or so I thought. I flip-flopped, really. One day I didn't care, the next I thought it might be nice to walk to my death.

Everything seemed to be geared around what I would do when the day came. Would I wheel or walk?

———

"Morning, we have a big day today," Anthony said when he came into the room.

"Yeah, not looking forward to it," I replied, pulling myself up using the bar hanging above me since I'd refused to entertain the hoist anymore.

Hannah's trial had started. She had been charged with conspiracy to commit murder. Although it appeared Anna was the intended victim, the charge hadn't changed. Samuel had kept me informed on a day-to-day basis. He was the only one I allowed to see me. He visited the previous week so we could get my memory refreshed on any statements I'd made. It had been hard, because although my memory prior was still sketchy, things were coming back to me, though that day was still clear as crystal. However, the defence had the ability to muddy the waters if they kept going back and forth over things.

I had been assured that wouldn't be the case, considering the extent of my injuries, but I wasn't sure. A monitor had been set up in my room, Anthony and my lawyer were the only people allowed in. I'd showered and dressed and sat in a chair. I could see myself at first. I hadn't shaved in weeks, growing a full beard. I didn't like it, but I couldn't be bothered to deal with it, either.

I had no idea who was watching the monitor other than they could see me, but I wouldn't see them. This was to help me concentrate and not get distracted. I could hear them, of course. When the judge spoke, I answered. I didn't deviate from my statement at all, and I tried to keep any emotion inside. I found that hard and had to stop a couple of times to regather myself, especially when I had to detail my lasting injuries. In one way it felt good to let the bitterness out, in another, not seeing the reaction, it made me feel vulnerable. In addition, it bought back all the feelings of hurt and pain, the insecurity and self-loathing that, although I hadn't realised it, had started to subside.

When my time was done, I asked to go to the bench.

By that point, I was wheeling myself. I had enough upper body strength to transfer from bed to chair and back again. I had even played a couple of rounds of table tennis, getting my arse whooped by a youngster.

I moved to the bench, and I wanted to kick the wheelchair away, get it out of sight. It couldn't go over the edge, there was a fence and below the fence, mounted to the cliff side, was a net. I wondered if that had come about because someone had thrown themselves over the edge.

I sat for a while and closed my eyes, just breathing in the fresh air.

I felt someone sit beside me and was instantly annoyed. I had a reputation for being a loner, not wanting company unless I instigated it, and I was always afforded that. Until then.

I opened my eyes and mouth to speak, but didn't.

Beside me sat a woman with long dark hair. Both my wife and Anna had long dark brown hair. She had blue eyes. Eyes so full of sadness and brimming with tears.

"I'm sorry to interrupt your thoughts," she said, in a soft voice.

"You haven't," I replied, lying.

"I just needed to sit here for a minute before I left." She closed her eyes and breathed in deep. "This has to be one of the best places on earth," she added.

She opened her eyes, and I looked out to sea. The sun shimmered on the calm water creating silver swathes of light. The sea was a dark blue, and on the horizon was a ship. Probably a cargo ship by the size. It looked stationary, but I knew it wouldn't be. Other than that, there was nothing. Just the blue of the sea meeting the blue of the sky.

"It certainly calms my mind," I said, not knowing why I said that, but suddenly recognising it as true. I didn't know who she was or why she was sitting with me.

"We all need that, don't we? I just wish my husband had got to this point."

There was such sadness in her voice, but also resolution and acceptance.

"He died here two years today. I come here just to sit and remember him. I guess I won't do that forever, but for now, it helps. I also volunteer here. I think it keeps me close to him somehow."

I looked at her.

"I'm sorry, I shouldn't have said that. I'm disturbing you," she said.

"No, please, stay. Tell me about your husband," I asked, knowing she needed to.

She smiled. "He was an amazing man, although I would say that. He was also a total shit when he wanted to be." She chuckled and I joined in. "I loved him though. He was in the navy, a pilot."

She paused and we sat in silence for a moment. She turned to me.

"If he'd have died in war, I could've accepted that. Is that odd?" she asked, and I shook my head because it wasn't. "But he took his own life, here, while recovering. I don't understand it. He was walking, talking, and coming home. Instead, he swallowed as many pills as he could, and he was found here, dead."

I went cold. That was how I intended to end my life, although I hadn't told a soul.

"Why would he do that?" she asked.

"His mental injury was far more painful than his physical," I said gently.

She nodded and then turned to look back out to sea.

"I wonder if he thought of us when he did it? It's the one thing I've always wanted to ask him. Did he sit here with his pills and water, thinking about us at all? Did he wonder how we'd cope without him, how destroyed our lives would be? My daughter has never recovered from it. I fear she'll be joining him next. Do you know the most painful thing? The abandonment. If only he could have opened up to me. I wouldn't have tried to change his mind, if he was that set on not coming home, and I know that sounds strange. But I could have reconciled that beforehand. I could have sat with him, even! Not knowing how he felt, not wanting me to be with him... That hurt more, I think."

I felt like I'd been stabbed in the heart. I was immediately cold to my bones. I reached out and took her hand. I think the hand-holding was more for me than her. She let me, but still continued to look out to sea. A lone tear rolled down her cheek.

"Why was he here?" I asked.

"A malfunction in his plane. He tried to eject and at first it didn't work. He went down with the plane, only managing to get out at a couple of thousand feet. He hit the water like a brick."

Her brutal summing up of her husband's accident had me wincing.

"He was pulled from the water, broken, but alive. That was five years ago. It took him three years to get to the point of coming home. I guessed that was too long," she said.

Three years. That was an immense amount of time to be in pain and trying to heal.

"My name is Emma, by the way." She had turned to me.

"Jacob. I'm sorry, Emma, for your loss."

She looked down at our joined hands. "Are you married, Jacob?" she asked.

I couldn't answer, I felt a swelling in my throat so large it blocked my airway. But I did nod.

I knew I wasn't strictly married in the legal sense, of course.

"I have to let her go," I said, finding the words.

"Why?" she asked softly.

I didn't answer, I returned my gaze to the sea. "I wonder if Jimmy thought that about me," she said. "I think I'd rather he left me than take his own life. He could have taken up with another woman if he wanted to. I struggle, Jacob, to know he sat here alone, died alone."

"I don't want to be a burden on her," I finally said.

She nodded. "I can understand that. I guess I'd feel the same." She paused and returned her gaze to me. "I hope I'd also have the courage to ask my partner if they wanted to be left as well. I think it's way easier to assume what our partners want than to actually ask, isn't it?"

I didn't speak. I couldn't. And then I could.

I didn't know Emma, but I poured it all out. I told her about Anna, Paloma, Nathan. I shared details about my first wife and child and how I felt when they died. I openly cried. She didn't interrupt me once. She just let me spew it all out.

I felt like I was a volcano. I'd been contained for so long and now I was fit to burst and my acid, my lava, poured from me. I told her how I intended to kill myself, exactly like her husband had done. And still she just sat totally unjudgmental.

I didn't know how long we'd sat there for, but the sun had begun to lower. A chill developed. We still held hands and we both cried.

Finally, I was spent. She looked at me and gently smiled. "I'm glad you've told me all this, Jacob. You've actually helped me understand a little of how Jimmy felt."

"Do you think you'll come back?" I asked.

"I don't know."

"I'd like you to," I said, and then regretted it. I shouldn't have involved her in my misery. She had her own life to lead. It also did occur to me it should have been Anna I'd unloaded to.

"Then I will. I'm not a saviour, Jacob. If I couldn't save my own husband, if I can't heal my own daughter, I can't help you. But I can listen. I can be a friend."

That's all I needed. A friend. Someone who didn't know me, who wasn't close to me, but understood, even if it was from the other perspective. Someone who wouldn't judge or expect anything from me.

Anthony walked across the lawn. I caught sight of him from the corner of my eye. I let go of Emma's hand. "I think the boss is here," I said.

She chuckled. "He's a good man, that one."

They greeted each other and I wondered if Anthony had cared for her husband. Emma patted my leg.

"I'll come back and see you, Jacob, if that's okay?" She looked up at Anthony.

"Of course, you know that," he said, smiling at her.

She stood and held out her hand to me. It wasn't a shake, just a hold. And then she left. It was only as she did that I noticed a small plaque she'd left beside her. I picked it up.

My darling James. Look out over the sea, remember me, remember us. Be at peace.

My hand shook and I passed it over to Anthony.

"She wanted that on the bench, we agreed."

"And I took that time away from her. She should have told me, and I would have left."

I hauled myself into my wheelchair and straightened my legs. He wheeled me back. I could have done it myself, but I was cold. I wrapped a blanket around my shoulders.

I sat on my own, as was usual, for dinner that night. Some of the other patients would pat my shoulder as they passed or smile, and all respected my space. I guessed that came from us all being in the forces at some point. We had an understanding. However, that night the restaurant was full. Anthony came in looking around. It was quite normal for the staff to eat at the restaurant. I looked over to him and gestured to my table.

"Join me if there are no spaces," I said.

"Are you sure?" he asked.

I nodded. He sat and placed his phone on the table. Shortly after, a plate of food was delivered. "I didn't know you had telepathy as one of your skills," I said.

"Ah, see, I can surprise you." He chuckled. "I'm pretty boring and have the same meals all the time. And I think she likes me," he said, giving me a wink.

The waitress slapped his shoulder and walked away. I chuckled.

"I was thinking about Emma," I said.

"Go on," he encouraged.

"She said that she wondered if Jimmy had thought about her and the kids when he took his own life."

Anthony placed his fork back on the table. "He left her a note. She never read it. She tore it up and threw it on the fire."

"Did you know him?"

"Yeah, I cared for him. He was very troubled."

"In what way?"

Anthony sighed. "I can't divulge everything, but he recovered the use of all limbs but when he ejected, he hit the canopy and sustained a head injury. He bailed out so fucking close, I'm amazed he survived. Anyway, he was prone to outbursts of anger, and there was a fear he could be dangerous. He couldn't help himself, so we were never sure if he really would integrate back into his family safely."

"Did she know that?" I asked. She hadn't mentioned that at all.

"Yeah, but I guess she didn't want to believe it could be a problem. He just wanted to end it and he was so angry he hadn't died that day."

"She said it took him three years," I said, wanting confirmation.

Anthony nodded. "Yes, it was hard work for him. He didn't want to do it. We can't keep you here, you're all free to leave, but with him, I guess, deep down he was scared. He knew he could hurt his family if he lost it so he... I guess he institutionalised himself to a degree. When it came to the push, making him leave, as such, he took his life."

"Man, that sucks. Who made him leave?"

"No one actually *made* him leave, but he couldn't stay forever. What we do here, Jacob, is prepare you for life at home."

"What if someone doesn't want to go home?" I asked.

He shrugged his shoulders. "I don't know. I'm guessing that person may have to move to a facility that offers long-term solutions."

I sipped my water, and he took a couple of mouthfuls of his pasta. "Are you talking about yourself, Jacob?" he asked.

I stared at him. "I'm not sure now."

He smiled and nodded. "Perhaps this is something you need to discuss with Mike."

Mike was my mental health therapist. I enjoyed my time with him, but he was well aware of how often I'd divert the conversation. Maybe I needed to get honest. It wasn't like anyone could talk me out of my plans.

"Maybe. We'll see."

I left Anthony to his meal and wheeled back to my room. I sat by the window looking out, seeing the empty bench, and picturing Jimmy there. Picturing myself there. I wondered if he'd slumped to the side or fell off.

What were his last thoughts?

It had started to rain, autumn was closing in. I had been at the facility for a couple of months. Although, I'd managed to get my upper body strength where I wanted it, I still wasn't walking. I could move my legs, however. I could swing from the hip and did this while holding myself up between bars. It wasn't enough to walk, I think I'd lost so much muscle, it would take a while for that to build up.

I caught myself short. Why was I thinking about my legs when I didn't plan on using them?

I pulled myself into a standing position using the window frame and held myself there. The muscles in my stomach protested and I snorted. I fought through it.

CHAPTER TEN

I sent a very rare text message to Nathan, asking him to come and visit me. I gave him the address. He replied almost immediately, telling me he'd be on the next available ferry. I told him to call James and arrange a flight, they could land at the facility and visit that afternoon. I hadn't checked with anyone, of course, before sending the message.

"Anthony, someone is coming to visit me, they'll fly in by helicopter. Can they land here?" I asked.

"I have no idea. I don't see why not. There is plenty of unused land. I'll check it out. Now, are you ready for your shower?"

"Yeah, but I'm doing it myself."

I hauled myself from the bed to the wheelchair and took myself into the bathroom. There were rails along the wall and a wet chair. A fucking awful white plastic thing with holes in the seat that water could run through. Those holes also pinched my bollocks at times. It was undignified for sure. I transferred to the chair and then into the shower where I turned it on. The one thing that pissed me off the most is that no one had thought to have the controls outside the shower. Cold water hit me, and I yelped. Once it warmed, I pulled myself up. I had been pulling myself up against the window fifty times in each session. I did at least four sessions per night. I went to bed with a stomach cramping from the effort, but I wasn't giving up.

I held on with one hand and washed myself with the other. It was more exhausting than I thought, and once I nearly slipped. My hand came loose from the soap suds. I thought I was about to land on my arse, and I'd need to call for help.

I'd had some training in how to get from the floor to a chair, but I hadn't had to do it for real.

When I was done, I lowered to the chair, and then wheeled out of the shower cubical. I grabbed a towel and dried as much as I could reach. I placed a second towel on the wheelchair and transferred.

Getting dressed wasn't so much of an issue. I could pull my shorts over my feet and up as far as my thighs. Only then did I need help. As I pulled myself up off the chair, Anthony slid them up. We did the same with sweatpants.

I hated every second of it.

"I need to do this myself. Think of a way," I said, grunting with the effort of getting socks on.

I pulled a T-shirt over my head, and I was ready for breakfast.

Emma was visiting that morning, and I was looking forward to it. She'd been to see me once since our initial chat on the bench. She'd shown me pictures of Jimmy and her daughters. I'd shown her the smudged image of Anna and Paloma. I bolted down breakfast and returned to my room to wait.

"Morning, Jacob. I brought you cake," she said as she entered the room. "I've asked for tea as well."

She liked to feed me, she said I was losing weight and needed to bulk up. I had laughed at that. I could eat for England and not put on weight.

"Emma, I need to tell you something. You know I wanted to end my life..." I paused as she turned sharply to me.

"*Wanted*?" she said. "As in past tense?"

I nodded. "I don't know what I was thinking, to be honest. I want to be around for my daughter."

"And Anna?" She came to sit opposite me by the window and handed me some cake.

"I still think she'd be better off with Nathan, but... I don't want her to be with him. I'm just not sure what kind of a husband I can be."

"What do you think will be so different, Jacob?" she asked gently.

"I don't know," I sighed. "I can still get... Intimate with her," I added.

"Well, that's good, but you know what? It's only men who think that's the be all in a relationship. I'm sure just having you home would be enough for her."

I liked to talk about Anna to Emma. I didn't feel I was betraying anyone or breaking any confidences. I had no sexual attraction to Emma, and she had none towards me.

"I'm meeting with Nathan later," I said.

"Wow. What's brought this on?"

"You, mostly. Something you said to me when we first met. You said, you wondered whether Jimmy was thinking of you before he took his life. You said the abandonment was the worst. It's stuck with me. Anna messages me every day and I can't seem to answer them. But I need them. I have to know how her day has been, what she has been up to. I try to read her mood in her words, and I can't, that frustrates me."

"You could call her," she said gently.

"I could, and I don't know why I don't. I pick up the phone time and time again. I hover over her number, and I don't press. I talked to Mike about it yesterday."

"What did he say?"

"He thinks I'm suffering from PTSD, but I don't agree. Look around this place, Emma. Some of those guys have suffered way more than me. Some have limbs blown off, have held their mates while they died. They have PTSD and to label me with the same, feels like an insult to them."

"I can understand that. But you know any kind of stress disorder can affect any type of person for any reason, and at any time. Trauma is trauma, Jacob. Anna went through a trauma, I went through a trauma, you have, also. Someone tried to kill her, you took the brunt of that. Maybe it's okay to accept that has a lasting effect."

I stared out of the window and took a bite of my cake. A porter came in with a tray and placed it on the small table. Emma picked up her black tea.

"I hadn't thought about it like that. Do you think I've been selfish?" I asked.

"I think, in your situation, selfishness is what pulled you through initially. It's okay to think only of yourself sometimes, Jacob."

Other than Anna, Emma was the only other woman I could sit in silence with and not feel uncomfortable. We both sat looking out to sea, eating cake, and drinking tea. I hadn't the heart to actually tell her I hated tea.

"How's the training going?" she asked.

"I showered myself, and my bollocks didn't get stuck in the holes," I said, and then laughed.

"I'm pleased to hear that," she replied, laughing as well. I'd previously told her how much I hated the wet chair.

"I'm gonna go home, Emma," I said.

She stared at me, and tears filled her eyes. "Oh, Jacob." She stood and leaned down to hug me. I accepted her hug and wrapped my arms around her.

When she stepped back, she smiled. "I'm so glad to hear that." She sat back down.

"Not yet. I'm going to walk into my house."

"Will you let Anna know?"

I paused. "I don't know. I'm afraid to build up any expectations in case I fail."

"Jacob, have you ever failed at anything?"

I stared at her and smiled. "Nope. Will I still see you when I'm home?" I asked.

She smiled back at me, and then sighed. "Probably not." She had spoken quietly and there was a sadness to her tone.

I nodded, understanding. I was going back to something she had been denied. I'd guessed that would be kind of painful. She would have loved Anna though.

"Will I see you before I leave here?"

She nodded. She lived on the island, not too far. She had moved here from London when Jimmy had been sent here. She couldn't buy, she wasn't a Jersey Being as the locals were called, but she rented a little cottage from an elderly couple and looked after them as part of the rent. Her daughters hated being away from London.

"I might move back to London. Maybe it's time for us both to stop putting our lives on hold."

"I think Izzy might like that," I said, referring to her daughter.

She took a deep breath and sighed. "You know, I think we've been good for each other. I also think we need to hold each other accountable. I'll move back when you leave here. I'm going to write a plan and so should you. When I come next week, we can swap plans."

I laughed. "This isn't school."

She rose, kissed my cheek, and said goodbye, reminding me to write my plan before her next visit.

I wondered what Anna would make of her. I didn't know Emma's age, about the same as mine, I guessed. She was naturally blond with tinges of grey. She fiddled with her wedding ring constantly, as if it was a source of comfort for her.

I had no idea of her financial situation, but I knew she would be getting just an army pension, perhaps a payout because of the malfunction, but it wouldn't be a lot. Service personnel sacrificed their lives for a paltry sum sometimes.

I picked up a pad and pen, and I thought.

Walk was the first thing I wrote. Underneath, I then added all the exercises I'd been encouraged to do but hadn't done.

––––––––

I was sitting in my room after having a physio session when Nathan walked in. Although I hadn't seen him for several months, he hadn't changed at all.

"Jesus, ate a bear and left the arse hanging out?" he said, striding across to greet me.

I stood, using the rail that had been placed on the wall

beside me. I held myself steady. He stopped abruptly and smiled.

"Well, fuck me, you're finally making an effort."

I laughed and he hugged me. I couldn't hug him back properly; I was holding on for dear life.

"It's good to see you," I said genuinely.

"Your voice has changed," he replied, staring at me.

"Has it? I don't hear a difference," I said. We sat and he continued to stare at me.

"You look the same, but different. I still wanna punch your lights out for what you've done though."

I waved my hand over my face. "Go ahead, my friend. But I can tell you that you can't hurt me more than I want to hurt myself."

I saw him close his eyes and swallow hard. "How are you, Jacob?"

"Struggling, mentally. I had planned to end my life, but I'm changing my mind on that at the moment. I'm working hard to walk. I'm having therapy, that helps but it also brings up a lot of shit from my past. And I'm talking about my wife as well."

"That's a good thing, isn't it?" he asked.

Anthony walked into the room. "Sorry, forgot you had company. I'll cancel physio."

"No, it's okay. Nathan can come with us."

I pulled myself up and Nathan reached out to help.

Anthony placed a hand on his arm, telling him not to. I transferred to my wheelchair, and we left the room.

"Lots of vets here," I said, as we passed some sitting in the day room.

I explained each area as we passed it. Eventually, we ended up in the gym.

"Jacob, good, you're here," Carl called out from across the room. "We're on the bars today."

We rotated around the gym. Some days I did weights, both arms and legs since I could move them from the hip. Carl would strap my legs together and brace them straight. I would lift weights with them. Other times we'd be on steps. It was a very short flight, and I would have to drag my legs up them.

That day, we were on the bars. I wheeled to the bench and picked up my gloves. As I put them on, I saw Nathan looking at my hands.

"Hard work," I said, showing him the blisters and cuts. I slipped on the gloves and then wheeled to the front of the bars.

Anthony stood behind the chair and put on the brakes. I pulled myself up into a standing position. Carl held my waist and lifted me. First, I did some dips, lowering to my shoulders and raising until I was off the floor. We did that until sweat rolled down my back. Carl helped me move to the lower bars. I rested my forearms on them and concentrated. I bit down on my lower lip as I focussed. It took a lot of effort but once I got my hip to swing my leg, I could move. I *walked* the length of the bars. One leg was better than the other I'd found, and as much as I tried not to, I tended to favour that one and concentrate more on it. I had a thought that if one worked well, the other would follow. Of course, it didn't work that way, as Carl continually told me.

"Jacob, left leg," he called out.

I struggled forwards, putting all my effort into my weaker leg. I, stupidly, looked up. I stumbled and my sweaty arm slipped from the rail. I fell.

Nathan rushed forward and Carl held him back. "I can do it!" I growled in frustration.

I dragged my body to the end and used the uprights to haul myself up. I punched my thighs, earning a sigh from Carl, and then I started again. I walked those bars four times, until my upper arms shook with the effort and my lower were bleeding from sliding across the wood.

"I think that's enough today," Carl said, and I slumped into my chair. I pulled my legs into position, placing my feet on the rests.

Anthony gave me a towel and I wiped my face and arms with it. I removed the gloves and looked at my palms. They were sore but I wouldn't change the gloves. I wanted to feel that soreness. It was an indication that I was working.

In silence, we made our way back to my room. "I'll have a quick shower then we can have a beer if you like," I said.

"Sure, mate, that sounds good," Nathan replied. His smile didn't reach his eyes.

While I showered, I could hear him talk to Anthony.

"That was hard to watch," he said.

"Yes, but way better than he's been before. He's working hard to get those legs going now."

"Will he walk again?"

"There's no reason why he won't. If he stays as determined as he is right now."

"What's changed?" Nathan asked.

"That's a question for him."

I wheeled from the room with just a towel around my waist. Nathan watched Anthony dress me, and although I was embarrassed by that, I didn't shy away from it. It was time for Nathan to know exactly where I was at in my life.

I winced as I straightened to pull my T-shirt over my back. I knew Anthony had seen the bruises on my ribs that were forming, but he didn't say anything. I hurt from my falls, and today had been the third. I was rushing, I knew that. When I looked at myself, somehow it threw me off balance.

"Beer?" I said.

Nathan followed me. We headed to the restaurant and to my usual table. He picked up a menu.

"Blimey, this looks good."

I nodded. "Let's eat as well, I'm starving. That workout leaves me hungry," I said.

Nathan laid his menu down just as a waitress arrived to

take our order. "Afternoon, Jacob, what can I get you?" she asked.

"I'll have the steak sandwich. And a beer."

Nathan ordered the same.

"I don't know what to say, mate," he said.

"Catch me up on the news," I offered.

He told me Harvey and Taylor's lives were still splashed all over the news. There were parliamentary inquiries and more people had been arrested. It seemed the ring was collapsing and was way larger than we'd imagined. Hannah was waiting for a sentencing date, and Daniel was out in Iran looking at a new contract. I was pleased he'd placed Daniel beside him.

"How's Philip?" I asked.

"Good. Bossy, as usual."

I then asked about others.

"Are you going to ask about Anna?" he said.

I sighed and looked around the room. I was given a temporary reprieve when our sandwiches and beer arrived. I sipped and took a bite. All the while he stared at me.

"How is Anna?" I asked.

"Missing you madly. Drowning, dying inside each day you don't reply to her."

I focussed my gaze on the beer label.

"Still in love with you. Still wants you home. She's sold her house, and her business is going as well."

I looked up sharply. "She's done what?"

"She's selling her business. She wants to be a stay-at-home mum. She's also delayed Paloma's christening, insisting she won't do that until you are there."

I nodded. "And Paloma?" I asked.

I watched his face soften. He loved my daughter as if she were his own. "She's amazing. Bolshy, looks like you, sadly. She's sitting up, I reckon she'll be crawling soon. She demands things, like, she holds out her arm and her hand is all grabby." He laughed as he spoke, and I couldn't help but smile.

"Do you have a picture?"

Anna often sent me pictures, but I wondered how much they were doctored. Nathan grabbed his phone from his pocket. He opened up his photos. "Swipe left," he said, as he handed it over.

I scrolled through pictures of my daughter awake, sleeping, in the pool, angry and waving her fists in the air. Then I saw pictures of Anna he had taken, without her knowing by the looks of them. She was looking wistfully into the distance; her hair was blown out in the wind. She had tears in her eyes. I scrolled on some more. There was one of her face; she looked sad and tired.

And the last one, the punch to the gut was one of her asleep on the sofa. She held my sweatshirt to her face, and I could see the sodden rings where she'd cried herself to sleep. I stared at that image until my eyes blurred with my own tears and another headache started to form.

"I love her so much, but I'm scared, Nate. I'm scared to fail. I'm scared, if I can't look after myself, she'll get bored of that. I'm scared I'll never walk my daughter down the aisle at her own wedding."

My hands shook as I held the phone. "Send me this?" I asked.

It was the one image of Anna I needed. The one that tugged at my heart so much it would spur me on. The sight of her holding my sweatshirt, not letting go of me, it seemed, would be what I needed in my dark nights with damaging thoughts.

He took the phone from me and immediately sent it. He didn't shut it down; he placed the phone on the table and left that image on show, facing me.

"We all miss you," he said.

He then coughed. He didn't do emotion, not publicly anyway, and I wondered if he was embarrassed by my open tears.

"You understand why I'm here, don't you?" I asked.

"No, I don't. You've never actually told us," he said.

I nodded. "I left the hospital because I knew I couldn't go home. I couldn't allow Anna to wipe my arse, wash me, dress me. I didn't want that for her. I was in a low place, mentally. I hated every fucking second of being alive and, in my mind, I knew I was going to end it. I couldn't do it there, so I decided to come here."

I swigged on my beer. The only other person I'd told this to was Emma.

"I was going to save up my pain meds and take them all in one go. End my life here. It's why I signed what I did over to Anna so she would have security. I changed my will as well. The business goes to you, obviously, she gets all my money and property."

"You think she'd want that rather than you?" he asked, his voice rising in anger.

"Yeah, back then I did. Do you remember when we were in Iran. We'd spent fucking days holed up in that house, running out of ammo and thinking we were going to have our fucking throats cut while watching each other. Remember that? What did we say to each other?"

He stared at me and swallowed loudly. He bit down on his lower lip, then sucked it into his mouth. He looked over my head before reaching into his pocket. His closed fist rested, palm up, on the table. I did the same.

When he opened his fist, I did the same.

We both held a bullet each.

"We said, we'd rather die. We were happy to take our own lives. We kept back one bullet for when we ran out, and we'd load our guns and look at each other while we blew our brains out. Do you remember how that felt?"

He nodded. "Calming," he said, sighing heavily.

"Yeah. When we knew *we* were in charge of our destiny, we didn't feel so despondent."

Slowly, he nodded. He closed his fist and returned his bullet to his trousers. Why we always kept them on us, neither of us really knew. They had become a talisman, I guessed.

"One day, we'll throw these in the sea."

His smile was slow to form. "What happens now?"

"I'd appreciate it if you didn't mention any of this to Anna," I said, and his smile fell. He shook his head. "Hear me out, please. I don't know how long this is going to take. I don't know what my future is, even. I'm not even halfway through this journey yet."

"Why does that mean she can't know anything?" he asked.

"Because if this fails, it's back to plan A." I rolled the bullet in my palm.

"I'll never forgive you if you do that," he said.

"I know, and maybe that anger will be what Anna needs."

He slammed his palm on the table. "She needs you!"

"She needs us both. Right now, I can't do it. I can't be the half-man."

His shoulders slumped and he picked up his beer. He took a sip. "Can we get a cold one?" he asked, looking over towards the waitress who had stood looking at us after his outburst.

She nodded and disappeared, returning with two cold beers.

"Let's get out of here," he said.

He walked and I wheeled myself beside him. We left the building, and he sat on a bench on the terrace.

"Bear with me, Nate," I said.

"Only for so long. I can't watch her slowly dying without you, Jacob. It fucking kills me. You know how I feel, and it hurts, mate," he said, his voice was strained.

"Just for a little longer." I knew what I was asking was hard and was a risk.

He stared at me for an age before he nodded. "I owe you, but consider this, once your home, it's all fucking paid. This isn't fair, but you're my brother so I'll do it, but that's it."

He swigged back his beer and then took out his phone. He sent a text. He stood and placed his hand on my shoulder.

"We miss you," he said again. He walked away then.

I watched as he crossed the field and then disappeared. It was a few minutes later that I heard the rotor blades churn and saw the helicopter lift into the air. The nose dipped as they flew over me. I shielded my eyes and watched.

I finished my beer before returning to my room.

CHAPTER ELEVEN

For the next few days, I worked hard. I fell often. I banged my head and ended up in bed with migraines, with only my insistence I wasn't attending the hospital keeping me there. Only Anthony and Emma were allowed to see me. I sat in the dark with ice patches on my forehead, popping pills as if they were sweets. It was the longest time I'd had such constant pain.

"Hey, I'm not staying long, and I don't want you to talk. I have this," Emma said, placing a cold bag in my hand. "It's for migraines."

I patted the bed and she sat. "Nathan came," I said, wincing as I spoke.

"Don't talk, you can tell me later. I hear you started to make your plan. I've written mine. When you're better we'll compare," she said. "And I've given notice on the cottage.

Now, I've left cake on the side, and I'll pop back in a couple of days."

She kissed my cheek and left. I knew what I was going to do to help Emma and her kids, and I felt guilty I was thinking this without consulting Anna. I knew Anna would have agreed, however.

When I was able, I tried walking again. The next fall I had set me back. I landed heavily on my wrist and broke a bone. I was furious with myself. There was an internal inquiry and I cursed at the director of the facility for blaming Carl. I had made the decisions; I had let go when I wasn't ready to. It had nothing to do with Carl. I even offered to sign a declaration that I wouldn't fucking sue them. Carl kept his job, but I knew he wasn't happy. Worse, he was hesitant with me.

"You should fuck this place off and start up on your own," I said to him one day.

"Well, that's always been the dream," he replied, strapping my legs for weight training. I might not be able to work with my arm for six weeks, but I wasn't staying out of the gym.

"Do it, Carl. They don't fucking appreciate you here."

He chuckled. "If only I had the money," he said.

I looked at him. "I do."

He frowned at me. No one knew much about me in the facility, only I could afford to be there as a private patient rather than referred and paid for by the NHS.

"I do," I repeated. "I can set you up, Carl, wherever you want to be."

He looked around him. "Well, let's talk about this another time," he said, catching someone looking at us.

I followed his gaze. "Another time, for sure."

We continued to work on my legs.

Not being able to use one arm frustrated the hell out of me. I pulled myself up on my bars in my room, often. When I was alone, I used my broken wrist, crying out in pain, but not giving in to it. I wheeled myself in and out with just the one arm. And I met with Emma.

"You are never going to believe this," she said, as she bustled in, yet another cake in hand.

"What?" I asked.

"I found a house. I'm going to apply for a mortgage, I haven't done that in years." She seemed so excited.

"Tell me about it," I said.

She sat and cut up the cake as she told me all about a little house on the outskirts of London, bordering Kent. She showed me details on her phone and said that she was going to view it over the weekend.

"It looks amazing. Send me the details so I can have a proper look," I said, she did so.

I forwarded the image to Samuel. If she liked the house, it would be bought for her. It wasn't an act of charity, and I would make it look like a foundation for lost servicemen paid for it, rather than me.

I highly doubted she had any idea of the impact she'd had on me and my decision for the rest of my life. It was the least I could do to thank her for that.

She had saved my life, basically.

———

Every evening I read the text messages from Anna. They kept me going and every evening I typed a reply and deleted it. I couldn't understand what was holding me back, and I felt a total selfish prick for not replying. I tried my hardest, even in the dead of night when I couldn't sleep because my bones hurt, my muscles ached, and my head throbbed. I would reread everything she sent me, over and over. And each time it hurt my heart that I was paralysed in responding.

I stared at the image Nathan had sent over. It haunted me day and night, and it drove me on. I pumped iron; I dragged my body across a mat chasing a fucking cone as part of physio. I swam, a lot. I'd always loved to be in the pool at home, and when my first session came in the water, I'd looked forward to it. I remember they had wanted to put me in fucking armbands, and I'd kicked off big time about that. I could swim, I didn't need my legs for that.

I'd wheeled a wet chair down the ramp and slumped forward into the water. At first, I had sunk under, forgetting I couldn't stand without holding on. When I surfaced, I saw a worried Carl about to get in with me. I laughed. I floated on my back and then I swam only using my arms. It gave my stomach muscles a good workout, I was having to hold up the bottom half of my body.

I swam lengths, every single day. I had the six pack of my youth, and my shoulder and arm muscles were defined. To the point, I had to order in some new T-shirts as the sleeves were too tight.

I'd seen plenty of Para-Olympians and often marvelled over their upper body structure. I was starting to look the same.

"You could enter the Invicta Games," Carl had said one day. "I bet you've got some speed on that swim."

I laughed, holding on to the edge of the pool. "Too old for that," I said.

Being in the pool gave me freedom. After a month of swimming every day, something else happened as well.

"Look at your legs, Jacob," Carl said quietly.

I glanced down. I was treading water, totally unconsciously.

I looked up, sharply. "What the fuck?"

He smiled and nodded. "Yep. When you're not concentrating on it, it's working."

As he said that, my legs stopped. I tried not to be disappointed. "Maybe we should have got in this fucking pool in the first place," I said.

"It happens when it happens," he said. He stood by the side with my wet chair and a towel. My session had ended, and it was with great reluctance that I left the pool. I show-ered myself, and I dressed, still with a little assistance, but I was learning to pull my shorts and trousers up with one hand and without getting my cock or balls in a painful twist.

That night I lay on the bed. It was hot and I was both excited and frustrated. I texted Nathan.

"My legs moved in the pool. I didn't know I was even doing it. I was treading water."

He replied almost immediately.

"Mate, that's fucking brilliant!"

"I know. I'm going back in there in the morning. I want to be full-on swimming by the end of the week. If I can do that, I can walk unaided."

"I gotta see this."

"Come over," I said.

"Can I bring anyone?" He had asked me that question before.

"I'd prefer not, and I'd prefer you didn't tell anyone."

I'd asked Nathan not to tell Anna he had seen me. He had argued he couldn't agree but then gave in. My reason was to avoid any hurt for her. I could imagine it would be awful to know I had him visiting and not her. I wanted to slap myself every time I had thoughts of excluding her, and I was pushing Mike for an answer as to why I was doing it. We were exploring fear and my ability to distance in preparation for the worst. I did that a lot. In my army days, if someone was badly injured, I kept my distance. It hurt them that I never visited, but most understood. In the same situation, they'd have done the same.

It was about never having to say a final goodbye.

I put the phone on the sideboard. I was frustrated and hot. I wanted to simply get out of bed and open a window, but the effort that would take would have me even hotter. It was the simple things that annoyed me the most. When I couldn't lie anymore, I sat up and slid my legs over the side of the bed. I pulled my wheelchair close and transferred. I wheeled myself along the corridor. The night staff looked up and smiled at me. No one questioned where I was going. I headed to the pool.

The main lights were off but the pool lights were on. The water glistened. I transferred to a wet chair and slowly wheeled down the ramp. When I reached the end, I put on the brakes and pushed myself off the chair. It was more like a sitting dive. At first, I just used my arms to propel me through the water. However, when I reached the end and turned, I started to kick my legs. They were very uncoordinated to start with and I did my best not to think about it. I counted; I recited a poem. I sang. I did everything I could to avoid thinking.

I swam twenty lengths of that pool in the quickest time I'd ever done. It didn't even raise my heart rate. I stopped at the deep end, just keeping my body still. I thought about the times Anna and I were in our pool at home. How she'd wrapped her legs around my waist, the feel of her wet naked skin. It aroused me. I could feel my cock harden in my shorts.

I swam another twenty lengths, and then another.

I laughed; the sound echoed around the room. I stood in the shallow end and let go. I held my balance. I lifted one leg and took a step. It was hard work pushing against the body of water, but I did it. I took one step, and then I took another. The water was supporting me to a degree. There was a definite weakness on one side, but I walked the short length of the pool back to the chair. I knew I'd be pushing my luck if I tried to walk up the ramp, so I sat and wheeled myself back out. Still wet, I transferred, and then left the pool room.

"Hey, you okay, buddy?" I heard. The night porter strode towards me as I wheeled back to my room.

"Yeah, fancied a swim. It's too hot tonight."

He chuckled. "Yeah, know what you mean. Well, if you need anything, just shout."

I thanked him and continued to my room.

I grabbed a couple of towels from the bathroom and headed to my bed. I dried my top half and my legs, laid the towel on the bed, and transferred. I slipped off my shorts and wrapped the towel I'd sat on around my waist, then laid down.

I slept well, I thought. I know I woke refreshed.

"Morning, been swimming, have we?" I heard. Anthony strode into my room.

"Yep, and I have something to show you."

I smiled as he helped me dress.

"After breakfast. I believe you have a visitor this morning as well," he said.

"Yes, Nathan is coming."

"Excellent. You know, Jacob. I think you'll be going home sooner than you think," he said.

I stared at him, and then nodded. "I think you're right. I will miss this place though."

"It's safe here, isn't it? You have all the help. When you get home, you'll have a transition period, I imagine. You'll need time to re-establish yourself and find new routines."

He had verbalised all my fears.

I nodded. "I'm not looking forward to that part."

"Why not get someone in to help initially. I know when a few of the long-term guys have left, they've employed an assistant to help them reintegrate."

I hadn't thought of that. "Would you do that?" I asked.

"Do what?" he asked, walking beside me as we headed to the restaurant.

"Would you come back with me, for a couple of weeks?"

He stopped and looked at me. "I don't know if I'd be allowed."

"Could we ask?" I felt like a child talking to a teacher about extra help.

"I guess so. It makes sense since we're already in tune with each other."

We continued our way to breakfast.

While I ate, I saw the helicopter fly over. It was five minutes later when Nathan walked into the restaurant. He sat and ordered a cup of tea and some toast.

"You are paying for this, aren't you?" he said once they'd sat it in front of him.

"Obviously."

"So, what's so urgent?" he asked while chewing on toast.

"A couple of things. There's a woman who comes here to see me—"

"What?" he said, his mouth hanging open.

"It's not like that. She came here to remember her husband. He took his own life. Anyway, we got chatting and she comes back to visit me. There is absolutely nothing in it. She lives locally and is moving back to London. I'm going to instruct Samuel to buy her a house."

There was a long pause while he stared at me.

"Are you for real?" he said, putting his toast back on his plate. "Your partner is sitting at home without a fucking clue what's going on. I'm lying to her, and you're playing fairy fucking godfather to a random?"

I expected a response, but not one as strong. "She isn't a random. She's a woman who lost her husband."

"I know a woman who has lost her husband as well. She's called Anna!" His words stung.

We stared at each other until I lowered my gaze first. "You're right. I didn't think this through, but I've committed to it now." I rubbed my hand over my beard. "And this is coming off today," I said.

"Oh, well, that's grand then," he replied sarcastically. "Honestly, mate, it's great you have someone to talk to, and I'm sorry she lost her husband, but you doing nice things for her when your own wife is crying herself to sleep still isn't fair."

I nodded and sighed. We fell silent for a little while. "I'll make it right."

"You fucking better. Now, what was the surprise?"

I smiled. "Wait and see." He didn't quite smile back.

I didn't want awkwardness with him. And when I saw Emma walk in, I closed my eyes. She came straight over.

"Hey, thought I'd pop in early. Sorry, I didn't realise you had company, I'll come back later," she said, smiling at me and Nathan.

"Emma, this is Nathan," I said. She turned to him.

"Oh, it's so nice to finally meet you. Jacob talks about you a lot."

He stood and took her outstretched hand. I held my breath.

"It's nice to meet you too. He's just told me about you, I'm sorry you lost your husband. No need to rush off."

I sighed in relief. Emma sat and pulled out yet another cake.

"She brings me cake every time," I said.

"Then she can come again," Nathan said, sliding the cake towards him.

If ever I'd wanted to kidnap Nathan, it was simply a matter of waving a coffee and walnut cake under his nose. And that was exactly what Emma had brought. I laughed.

"Do you want tea?" he asked her. He waved to the waitress and indicated to bring another tea.

I stared at him quizzically. This was the woman he was berating me about just a few minutes earlier.

"It's been nice getting to know you all through Jacob. I'm pleased that you're looking after Anna. Hopefully, he'll be able to get home soon," she said, smiling at me.

"That's the plan," I answered.

"So he told you about Anna?" Nathan asked, and I knew he was fishing.

"Of course, why wouldn't he? And Paloma, and Sadie and Bill. And you, of course."

That seemed to satisfy him a little. "Well, Jacob here has a surprise for me, maybe you want to stick around for that."

She looked over to me and frowned. "A surprise?" she asked.

"Drink your tea."

She gulped down the hot liquid and frowned. They stood and I pushed myself back from the table. They followed me to the pool. I wore my swim trunks under my sweatpants, so it was a quick change poolside and then a transfer to the wet chair. Carl was on standby, and I hadn't told him what I intended to do.

I wheeled down the ramp and dove into the pool. I swam, kicking my legs away from them. Each time my head came out of the water, I could hear them shout encouragement. I did my warm-up twenty lengths and then stopped at the shallow end farthest from them. I walked over to where they stood.

"Fucking hell, mate, you're walking!" Nathan said. Emma had her hands over her mouth, and Carl was clapping.

"Back again," Carl said. I walked back the way I'd came.

I walked the short side three more times, and then swam again. I floated mid pool and laughed out loud.

"I fucking walked," I shouted.

By the time I got out, I was tired, but elated the previous night wasn't just a fluke.

I stared at Nathan. "I'm coming home," I said, and he nodded.

Once I'd dried off, I joined them both in my room. They had walked ahead of me and were sitting in the armchairs facing the window. Emma was talking about her husband and Nathan seemed enamoured. He stared at her and smiled. He laughed at something she'd said and leaned towards her. I smiled to myself and joined them. We had more tea and ate the cake. Well, Nathan ate most of the cake and then wrapped the rest to take home with him.

"Jacob said you're moving to London," he said, as he stood to leave.

"Yes. I've found a lovely house, viewing it tomorrow. It's time to move on. I've laid my Jimmy to rest and my ghosts with him. He'd want me to stop coming here, I'm sure." She smiled over to me as she said that.

"Well, if you need any help," he said, and handed her his card. I raised my eyebrows at him, he ignored me.

"Thank you. It might be nice to have some friends in London," she said.

We had thought that once I'd left, we wouldn't see each other again. What we had was friendship born from a need for comfort in a place of distress. But looking at Nathan as he stared at her retreating body, I wasn't so sure.

When he finally turned back, he saw me looking at him.

"What?" he asked, and I shook my head, laughing.

"So when are you coming home?" he asked.

"As soon as I can walk through the door. I don't think it will be long."

———

It was another month before I was able to walk with just a stick. I'd started back at the bars, walking the length with both arms on the rails, then one arm, then one hand, then nothing. I found it easier inside the wooden poles but often lost my balance when they weren't around.

I managed to walk up and down three steps, progressing to the mini flight of six in the physio studio. I had to hold the rail, but it was progress.

"I don't want the chair anymore," I said when Anthony came into my room one morning.

"Okay, that's huge progress," he said.

"I also want to shave this off," I replied, running my hand over my beard, having not shaved it when I'd told Nathan I was going to.

"Okay," he said, stringing out the word.

Whether I was conscious of it or not, I was preparing myself to leave. Nathan had messaged to tell me he'd met with Emma in London, she loved the house, he'd taken her out to dinner. At first, I was concerned. I didn't want him to neglect Anna, and then I pulled myself up short. It had been me who had neglected Anna for so long.

After I shaved and dressed, I headed out for breakfast. I still sat alone; it was my time to read the latest news from home. Except, it hadn't arrived. At first, I didn't worry. Anna was probably busy, but as the day moved on, I began to get concerned.

Had I pushed her too far?

I asked for a chat with Mike.

"I'm concerned that Anna hasn't texted me," I said, when I sat in this office.

"What concerns you, specifically?" he asked.

"That I've left it too late, that she's moved on," I said.

"You know there is only one way to know that for sure," he replied.

"What if she has?" I asked.

"I can't answer that, but what if she has? What will you do about that?"

"I'd fight for her." My voice had hardened, and I felt a punch to my gut.

"Will you win that fight?" he asked. I looked up abruptly at him.

"Why wouldn't I?"

"Do you win every fight, Jacob?"

I stared at him. "Yes, when I want it enough."

"Then I'm glad you want this enough. How are you going to do this?"

I fucking hated his questions, but understood, he wasn't there to give me answers. I had to find those.

"I have to call her. I can't."

"Then perhaps you could find another method to contact her."

"I'll text her... later."

"Why later?"

"Because I'm afraid she doesn't want to wait any longer."

I was going around in circles.

"The fear is real, we're not going to dismiss that, but you also know how to manage that fear. Can you do that?"

I looked directly at him. "I'm going home, Mike. I want to

take Anthony with me for a couple of weeks to help me rein-tegrate. And I'm going to marry her."

"I'd suggest you call her first," he said.

I smiled. "No, I'm going to walk through the front door unannounced."

"If you think that's the best way, then I applaud you. I think if you speak to the director, you can hire Anthony for a couple of weeks since you have such a bond with him."

He smiled at me. I liked Mike. I hadn't at first, and he irritated the fuck out of me when he wouldn't give me the answers, but he was someone I knew I'd continue to work with. We would move to Zoom consultations as and when I felt I needed them.

Not getting those two text messages from Anna spurred me on. More so when she didn't text to wish me goodnight.

I held my phone in my hand later that evening and trembled. I sent a message.

Hey, I missed your texts today. I don't deserve you, I know that, but they give me hope.

I didn't know what else to say and pressed send before I could add or delete any more words.

As the minutes wore on, I became despondent. I had no idea if she'd seen the message or not, if she was debating whether to reply or not. In all my fifty-three years, I didn't think I'd felt as nervous.

I was ecstatic when she did reply.

It's so good to hear from you, Jacob. I'm sorry

not to have texted today, but I can catch you up on news now. Paloma and I are off to Sandgate for a weekend break, just me and her. I want to sit on the beach and read. I think she has a tooth coming through, she's been a little grumpy and it doesn't help that it's been so warm here. She's eating 'proper' food now, still has her bottle at night and is growing. She's going to be tall, and she looks so much like you. I hope you got the photograph I messaged.

I hope the weather is nice where you are and that you're getting out. Sadie and Bill send their love and hugs, as does Nathan. We all look forward to you coming home when you're ready.

We love you, Jacob, sleep well xxx

I held the phone and read the message over and over until my eyes blurred with tears.

She was looking forward to me coming home. It was all I needed to know. I rested my head back on my pillow and cried some more.

The following day, I received another text from Anna.

Hi, Paloma and I have arrived at a lovely cottage on the beach at Sandgate. I'll send you some pictures. We're sitting in the garden and the beach is just beyond the gate, it's adorable

here. Maybe you could come here with us some time.

We're only staying for a few days and I'm sure we'll both benefit from the sea air, I guess those Victorians knew their stuff, huh? Anyway, Paloma woke this morning with two teeth! Two tiny little teeth poking through at the front. She was smiling away, showing them off to me. She's been eating a slice of cold apple this morning to soothe her gums ha ha I hope you have a good day, Jacob. Love and hugs from us all xxx

That time I replied.

Give Paloma a big hug from me, tell her Daddy loves and misses her. Explain to her that Daddy needed to find himself and tell her to look after Mummy. You found me once, Anna, and I'm glad you did.

I needed to find me now; I needed to find the new me who can live with my injuries. It's been tough, but I'm getting there. I abandoned you when you needed me the most. I appreciate your updates and I just want you to know that it pains me greatly that I'm not with you, I just can't right now.

Now I've found Jacob, the one you deserve, I just hope I haven't left it too late for us.

She replied:

Thank you for replying and for opening up a little. Just keep in mind, the Jacob you want for me, might be way more than the Jacob I need. I miss you xxx

I worked hard all day, only breaking for lunch, before I slumped on my bed utterly exhausted and with blistered feet. I missed dinner so Anthony brought some to my room.

"Hey, I thought you might be hungry," he said.

I'd moved on to a more protein-based diet to help with my fitness. The smell of steak caused my mouth to water. I hadn't realised I was actually hungry.

I sat up in bed, a far easier exercise than it had been, and took the tray from him.

"The director has agreed I can accompany you home for a couple of weeks, did he tell you?" he asked, as I took a mouthful.

I swallowed quickly. "Not yet, that's great."

"I'm sure your kind donation to expand the centre helped," Anthony laughed.

"I would have done that even if the answer had been no."

I had been so impressed with the centre and so upset to learn how hard it had been to get into. There were rehab places in England, of course, for returning soldiers, but nothing that offered the full range of facilities this one did. I had spoken to Samuel about setting up a fund that could be accessed by those less fortunate to pay for their treatment, and I'd donated a million pounds in the hopes the centre could either expand or set up a satellite unit elsewhere. I also pledged my continued support. I named the grant after Jimmy. I hadn't told Emma that, I would, after the fund bought the house she'd fallen in love with. I had planned to keep it anonymous initially, but after learning more about Emma, I wanted her on board to run the charity. She'd fund-raised for various ex-military charities for years. She'd fought on behalf of widowers to get what they deserved before her own husband had died.

We were all getting a second chance, I thought.

"Is it time for me to get rid of these?" Anthony asked, and I looked up from my plate.

He held the small pot of pills I had been collecting in the bathroom.

"I hadn't noticed them gone," I said quietly.

"We knew what you were doing. These are placebos," he said, shaking the pot.

"That's not... Are you allowed to do that?" I asked.

"Yeah. We're not here to help you kill yourself, and once you got to the stage that you didn't want to, of course we have to remove these. Someone else could have gotten hold of them."

I stared at the pot for a little while, my hunger gone.

"So you replaced the pills with a fake?" I asked, finally smiling.

He nodded. "I think we should have a ceremonial disposing of them, don't you?" he asked.

I stood. "This way," I said.

We walked to the bench. Jimmy's plaque had been screwed to the back and I gave it a small nod of respect. Anthony handed me the pot and I unscrewed the lid. I stared in it for ages. Pills of different shapes sat at the bottom. I picked one up and threw it over the fence. I did the same with every pill until I finally threw the pot. I brushed the pill dust from my hands and then smiled.

Anthony patted me on the back, and we returned to the room.

CHAPTER TWELVE

I worked the hardest I ever had. I was walking with a cane. I hated the cane, and vowed I'd get rid of it as soon as I could, but it helped with the slight unbalance. I saw a neuro consultant who ran some checks. It was believed I would have some permanent damage to the brain, but it would be nothing I couldn't live with. I still got the headaches, but they were becoming less frequent and less severe. The balance issue couldn't necessarily be explained and that frustrated me. If I knew, then I could work on it. But the brain didn't always give up the answers. One said it was muscle atrophy, another said it was nerve damage from the broken spine. I'd also have some scans on my ears to see if something there was causing the problem. Whatever it was, I was going to overcome it.

"Hey, how are you?" Emma asked as she walked into the room. She didn't look her usual bright self.

"What's up?" I asked immediately.

"Nothing."

"Yes, there is," I replied.

"I'm just a little sad today. That's allowable, isn't it?"

"Will you miss this place?" I asked.

"Yes, I will. I've said that I'll come back and volunteer every now and again. But I'm leaving Jimmy here and that's hit me hard this morning."

"He's inside you, Emma, he'll be wherever you are."

She smiled. "You are a good man, Jacob. Now tell me about this job again."

I'd already told her about the charity I wanted to set up and I'd found a way around buying her house without her feeling awful about it. The fund would buy it and it would be the head office, as such. Although it would be gifted to her at a later date.

"So, people can apply for a grant to fund their treatment here, or in a satellite facility I want them to set up. You run the charity. You, and a panel, assess the applicants and grant what's needed to them."

"I'm not qualified to do that," she said.

"You don't need to be. There'll be a panel of consultants as well. In fact, most referrals will come from hospitals or consultants anyway. And Nathan can help you."

She blushed and I laughed.

"You're blushing," I said.

"Oh... Stop it, Jacob. I'm not. I'm too old for that lark," she said, but fanned her face. "Menopause," she added.

"Too old for dating Nathan, or too old for blushing?"

She laughed. "Is it wrong? It feels wrong." She had quietened.

"There is nothing wrong about it, Emma."

"It's only been a couple of years, nearly three."

"Is there a time limit on it?" I asked. "Would Jimmy want you mourning him for the rest of your life?"

"Yes, I think the bastard probably would have," she said, laughing. I chuckled.

"I can't wait for you to meet Anna."

I just knew Anna would understand and even appreciate the friendship I had with Emma. I could never do the same, I knew. I wasn't as selfless as her. Anna wasn't the jealous type, I was.

"I can't wait to meet them all. Now, what's the plan?" she asked.

"I'm going home in a couple of weeks when the paperwork for the donation and whatever is done, and Anthony is freed up. What about you?"

"I've sorted out a van to move my things, the girls are absolutely over the moon. They got their uni places sorted, fully funded, thank you," she said, smiling at me. Again, the charity had provided for her family.

"Nathan would be happy to help," I said.

"I'm sure he would, but I can do this myself. I need to do this by myself."

I understood that. She left a cake and headed out. I heard her chat to everyone she met on the way until she was out of earshot.

I sent a text message to James and Daniel.

I'm coming home. James, can you collect me on the 17th mid-morning, and Daniel, can you meet us at Bigging Hill? James will give you an ETA.

I didn't add anything further and promptly received two replies.

Of course, I'll file a flight plan. Good to have you home. James.

Yep, boss, catch you later.

I smiled at the boss reference, that had been Nathan for the past six months. It was going to be difficult to take over. In fact, just going home and taking back my wife was going to be difficult.

I knew I could never make it up to Nathan for all the things he had done. He'd lied to Anna, something he hated doing, constantly. He'd told her he had only seen me once when it had been more. I would tell Anna everything, about Emma, about my discussions with Mike, my fears, and injuries. Everything. I hoped she wouldn't hate me for any of it.

Nathan had done everything I had asked of him. I'd used

our friendship to blackmail him, in some ways. I'd hurt him, everyone, along the way. It couldn't be as simple as just stepping back into my old life, which is one reason I wanted Anthony. It wasn't just to help me reintegrate into my home, navigate the stairs and all that shit. It was to have an ally to help me. Someone who understood how fragile my mental state had been and knew I'd done what I thought was the right thing at the time for my survival.

I was a very instinctive person. It's what had made me a good soldier, a good businessman. And it got me through those dark times. I reverted back to type when necessary, so Mike had said. Acting on instinct, being in survival mode, until I couldn't do it anymore, it had exhausted me. It was only then that I could see a clearer way forward.

As the days approached my last, the nerves kicked in. Emma had already left but had messaged with photographs of the house. Although she and Nathan had shared a couple of meals together, that seemed to have cooled. I would have to work on Nathan with that one, I thought. He had distanced himself from me as well. I knew why, I was back, and he had to relinquish the reins, so he thought. He didn't have to though. He had spent so much of his time looking after Anna, now he didn't need to, he could continue to spend that time in the business. I intended to have many conversations with many people. My life was going to change, dramatically. I was going to step back from the business entirely. My place was with my wife and daughter, making more babies, and being the family she deserved. I didn't need to work, hadn't done so for years. I could wind the company down, but I wouldn't. I had too many people relying on me for work.

———————

When the day finally came, I woke earlier than normal. I was nervous. I showered and shaved, dressed, and sat on the end of my bed. I looked around the room.

The cream walls had paintings of the local area framed and hung to take away from the blandness of the colour. The grey carpet was worn in some places but warm underfoot. The grey curtains were tied back and matched in colour. The television mounted on the wall hadn't been turned on at all. I'd had no desire to watch anything. Not that I watched it much at home, either.

The double bed was comfortable, but I wouldn't miss the rails that could be raised or lowered to stop me from falling out, or the handle that hung from the ceiling and was currently wound up to keep it out of the way. I wouldn't miss the wet chair, not that I'd used it of late. Or the wheelchair that still sat in the corner despite me asking for it to be removed. It was a reminder of how far I'd come. There had been talk of getting me an electric chair at one point and I'd point blankly refused that. My resolve to get out of it, was what had kept me going. That, and Anna's texts.

My suitcase was packed, I'd donated all my toiletries to

my fellow *inmates*, and I was ready to go. I hadn't told Anna I was coming home that day, only Nathan knew, and he was under strict instructions to not tell her. I'd wanted it to be a surprise.

"Ready?" Anthony said. He walked in my room dressed in a polo shirt and jeans. Not his usual uniform.

"No, and yes," I said, chuckling.

"Nervous?" he asked.

I nodded. "Yeah. Although I don't know why."

My level of honesty with him far exceeded any level of honesty I'd had with anyone, including Nathan. I wasn't sure why that was. Nathan was my closest and oldest friend. I'd married his sister, but there were times when I felt I couldn't open up to him. I couldn't divulge my inner feelings. I knew I wanted to change that.

"I can imagine you'd be nervous. It's a massive change you're about to embark on."

James flew over the top of us and landed in the field next door.

We stood and he grabbed my suitcase. I wouldn't be able to manage that and a cane. I said goodbye to a couple of people and, with the director waiting to see me off, I made my way to the back entrance. I was pleased to see Daniel had accompanied James. He stood on the terrace waiting for me and rushed forward to take the cases from Anthony.

"All right, boss?" he said. "Got a gammy leg there, have you?"

"Yep, and yep," I said, laughing. I introduced him to Anthony, and, without a backward glance, I walked to the helicopter.

It was slow going, I hadn't practiced on uneven grass, but when I got there, and without help, I climbed up the steps and took my seat. Daniel helped Anthony buckle in, then took his place next to James.

With just a welcome and then a few reminders to belt up, we were in the air.

It took an hour and half before we landed in Bigging Hill. Daniel rushed off to get the car and James helped unload the bags.

"It's good to have you back," he said. And I smiled my thanks. "It's good to be back."

When the car arrived, I slid in the back with Anthony beside me. Daniel looked at me in the rear-view mirror and smiled. "Ready?" he said.

"As I'll ever be," I replied, and we started the journey back to Hampshire.

I was quiet for most of the journey, only livening up the closer we got. My nerves were shot, and I could feel a headache approaching. I reached into a small bag for some pills. Anthony looked at me, watched how many I shook out, and then handed me a bottle of water from the side door. I swallowed the pills and gulped the water. I rested back and closed my eyes, hoping they'd kick in quick.

Daniel stopped outside the gates and waited for them to

open. If anyone was watching any monitors, they'd have seen the car approach. By the time we rounded the top and stopped, Sadie was at the front door. She clasped her hand to her mouth, dropping the tea towel she had been holding. As she bolted in, Nathan walked out.

"Ready?" he asked, opening the car door.

"No, but I'm glad to be here."

I looked over his shoulder to see Anna holding Paloma. She stood just outside the door. Her knees were dirty as if she'd been kneeling in mud. Tears ran down her cheeks. I slid from my seat and Nathan held out a hand. I swiped it away. I hauled myself up and, when handed my cane, I walked towards her with Nathan beside me, then turned to him.

"Thank you," I said.

At first, he didn't respond. Then he looked at Anna. He nodded. "I won't do it again though," he said before smiling.

He took a step forward and embraced me.

"I won't ask again, and I appreciate how hard this has been for you," I said.

Finally, I looked at Anna. "I owe you so much. I have a lot of making up to do if you'll allow me. I won't presume to live here with you, this is your house. We can spend some time getting to know each other again, if that's what you want."

Sadie came to stand next to Anna, and I could see Anna shaking. She handed our daughter to Sadie and then walked towards me. "Oh Jacob," she said, her voice cracking with emotion.

"Welcome home," she said, and then wrapped her arms around me.

She cried into my chest, and I didn't hold back my tears. I rested my face into the side of her neck, and we just held each other.

"I've missed you so much," she said, and all I could do was nod. "Let's get you inside, shall we?"

"I need to hold my baby," I said, looking over at Paloma. Anna had been right, she looked exactly like I did. Same eyes and same colour hair.

Daniel handed me the cane and we walked up the steps to the front door. I had to take my time because there were no rails to assist me. I took one step at a time. I rested my cane against one of the canopy pillars and Sadie handed me my daughter.

At first, she stiffened. Had she reached for Nathan, I think I would have been devastated. She looked his way, but then back at me. Then she touched my face. Her muddy hands rested on my cheeks and her hazel eyes stared at mine. She settled in my arms. I wasn't aware of the tears still coursing down my cheeks until they started to drip onto her dress. She gurgled, waved her hands, and kicked her legs. She smiled at me, and I just melted.

I fell hook, line, and sinker, totally and utterly in love with her. And I cursed myself inwardly for not being around for her. I felt a physical pain in my chest when I looked at her.

"Daddy's home," I whispered, praying she would have some sense of who I was, and what that meant.

Never, would I leave my child again. Ever.

I handed her back to Anna and we walked in. I paused in the hall. Nothing had changed since I'd last seen it, other than a small pile of Paloma's shoes by the door and a pram.

I remembered the man standing behind me. I gestured him forward.

"Anthony, this is my family. You've met Nathan, this is my baby, Paloma, and my wife, Anna. Well, I say wife..." Anthony shook their hands. I then introduced him to Sadie and Bill. "I need Anthony to stay a little, while I adjust to a different surrounding, is that okay?"

I was a little hesitant in asking. It was her house, after all.

"Of course it's okay! Let's all just sit for a while," she replied, and I instantly relaxed.

We walked into the snug and I smiled at the familiar surroundings. I aimed for the chair I usually sat in and lowered myself. I sighed. I was home and there was no feeling like it. Anna sat on the footstool in front of me.

"I reckon we should decorate that thing," Nathan said, taking the offered cane as he sat.

"Yeah, in what way?" I replied.

"I don't know, paint it pink?"

"No fucking way. It's bad enough having to use it," I said.

"Well, I'll do it anyway, it's not like you can run after me to stop me, is it?"

I laughed, a real belly laugh, Nathan joined in. It felt so good to be home!

"I can still hurl it at you," I said.

I noticed Bill standing in the doorway.

"Good to have you back, Son, but those peppers won't plant themselves," he said, and touched the corner of his eye with his handkerchief. He nodded and then left us.

"I'll put the kettle on," Sadie said, scuttling after him. It was obvious they were trying to give us some space. "Anthony, let me show you to your room," she added.

And then there were just the four of us.

"Can I hold her again?" I asked.

Anna placed Paloma on my lap and, as before, she looked up at me.

"She's beautiful," I whispered. "Where do we start?" I asked, looking at Anna.

"Let's just take it slow, huh? You tell us, when you're ready, all that you want to. There's no rush."

I knew she didn't really mean that, I was sure she had a ton of questions busting to get answered. But that was Anna all over. She was the most selfless person I'd ever known. She had put her life on hold waiting for me, and she would still do that, waiting until I was ready to tell her everything.

I would tell her everything, of course. I'd have no secrets from her.

"I told Nathan I wasn't coming back, and I asked him to look after you. He... Well, you know, I'm sure." I looked between her and Nathan. "I thought I was doing the right thing, back then. Letting you go. They'd told me I might not walk again, and I couldn't bear the thought of being a burden, of having you give up your life to care for me."

"You should have said, and not made that decision for me," she replied gently.

"I have a lot of talking to do, of explaining. I know that. I can't do it all in one go. I get fucking tired easily, and I get these headaches, they put me on my back sometimes."

"I think we all have some catching up to do. Right now, though, it should be you two," Nathan stood.

"Will you come back later?" she asked, and for the first time I witnessed how reliant she had been on him.

He nodded. "Well, I do sort of live here now as well," he replied, laughing.

I frowned. "I needed him," she said, and I nodded. I got it. He'd done what I'd asked him to do, but there was a small part of me that didn't like to actually hear it.

Nathan placed his hand on my shoulder. "As I said, it's good to have you home."

He gave Anna a smile and then left the room. She stared at me, she bit down on her lower lip and sighed. She then rose and knelt down in front of me. "Whatever we have to do, we will, as a team," she said.

I placed one hand on her cheek. "I don't deserve you."

"Yes, you do. You deserve me, and her," she said, looking

at our child. "You deserve Nathan and everyone else who loves you."

She turned her face to my palm and kissed it.

"Have you found Jacob?" she whispered.

"Yeah. I'm the man you loved. I thought I needed to be something, someone, different, but I'm not. I just have a fucking limp that I hope will go, but I'm back, and I promise you, I won't ever leave you again. It's been the hardest fucking months of my life, worse than when I lost my wife. I didn't know if you'd still want me, and it was only when you didn't text that I finally knew I was pushing you away. That missing day was all I needed to see the light, to understand how selfish I was being.

"I found myself, Anna, and I have so much thanks that you allowed me the time to do it."

She wrapped her arms around my neck and, with Paloma between us, kissed me. At first it was gentle but as her desire, and mine, rose, it became more feverish. We had to pull apart for fear of crushing Paloma.

"I found you once, and I've found you again," she said as she pulled back from me. "And this time, I'm not letting you go. Marry me, Jacob, make us complete."

I thought I'd misheard her and frowned. She stared at me with a broad smile. I was meant to ask her, not the other way round! I nodded and then laughed so suddenly, it surprised Paloma who screamed.

"Will you marry me?" she said, still on her knees.

"Yes, tomorrow, or however quickly we can." I kissed Paloma and then leaned forwards to kiss her again.

"And know this, even if my leg is damaged, no other part of my body is. I've waited a long time to fuck... No, to make love to you. To make you mine again, claim you back."

She stood and took Paloma from me. "Then we ought to start now," she said, holding out one hand to me.

I wanted nothing more than to hold her naked body in my arms. For her to see the scars on my body from the broken bones that had healed. I wanted her to feel my heart beat strong. I needed her, I needed to be inside her, to make her come and call out my name. We walked up the stairs and while I headed for the bedroom, she placed Paloma in her cot in the nursery. I didn't want to just ignore my child, but my need for her mother was far greater.

When she joined me, we stood facing each other initially. I slowly undressed her, and she did the same. We explored each other's bodies. I kissed her stretch marks, and every inch of skin on her body. I fucked her, we made love, we lay facing each other, and we talked. I told her about the facility, about Anthony, and Emma. She wept for Emma and told me she would love to meet her. We made love again. I heard Sadie talking to Paloma through the baby monitor, she'd picked her up and was taking her downstairs. I silently thanked her.

I don't know how long we spent pleasuring each other, but it wouldn't get close to making up for our missing six months.

We slept for a little while, totally at peace in each other's arms. And we cried together.

"I think we've found each other again," she whispered.

"And this time, it's for keeps," I replied.

I had every intention of getting straight on line to find the quickest way I could marry her. I wanted her to wear my ring, and to carry my name. I wanted more babies, and a life of travelling, fucking, and loving one another.

While she slept, I lay beside her and just stared. She was as beautiful as the day I met her.

"I love you a million times more than I loved the thought of you," I said, knowing she wouldn't hear me.

I had a lot to do over the coming months, and I knew she'd be beside me each step of the way.

I'd found my soulmate in Anna.

I'd found my peace in me.

I'd found I could let go of the past.

I rose and used the bed to steady me. I reached inside the drawer of my bedside cabinet and pulled out a tiny white leather box. I opened it.

Lying on a white silk pillow was a bangle of gold. An adjustable one that would grow with the child. I picked it up.

I pulled on sweatpants and a T-shirt and grabbed my cane. I navigated the stairs and only stumbled once. Sadie had rushed towards me.

"It's okay, I've got this," I said.

She had been sitting in the kitchen with Anthony. I

walked past them. Anthony asked me if I needed help, and I shook my head. I walked straight to the pool and stood looking at my reflection. I held out my hand and I let the bangle slide off and into the water.

Both my daughters were individuals. They deserved to be recognised as such. Sitting by the pool was my favourite place and I intended to erect a small headstone in memory of my wife and daughter. I'd honour them by getting on with my life and loving my second wife and daughter, knowing I'd have the permission of both to do so.

I wiped a tear and headed back in. I told Sadie that I'd sort dinner later if she wanted to head off home and offered to show Anthony around the house.

"Sadie has kindly offered to cook for me. I think you two need today and tonight alone."

They left and I made my way back upstairs. She was still sleeping when I climbed back into bed, and I shuffled down. In her sleep she reached out for me. As she did so, I noticed the sweatshirt under her pillow. She wasn't holding on to it as she had been in the photograph. I reached for it and placed it in her hand.

Without waking, she pushed the sweatshirt aside, shuffled into me and wrapped her arm around my waist. Her head was tucked into my chest, and she inhaled.

She didn't need the sweatshirt, she needed me, and she had me. I wasn't going anywhere ever again.

CHAPTER THIRTEEN

It took seven weeks. Seven bloody weeks of planning, gaining the relevant licence, buying dresses before we could wed.

Personally, I'd have just opted to head to the local registry office and do it there, but no, everyone wanted a wedding.

"Stop being so grumpy and go down to Sadie's. You can't be here," Emma said. I rolled my eyes. She was bossier than Philip!

I grabbed my suit carrier and stomped off.

I'd ditched the cane a week ago. I was determined I wasn't marrying Anna with a fucking cane by my side. I still wobbled every now and again, but I was getting so much stronger each day. We were in the planning process of installing an indoor pool and gym in a purpose-built building in the grounds. I still swam every day in the outside pool, and

I realised just how beneficial swimming was for me. But I needed a bigger one.

I walked down the drive towards the gatehouse, past the huge marquee that had been erected the day before. There were vans for the caterers and entertainment parked on the grass, and I winced at the damage they might have caused.

Anna had had a ball planning her wedding. I tried to be as enthusiastic, but I didn't really care what canapes we had. She'd laughed at me when I told her I wanted her pussy rather than a mini duck wrap to eat.

My input had been to buy rings and Anna had no idea that I'd bought not only a wedding band for us both, but an engagement ring, an eternity ring, and a new bangle for Paloma.

I'd told Anna about the bangle lying in the pool and she thought I should have it mounted in a small headstone for my wife and daughter. I thought that was a nice idea, especially when she said Paloma could feel it and, later on, understand she had a sister.

I smiled as I walked. I had loved all the preparation really. I was just nervous, as any groom should be. Not that she wouldn't turn up, of course, but of being so overwhelmed when I saw her I'd cry.

Nathan had taken to calling me a soppy bastard such was my level of eye leakage.

"Breakfast is ready, I was just about to call you," Sadie said as she came to the back door.

Nathan, my best man, Philip, and Daniel, both ushers, sat around the table. Anthony would be joining us as soon as he arrived. He'd returned to the centre, but I wanted him at my wedding. James was collecting him and would be landing behind the house on the helipad. He'd already had several journeys that day. Dory had been with us for a few days, having flown in from Monaco, where she was staying with a cousin.

Emma and her daughters had been with us, and with Dory, all four were bridesmaids.

I'd been thrilled at how well Emma and Anna had gotten on. Their first meeting had been in London at a restaurant and Anna had run to her. They'd hugged and both cried. Anna had thanked her over and over for looking after me. I'd struggled to keep back the tears.

The thing that made me the happiest, however, was the relationship between Nathan and Emma. He was in love, finally, although he had told me his feelings for Anna were still there. Emma knew this and understood. We all knew nothing would come of it and we often joked about it.

"Jesus, it's like a fucking circus up there," I grumbled as I sat. Nathan laughed.

"You love it, mate, don't lie," he said, and I joined in that laughter.

"Got the rings?" I asked.

"Nope, no idea where they are."

"Don't fuck about," I replied.

"Yes, I have the rings. I've had the rings since you gave them to me and all the times you've asked if I have them. So quit with it, will you?"

Sadie had cooked up a huge breakfast, the full English. We knew we wouldn't be eating again until late afternoon, so we wanted our stomachs full, so she said. Bill was flapping about buttonholes, making sure they were watered and fresh. All the flowers had been delivered that morning. The marque was festooned, and even I had to admit the smell was amazing. The wedding coordinator had outdone herself in the short time she had to get the perfect day for Anna.

We ate, and we laughed. I'd never thought I'd remarry, and the boys took great pleasure in reminding me how much older than Anna I was. Particularly when we'd all dined out for my 'stag-do.' I'd been gifted Viagra, vitamins for old people, and energy drinks to keep in the bedroom.

"Everything set for you and Emma?" I asked. Nathan nodded. They were flying out to Dubai after the wedding. He was meeting one of our regular clients and Emma was accompanying him for a holiday.

Stepping back from the business was delayed. It was a good idea at the time and one I still wanted to do, but I'd chosen to go part time for a while. Anna thought I needed the distraction of work, I thought she believed I'd get under her toes.

I was taking a month off, however. We were off to Crete with Paloma for two weeks, and then Spain. For the first time in ages, I was revisiting my village and planning a new house there. Anna was very insistent that Paloma be bilingual, and we both felt living in Spain for some months of the year would help that. I was already talking to her in Spanish, singing Spanish nursery rhymes, and reading Spanish books to her. She didn't understand, obviously, but loved the sound of my voice. When I stopped, she'd grumble in her own language until I started again.

She was starting to say Papi and Mumma, but Anna insisted she didn't really know what the words meant. Although I swore she'd look for me when Anna asked her where Papi was. My kid was going to be a genius, I told her.

"Earth to Jacob," I heard.

I snapped out of my thoughts and back to the table. "Sorry, miles away."

"We saw," Nathan said. "Anthony's here."

I hadn't heard the helicopter fly over but rose to go and greet him. He knew all the men were at the gatehouse.

"Wow, this looks good. And so do you, my friend," he said, looking at the marquee. He dropped his bag and hugged me, finishing with a slap on the back. "And no stick."

"No stick. It's gone for good."

We walked back to the house, and he caught me up on the developments at the centre. Planning permission had been sought for an extension. Jimmy's wing would be able to house ten people and there was a family room for partners or kids to come and visit, stay over for a couple of days. That was one thing I thought missing. Although I hadn't wanted family there, some did. And hotels were expensive in that part of Jersey. I was after the cottage Emma had rented, but after the owner's death, the family was holding out hoping for a bidding war.

"Honestly, Jacob, you look so well. Tanned and healthy," he said, smiling. I'd seen him three weeks prior so hadn't thought I'd changed that much!

Sadie grabbed him for a hug, and the guys greeted him warmly. Although he'd only been with us for two weeks, he'd integrated so well, it was as if they'd known him for so much longer.

"Right, Son, I think it's time we got to the pub," Bill said. He laughed, and Sadie forbade him from getting drunk.

We were walking to the local pub for a couple of drinks before getting ready. We had two hours to kill, and the pub was the best place to do that.

I bought the first round and we all clinked bottles or glasses in a toast. Bill cleared his throat.

"Son, I just wanted to say a few words," he said. Since he and Sadie had taken the parents of the bride *and* groom role, he was allowed.

"These past months have been such a worry and I can't tell you how pleased me and Sadie are to be with you now and stand beside you while you marry Anna. It's the best thing you've done since I've known you." He coughed to clear his throat again. "We love you like a son, as you know, and to be part of this day.... Well, it's better than any other because there was a point I didn't think we'd see you again. Anthony, thank you for caring for my boy. Nathan, James, Daniel, thank you for being his friends. Philip, maybe one day you'll settle down and we can do this all over again," he said to his blood son. I laughed and Philip rolled his eyes, knowing that would never happen.

"I'm not a man of many words, or God, but I prayed, Jacob. My Sadie prayed every night for you, and we now can thank fucking God we don't have to do that again!"

We all laughed and raised our bottles and glasses to him.

By the time we headed back, I was ready. I was desperate to see my wife in her dress. To dance with my daughter in my arms.

———

Seeing Anna walk towards me holding Bill's arm floored me. I'd hoped that it wouldn't, that I'd stay strong. I pinched the bridge of my nose and closed my eyes.

She wore a white, off-the-shoulder, vintage lace gown. It had been Sadie's wedding dress, so I'd been told, and had been repurposed for Anna. It was stunning, just perfect for her. She carried a bouquet of white jasmine, the flower of my home region, Andalucía. I, and all the men, wore a red carnation, the national flower of Spain.

The musicians played 'Te Amaré,' and the soulful tones

of a singer sang in perfect Spanish the words Miguel Bosé had penned many years ago. I hadn't known she'd be walking down the aisle to that song; it was one of the greatest love songs of my youth. I held back the tears.

And then she was in front of me. Bill lifted her veil, and he kissed her forehead. A tear ran down his cheek as he nodded to me. Anna turned and handed her bouquet to Dory, her chief bridesmaid. I took her hand and lifted it to my lips. I kissed her knuckles gently.

"You are so beautiful," I whispered.

We turned to the official. We hadn't opted to write our own vows or anything like that. For us, we had said privately everything we had wanted to the past few weeks. There was nothing that needed to be declared in front of our friends. More importantly, I just wanted to get to the important part.

Finally, Nathan stepped forward and handed me three rings. Only then did I say my own words.

"With this ring I give you my heart." I slipped the solitaire engagement ring on her finger.

"With this ring I give you my soul." I added the platinum wedding band.

"And with this ring, I give you my love, eternally." I added the diamond encrusted eternity ring.

I then pulled another piece of jewellery from my pocket.

"With this band, I promise to be your daddy forever and I will love you fiercely for all my days." I walked over to Emma, who held Paloma, and placed the bangle on her wrist.

Anna let out a sob. When I returned, I held her face, stared into her tear-filled eyes, and then I kissed her. I didn't wait for her to put my ring on, I didn't wait for the officiant to 'pronounce' us man and wife, I just wanted to hold her.

When we were done, Nathan handed her my ring, and she slipped it on my finger. "I love you, Jacob with all the names. More than I did yesterday."

We walked towards the marquee to the same song she'd walked down the aisle to.

"Happy?" she whispered, as we stood to wait for our guests to join us.

"Like you wouldn't believe," I replied. I kissed her again. "I can't fucking wait to get this gorgeous dress off you."

"I think you'll like what you see underneath," she replied, giving me a sly smile.

"Can't we leave now?" I asked, pulling her closer to me, and nuzzling her neck.

"We could, but I'm starving," she replied with a laugh.

By then, our guests had joined us in the entrance to the marquee. We had some of her old work colleagues, the girl-friends that I didn't like but she had forgiven, my colleagues, the ones who had become friends, of course. And our *family*. Nathan carried Paloma and he was cooing and rubbing noses with her. Izzie and Liv—Emma's daughters—were trying to take her from him.

The photographer wanted the throwing of the bouquet picture, so lined the bridesmaids and some female guests in a half circle behind Anna. I'd thought it a terrible waste since the flowers were so beautiful. I hadn't expected what was to come, however.

Anna went through the motions of pretending the throw them over her head. At the last minute, she turned and walked straight to Emma. She presented her with the flowers. Anna laughed and Emma looked puzzled. That was until, to her side came Nathan. He knelt in front of her and opened a ring box.

"Marry me, Emma," he said simply.

Liv and Izzy screamed and danced around. Even Paloma joined in the screeching. Emma covered her mouth with her hand and held out the other. She nodded as Nathan slipped the ring on her finger.

"What the fuck?" I said, standing beside Anna.

"We planned this, wanted it to be a surprise for you as well," she said.

"It certainly is."

Nathan rose and everyone cheered then. He hugged Emma and as he did, he looked over to me. He had tears in his eyes.

"Soppy bastard," I mouthed, and he laughed.

I walked over to congratulate them. I waited until his soon to be stepdaughters untangled themselves from him, took Paloma from one, and then hugged him with one arm.

"Mate, finally," I said.

He nodded. "I know! Too soon though?"

He'd only known Emma for a couple of months.

"Not at all. When you know, you know," I replied.

"She floored me when I met her in Jersey. And I want to make her mine," he said, shrugging his shoulders. "And as for these two?" He grabbed Izzy and Liv for another hug. "You are all gonna be the death of me, and if you think you're bringing any boys home, you can think again!"

I let others congratulate him and walked back to Anna. She smiled and raised her eyebrows at me.

"Only you would share this day with another woman. You amaze me, every day, Anna."

"She's the sister I never had. I wanted this day to be special for her as well."

She stared at them, laughing until Emma looked around for her. She ran over.

"You knew! I can't believe it. I'm in my bloody fifties, how has this happened?" Emma said, and we laughed.

"He loves you," Anna replied.

The two women looked at each other. They shared a private moment, one that I felt I was on the outside looking in.

"Thank you," Emma said quietly. And then they hugged and kissed each other's cheeks.

We were asked to make our way into the marquee, and I collected yet more champagne along the way.

"Is this the cheap stuff?" Anna asked, and I chuckled. I got the reference.

"No fucking way," I said. "However, how about I present it to you as if it was?"

I held out one glass to her and as I did, I leaned down to kiss her cheek. I ran my lips over her skin, and down her neck.

"Mmm, you might need to stop that, but not yet," she mumbled. I chuckled and then bit her.

We sat and ate, we listened to an excruciating speech from Nathan that not only detailed some of our exploits in Gibraltar but mentioned nearly every disastrous relationship I'd had. I wanted to hold my head in my hands. When he talked about Anna it was with fondness, and not with the level of want he'd had before. She reached out to take his hand, stood, and then hugged him.

As the evening wore on, we danced. It fucking killed me, and I popped as many pills as I could without losing consciousness. Anthony constantly checked on me, Anna wanted us to leave. I was determined. I was going to dance with my wife, and then my daughter, and then both of them. I hadn't anticipated Nathan dragging me up for more *dad and uncle dances* as Liv and Izzy called them. By the time I got to sit down, I was done in.

"I am getting too old for this," I moaned.

"So am I. Shall we go?" Anna said, sitting on my lap. "I feel something far more appetising in your trousers than wedding cake," she added.

Sadie had Paloma for the evening so Anna and I could spend some alone time, as she called it. It wouldn't have bothered either of us to take her home with us, but, since we were off the following day, I thought she might be wanting that alone time with her *granddaughter* herself.

We waved a goodbye, gave and accepted hugs, and then I took my wife by her hand and led her back to the house. The closer we got, the darker it was. Anna led me behind the house to the pool. She placed my red carnation on the headstone that had been erected. She ran her fingers over my wife's and daughter's names.

"Thank you, Eleanor, for giving Jacob to me. For letting him know he could love us both and it was okay. I promise to look after him for all my days."

I let my tears flow freely.

When she stood, she stared at me. She reached behind her to unhook her dress.

"Swim with me?" she said. I didn't hesitate, I was naked before her.

Just before I entered the pool, however, I was floored for a second time.

"Jacob," she said, causing me to look at her. She wore no underwear but had a message written on her stomach. I frowned, and then read. Then read again.

I fucking shouted. I picked her up and dove into the pool. She laughed and coughed as we submerged.

"Are you sure, how far?" I asked when we surfaced.

"Just six weeks, so no telling anyone just yet," she replied.

She'd written on her stomach...

Daddy, I'm in here and I can't wait to meet you.

She was pregnant.

"It's a boy. This one is my son," I said.

"We have no idea yet." She laughed as she wrapped her legs around my waist and her arms around my neck.

I kissed her. I sucked the air from her lungs, wanting every piece of her. She did the same. She reached between us, grabbing my cock, and I was reminded of how horny she'd been last time. I chuckled as she lined me up and then forced herself down. I sighed. I was home. Being inside her was the one place I never wanted to leave.

"I want more," I said as I kissed her neck. She nodded.

CHAPTER FOURTEEN

Packing up the car was a nightmare. People came to see us off and got in the way. Finally, with Paloma strapped in, we left. Daniel drove us to the airport where we had a flight waiting. Both Anna and I were tired, we hadn't gotten any sleep the previous evening. We'd fucked in the pool and then again for most of the night. I talked to my son, and we dozed.

I held her hand and smiled at her as we pulled up outside the airport. We didn't have too many cases, we'd shipped what we wanted out to the villa before the wedding, but it was things for Paloma mostly. I carried my daughter in, through customs, and to the private lounge. We didn't have long to wait, of course, before we were sitting on the plane and taxiing. Anna settled back and closed her eyes, I played with Paloma, walking up and down the plane when the seat belt sign was released. When I sat again, Anna was smiling.

"You are very good at this parenting," she said, without looking.

"I have your lead to follow," I said.

For the rest of the flight, Paloma and I drew a masterpiece. Well, I drew, then held the pen in her hand so she could scribble and try to smash the table up.

Soon enough we landed, and we were in the car on our way to our boat.

I had a surprise for Anna. I'd chartered a yacht for a few days. I hadn't wanted to do it for long in case Paloma got bored, but I wanted to sail around Greece before we headed to our villa.

"What's this?" Anna asked as we walked along the jetty.

"Surprise. We're taking a mini cruise for a few days."

The captain and her staff greeted us, all were lined up on the jetty in their uniforms. We were shown around the interior and then the master bedroom. A cot had been placed in the corner for Paloma.

"This is wonderful," Anna said, walking around with the chief steward.

I'd already sent over a likes and dislikes sheet and detailed what we wanted to do for the three days. We wanted to sleep, make love, not that I put that on the sheet, obviously, swim, and visit some of the coastal villages.

A full itinerary was presented to us with a glass of champagne.

We changed into more suitable clothing and while

Paloma had a nap in the shade of the sun deck, Anna and I stretched out on loungers.

It was an idyllic few days, being fed wonderful food, having amazing picnics on isolated beaches that only boats could get to, and it was with sadness that our trip came to an end.

We thanked the crew as they moored up on Crete, gave a substantial tip for them, and slid into our waiting car.

My second surprise was just as good as the first.

When we entered the villa, it had been redecorated, and a full nursery set up in one of the bedrooms.

"This is why you kept moaning at me about luggage allowance," Anna said, laughing.

I wrapped my arms around her from behind, kissing my daughter's forehead at the same time.

"Yep. No need for luggage here."

"And what happens when we get to Spain?" she asked.

"There, we might struggle," I said, laughing and knowing full well we wouldn't. "Anyway, talking of Spain, the architect has sent some plans. Want to see them?"

We left the nursery and while Anna placed Paloma in her highchair and opened the fridge to prepare her lunch, I grabbed my laptop and opened it.

The Crete villa was a mini replica of our home in Hampshire. I hadn't wanted the same in Spain. Anna had left it totally up to me, with just an instruction that she'd prefer a modern look that was spacious and to remember it had to be child friendly. I had two children to accommodate. I smiled at the thought.

While Paloma ate, Anna and I looked over the plans. We both liked what the architect had come up with, although I wanted the pool to be larger. I didn't want a pool just to splash around in, but one to continue with my exercise. We added a children's shallow pool, water fountain to splash in, and an olive grove. Anna wanted for us to produce some of our own foods. She started the veg garden back home and wanted to pick oranges, lemons, and olives.

Barefoot, pregnant, and picking fruit wasn't how I imagined she pictured herself, but it got me hard just thinking about it.

Paloma loved Crete and the Cretans loved her. Every restaurant we attended, she was cuddled and kissed. She loved it, much to my dismay.

"She's going to be a proper diva when she's older," I said. "She loves all the attention."

I was worried about germs, and constantly wiping her face to rid her of the many kisses. Anna laughed at me.

"She'll have no immunity if you keep her away from germs," she said, taking her from me. "Now, pour me a wine and stop worrying."

That evening we went over the wedding photographs that had been sent to us via email. Paloma was asleep and Anna and I sat outside on the terrace. As we scrolled through, I paused at one.

The image of Anna taking a nap on the sofa before the wedding was in the same room as Anna taking a nap hugging my sweatshirt.

I still carried that photograph in my wallet, and I asked Anna to wait before scrolling for a moment. I walked to the kitchen and retrieved it.

I placed the worn photograph on the table and looked from one to the other.

"Where did you get this?" Anna asked.

"Nathan took it. He showed it to me when I was in the centre. He sent me a copy and I printed it off. I have stared at this image for hours and hours, Anna. When I got low, I looked at it, reminding myself that I was never as low as you, I was never as hurt and broken."

"Don't say that. That's not true," she said gently.

I looked again. It was the same couch, same pose, but Anna's face was totally different. Whereas she'd look wretched in the first, she was happy and relaxed in the second. There were no tearstains on her cheeks, no red nose, or puffy lips from hours of crying. Her cheeks weren't hollow, and her skin was clear.

"Can I have that photograph?" she asked. I hesitated. "Do you feel like you still need it?"

I looked one last time at it and then her. I shook my head. "No, I don't need it anymore."

She took the photograph from me and held it over the

candle. We watched it burn and then flutter to the floor. She reached over to shut the laptop closed and then stood.

"Swim with me?" she said and slipped her sundress over her head. She was naked underneath.

"What the fuck?" I said, and she laughed. She laughed so much she had to cross her legs to stop herself from peeing.

"What the fuck?" I said again, and she nodded.

"Twins?"

She nodded again.

She'd written just the one word on her stomach.

"When did you find out?" I asked. She hadn't mentioned a doctor's appointment.

"Had an ultrasound at the hospital. I wanted just a quick chat with the midwife about whether I'd need another C-section. We heard two heartbeats."

I picked her up and dove us both into the water.

Celebrating pregnancy news while fucking in a pool was going to become a tradition, I felt.

The End.

If you enjoyed meeting Jacob and Anna, then you might enjoy Mackenzie and Lauren. The Facilitator is super saucy, though!

mybook.to/TheFacilitator

ACKNOWLEDGMENTS

Thank you to Francessca Wingfield from Francessca Wingfield PR & Design for yet another wonderful cover.

I'd also like to give a huge thank you to my editor, Karen Hrdlicka, and proofreader, Joanne Thompson.

A big hug goes to the ladies in my team. These ladies give up their time to support and promote my books. Alison 'Awesome' Parkins, Karen Atkinson-Lingham, Ann Batty, Elaine Turner, Kerry-Ann Bell, Lou Dixon, and Louise White – otherwise known as the Twisted Angels.

My amazing PA, Alison Parkins keeps me on the straight and narrow, she's the boss! So amazing, I call her Awesome Alison. You can contact her on AlisonParkinsPA@gmail.com

To all the wonderful bloggers that have been involved in promoting my books and joining tours, thank you and I appreciate your support. There are too many to name individually – you know who you are.

ABOUT THE AUTHOR

Tracie Podger currently lives in Kent, UK with her husband and a rather obnoxious cat called George. She's a Padi Scuba Diving Instructor with a passion for writing. Tracie has been fortunate to have dived some of the wonderful oceans of the world where she can indulge in another hobby, underwater photography. She likes getting up close and personal with sharks.

Tracie likes to write in different genres. Her Fallen Angel series and its accompanying books are mafia romance and full of suspense. A Virtual Affair, Letters to Lincoln and Jackson are angsty, contemporary romance, and Gabriel, A Deadly Sin and Harlot are thriller/suspense. The Facilitator books are erotic romance. Just for a change, Tracie also decided to write a couple of romcoms and a paranormal suspense! All can be found at: author.to/TraciePodger

ALSO BY TRACIE PODGER

Books by Tracie Podger

Fallen Angel, Part 1

Fallen Angel, Part 2

Fallen Angel, Part 3

Fallen Angel, Part 4

Fallen Angel, Part 5

Fallen Angel, Part 6

Fallen Angel, Part 7

The Fallen Angel Box Set

Evelyn - A novella to accompany the Fallen Angel Series

Rocco – A novella to accompany the Fallen Angel Series

Robert – To accompany the Fallen Angel Series

Travis – To accompany the Fallen Angel Series

Taylor & Mack – To accompany the Fallen Angel Series

Angelica – To accompany the Fallen Angel Series

Robert's Fall – To accompany the Fallen Angel Series

A Virtual Affair – A standalone

The Facilitator

The Facilitator, part 2

The Facilitator, part 3

Letters to Lincoln – A standalone

Jackson – A standalone

The Freedom Diamond – A novella

Limp Dicks & Saggy Tits

Cold Nips & Frosty Bits

Posh Frocks & Peacocks

My Lord – a standalone

CEO January

CEO February

CEO March

CEO April

CEO May

CEO June

Finding Jacob, Book 1

Finding Jacob, Book 2

Thrillers written under the name T J Stone

Gabriel

A Deadly Sin

Harlot

Paranormal written under the name T J Podger

The Second Witch of North Berwick House

The Last Witch of North Berwick House

A Blood Like Mine

Printed in Great Britain
by Amazon

27624083R00169